THE CLOCKWORK CHRONICLES

EDITED BY JADE CINDERS

The Clockwork Chronicles

Hardback edition ISBN: 979-8-9851865-4-3
Paperback edition ISBN: 979-8-9851865-2-9
Electronic edition ISBN: 979-8-9851865-3-6

Published by Madhouse Books
Spring Valley, California
http://www.MadhouseBooks.com

Cover Art by Ambient Studios on Fiverr

TABLE OF CONTENTS

THE FACE OF THE FUTURE

KELLY A. HARMON

J eb Sullivan slipped the screwdriver into the seam of the faceplate on the clockwork man and pried the dented shield away from the brain cavity. He sighed. Samuel's mechanics were in worse shape than he thought they might be from the fall from the top of the forty-foot lighthouse. Jeb loosened nuts and bolts, removed two broken springs, and a handful of twisted cogs—some of the smaller ones were missing—and sand. Always, he found sand gumming up the works when he opened the machines.

But had this sand gotten in while the clockwork man had polished the glass at the top of the lighthouse—perhaps blown in on the ever-present wind coming off the sea? Or, had it entered after the seal broke around his face when he hit the rocky beach below? Jeb grabbed a soft towel and cleaned out the cavity. He would never know.

Either way, the mechanics were ruined. Samuel would never blink his eyes or raise his eyebrows again—at least not until Jeb could remake them. He knew it was silly to give the machines expressions—or names—but it made living with machines much more interesting. It gave them *personality*.

He checked Samuel's large neck spring—the heavy-duty wind-up that enabled the clockwork man to walk and lift his arms—and found that it had been severed from the cogs managing Samuel's shoulders. *How did that happen?* He wrapped his palm around the spring, lifting it gently to look behind it—and found a bullet. No wonder Samuel had fallen over the railing. He'd been forced over by the propulsion of a gunshot.

"Who the hell shoots at a clockwork man?" Jeb yelled.

A mechanical seagull whistled from her perch on the windowsill above the table. She careened down and deposited two tiny gears by Jeb's right hand before swooping back up to land on the window sill. "Bombs away! Bombs away!"

Jeb smiled. The birds were always bringing him interesting bits from outside. These must have been knocked loose from Samuel's head. He looked at the bird's markings. "Thanks, Trudy," Jeb said. "Go patrol."

Maybe whoever had shot Samuel hadn't realized he'd shot a mechanical man. Maybe his own life was in danger. And Jeb thought he'd been through with that nonsense when the war ended.

With a whistle, Trudy acknowledged Jeb's command, then pushed through the canvas flaps covering the small window high above his work table. Jeb had built it just for the birds. "Bess! Lila! Patrol!"

Two more mechanical gulls raised themselves on copper legs, whistled acknowledgment, and plunged through the canvas.

Jeb reached for the loose wire near the gears Trudy had deposited and unrolled a two-foot length before cutting it, thinking how to best repair Samuel. He'd have to cut the damaged portion from

Samuel's mainspring before reconnecting it, which would shorten the length of time Samuel could work. It was fitting, Jeb supposed, since Samuel was his oldest machine. He'd lack the energy that most old-timers had. That made Jeb smile until he thought about the dented faceplate. It looked like Sam had picked up some scars as well. *But don't we all, as we go through life?*

Jeb clipped the damaged portion off the top of the spring and started boring a hole into the end that remained. Trudy pushed through the oiled canvas flaps on the window. "Intruder," she sang. "Intruder."

Jeb looked up from Samuel's broken parts and gave the glass-eyed bird his attention.

"Friend or foe?"

"Suit and tie! Suit and tie!"

Jeb pulled off his magnifying lenses and stood, catching his balance on the table's edge as his prosthetic leg dragged. *Dammit. Sand in the knee joint, again.* He was certain.

He hadn't been expecting the representative from the Lighthouse Board until tomorrow, but it appeared that things had changed. He couldn't help the leg now.

"Well, let's see what he wants."

The bird whistled and flew outside again. Jeb walked to the door, his limp more evident than usual, and met the man at the top of the porch steps. He didn't recognize the agent, who was dressed more slovenly than any Board man he'd ever met. His jacket barely contained his paunch.

"I wasn't expecting anyone from the Board until tomorrow," Jeb said. He leaned against the porch rail, preventing the man from climbing the stairs—and more importantly—resting his leg. Trudy came to light beside his elbow on the railing, her red eyes gleaming in

3

the sun.

"Caught an earlier train," the man said, setting his briefcase on the first step and eyeing the clockwork seagull warily. "I thought I'd get an early start." Which Jeb figured was as close to an admission as he would get to the man's sudden appearance being a "surprise inspection" from the Lighthouse Board.

What had they expected to catch him at?

"Well, as you can see—" Jeb spread his arms wide, "things are just fine."

The Board man tilted his head back and shielded his eyes, staring at the three clockwork men polishing the glass at the top of the tower. He turned back to Jeb. "There have been a few complaints about the mechanicals, but I have to admit I thought the problem was your leg. I wasn't expecting to see you walking." He bent and opened the briefcase, then brandished a sheet of paper that had been lying on top. "I have a letter here from a Mr. Vestal Baird who says you lost your leg in the war and can no longer walk."

Jeb swore. *Damned rotter.*

"As you can see, Baird clearly exaggerated, Mr...?" Jeb stood up straight and crossed his arms across his chest. The leg pained him. He itched to rub his stump where it joined the prosthetic—dragging the leg around when it wasn't working well was damned wearying—but he wasn't going to give the Lighthouse Board a reason to dismiss him. He needed this job.

"Forgive me." The man lifted his hat, then replaced it. "Whitsund. Mr. Arnold Whitsund, of the Lighthouse Board—as you know." Whitsund pulled a graying, crumpled cloth from his pocket and blotted his forehead. "Do you think we could get out of the sun?"

Jeb was reluctant to entertain the man—there was much to do, and now he had the added burden of finding out who was taking

4

potshots at his clockwork men—though he thought he might now know who it might be—Vestal Baird. "Since you can see that I've got full use of my leg, might it not be best to go file your report?"

"Yes, well—" Whitsund tilted his head up again. "There's the matter of the clockwork men. And the repair work that hasn't been done. Why don't we get out of the sun and discuss it?" Jeb opened his mouth to deny him, but Whitsund forestalled him. "I'm afraid if I go back without answers, the Board will find someone to replace you immediately."

Jeb sighed. He motioned Whitsund up to the porch, where two weathered chairs sat side by side. Jeb sat in the far chair, stretching out his left leg, hoping for some relief.

Whitsund sat in the chair closest to the porch steps, mopped his brow with the dirty rag again, settled his briefcase on his knees, and opened it. He took out a thin sheaf of papers and paged through them. "I think we have settled the question of your leg satisfactorily. Now, there is the matter of the clockwork men...?" He raised his eyebrows to indicate he required an explanation from Jeb.

Without knowing what the problem was, Jeb wasn't talking. Was there really a problem, or was Whitsund on a fishing expedition? "There's a problem with the clockwork men?"

A hint of anger flashed across Whitsund's face. He consulted his notes, lifting three or four letters out of the case to show Jeb. "Yes. A few men in the neighborhood feel that your clockwork men are putting them out of jobs. And some of the women are frightened of them—they don't wish to be attacked."

Jeb sighed and ran his hand across this forehead. He'd run into these worries while enlisted.

"Clockwork machinery is relatively new. There is always a modicum of fear and trepidation when something new is introduced

5

into existing conditions—people don't like change."

"But—"

"Tell the worriers to rest assured that the clockwork men will not attack the women. They have been built for a specific job, such as cleaning the windows or hauling whale oil to the top of the tower, and they can't do anything more. I'll be happy to offer a demonstration if they want to stop by Monday next." Jeb shifted in his seat, trying to ease the growing pain in his leg.

"And the out-of-work men?"

"Have lost nothing by my machines. Be certain to tell them that the Lighthouse Board has given me no means to pay for help to renovate this lighthouse. So, I couldn't have hired them anyway."

There was no use arguing that he'd rather the machines do the work anyway. The clockwork men performed menial labor that bored most men silly—and they did so without being told more than once. In his experience, unless the pay were more than decent, the men would be quitting on him left and right. No man wanted to stand in the blazing sun at the top of the lighthouse and clean glass for hours on end, no matter how much he needed a paycheck. Clockwork men didn't complain, worked sun-up to sun-down, and didn't take smoke or lunch breaks. Further, they didn't jabber like a pack of seagulls.

"But you hired men to help you with the lens—"

"And paid them out of my own pocket." *Because it would have been impossible of me to do the job my own—and the Board should have known that.* "When will the Lighthouse Board be reimbursing me?"

Whitsund's brow furrowed. "I couldn't say." He made some notes on a blank pad, licking his pencil every few words to keep the letters dark. Jeb waited in silence until he finished. Finally, Whitsund tucked the papers into the briefcase and pulled out a half-sheet of paper, written upon with an enumerated list. Jeb couldn't read it from this distance, but he knew what it contained: an accounting of all the lighthouse repairs he'd promised to do. The list was long, and he'd barely accomplished the first few items in the six weeks he'd been there—though not for lack of trying.

"Let's discuss the repair timeline," Whitsund said. "Do you want to take me through what you've accomplished?" He looked around with a judging eye. "Or shall I just tick off what I see? You've only a few more weeks to take care of the issues, or we'll have to replace you with someone who can get all the work done in a timely manner—with or without clockwork men."

Jeb stiffened. "Mr. Whitsund. I've rectified the most important problem this lighthouse had before you hired me—it's now in operation. Everything else is superficial."

"Not according to the people of Washington."

"Lifting that lens to the top of the lighthouse was a time-consuming, backbreaking job, requiring the help of several able-bodied men—" which is why the locals were complaining about being out of work now, he thought, there's no more work where that came from. "And there's the matter of the items that needed fixing to accomplish that monumental task—repairing structural flooring to support the two-ton Fresnel lens, the eradication of vermin in the oil shed, the rat-infested curtains needed to cover the lens in daylight, the—"

"Mr. Sullivan—"

"Did no one *keep* this lighthouse during the war, Mr. Whitsund?"

"We deliberately kept them dark so as not to aid the enemy."

"And after you removed the lenses to save them from enemy destruction, did you think to have a keeper in residence to make

7

certain things weren't vandalized?"

Mr. Whitsund drew himself up tall. "It would have been dangerous to leave keepers in residence."

"And more expensive, too—I'll bet. How soon will I be reimbursed, Mr. Whitsund?"

Whitsund packed up his briefcase. "I believe I have enough for my report, Mr. Sullivan. I think my superiors would agree that you can stay until the end of July—"

"August," Jeb countered.

"July." Whitsund snapped the case shut.

"But that's only one additional week."

"With your clockwork men, you shouldn't need the extra time at all. Good day." Whitsund stood and left.

"Well, dammit."

Trudy chirped from her perch in agreement.

Seated at the table, Jeb rolled up his left pants leg to mid-thigh and loosened the leather bands on the copper bucket that surrounded his stump. He felt an immediate sense of relief in the limb and then a flurry of pins and needles when blood rushed into the expanding flesh—since *tight* was the only way he could keep the prosthetic attached. Jeb sucked in a quick breath and held it, shoving Samuel out of the way and laying the copper leg on the over-crowded, wooden table in front of him, then massaged the scarred lump of flesh at the end of his left leg, squeezing almost painfully until the pins and needles disappeared.

He brushed off the ever-present sand, then poured a little liniment into the palm of his hands to warm before rubbing it into the most tender parts of his leg. When the menthol burn in the liniment finally replaced the ache he'd been feeling all day, Jeb turned to the copper-clad, mechanical leg on the table.

The artificial limb was four parts, jointed—right where his knee should be, so that it could bend and move essentially like a real leg—and again at the ankle, so that it could bend and move, essentially like a real foot.

The tubular casing on the lower half of the leg contained a heavy-duty spring attached to a flat metal plate through the lower joint. The tension kept the metal plate in a horizontal position. That—and the padding—helped him keep his boot on. But it was also strong enough to allow Jeb to tiptoe if he shifted his weight appropriately. With the shorter, stronger coil in the thigh portion of the leg, he could also walk up and down stairs. It was a little unnatural-looking, with him swinging his weight—his hips—back and forth, but the leg bent and lifted just fine. He wanted to experiment with a heavier spring to see if he could jump—or even run—but first, he had to iron out the problem with the sand, finish all the items on the Lighthouse Board's list, and stop Vestal Baird—or whoever it was—from taking potshots at his clockwork men. Or him.

Only then could he work on improvements.

Jeb flipped open the casing covering the knee joint. It looked fine—just like he knew it would, but the sand was insidious. He couldn't keep it out of anything. Even when he opened tinned food for dinner, he invariably found sand in his meal!

He turned the large key in the middle of the joint, testing the tightness of the spring. It was firm, as expected, which meant sand was gumming up the works. He'd have to take it apart to clean it properly. Could he blow the sand out? He reached for a bellows.

"Intruder! Intruder!" Jeb looked up from the table and spied Bess. "Friend or foe?"

"Uniform! Uniform!"

Surprised, Jeb lurched upright and looked out the front

window. "Baird." He still wore the tattered remnants of his army uniform. *What could he want?*

Hastily, Jeb sat and re-attached his leg, seeing stars when he pulled the leather straps tight around the stump bucket. He got to his feet again and hurried to the door, grabbing his shotgun from where it leaned against the door frame.

Then, Jeb opened the front door and stepped out onto the porch, keeping Baird standing in the sun. He carried the gun in the crook of his arm, the barrel pointed down. It wouldn't take but a moment to lift and aim at Vestal if he became a threat. "What do you want, Baird?"

Vestal pushed the brim of his dirty, foraging hat backward and tilted his head to meet Jeb's eyes. "Is that any way to treat an old army buddy?" He opened his arms wide, smiling at Jeb.

"Cut the crap, Vestal. We were *never* army buddies."

Vestal frowned. Shoving his hands into his pockets. "Not since you took my job." He took a step closer to Jeb.

Jeb tightened his grip on the gun. "It wasn't your job, Vestal. The captain asked for volunteers, and he picked me."

"I was the better man!"

"Captain didn't think so."

"Losing that job lost me my wife."

"If she left you over two dollars, she wasn't much of a wife."

"We lost the house!" Vestal's face turned red, and he jumped up on the first step of the porch, looking as though he'd like to take a swing at Jeb.

Jeb lifted his rifle and planted it in Vestal's chest. "One more step, and you'll lose your life."

Vestal stepped back onto the hard-packed sand at the foot of the porch. "How do you always come up smelling roses?"

10

"Lots of people lost things in the war, Vestal. It wasn't my fault."

"How are you still standing?" Vestal pointed at Jeb's leg. "I saw them cut off your leg—high enough up that you should be wearing a crutch 'stead of a peg. I figured you'd be living it up in one of those fancy wheeled chairs—set for life."

Jeb nodded. "I did get a small settlement from the army, but there was no way I was spending the rest of my days in a chair—wheeled or not. I want more out of life."

"Well, you couldn't have grown a new leg."

Jeb rapped on his ankle with the end of the gun. "Copper."

Vestal nodded. "You're still smelling roses, then."

Jeb sighed. "What do you want from me, Vestal?"

"Justice."

"Justice?" Jeb ran a hand through his hair. How the hell was he going to give Vestal justice? There wasn't enough justice in the world to go around. "My settlement's gone, Vestal. It didn't pay for the knee joint, let alone an entire copper leg. Even if I wanted to give you the money you missed out on, I couldn't."

Vestal sank down on the front stoop, looking out at the ocean. His voice was soft. "The money doesn't matter anymore, Jeb. The house is gone—Sarah is dead—"

"Dead?" Jeb felt sick to his stomach. He hadn't realized it had gone that way. "Vestal, I'm sor—"

"Save it," Vestal said, standing and walking away. "We're not done, Jeb. Not by a long shot."

Great, Jeb thought, watching him go. A war with Vestal was just what he needed in addition to the Lighthouse Board's time limit.

He was still standing there, staring out to sea, when dark clouds blew in off the water and lightning flashed. The sun behind him

11

nearly washed out the blink, but the resounding boom confirmed it.

"Shoot," Jeb swore and hurried to the lighthouse door. He'd have to light the lamp earlier, which meant an additional trip up the stairs in the middle of the night to replenish the oil. Even if he didn't have to tote the oil up himself, he still had to pour it into the lamp and trim the wicks. The mechanical men weren't sophisticated to perform such a task.

It was going to be a long night.

The next day dawned crisp and beautiful. The beach was littered with snails the size of chicken eggs and other sea bounties that had churned up during the storm. Too bad Jeb was too tired to collect any.

There was nary a cloud in sight. Jeb was grateful as he extinguished the lamps and cranked up the weights that turned the lens. The clockwork men could clean up the glass a bit—cloudy from all the salt spray blown around in the storm—and he could catch an hour or two of rest, even with that distant rumbling—almost a buzz— that he heard on the horizon. Still no clouds, though, so a storm was far enough away that he could catch some shut-eye without worry. The birds would wake him if there were a problem.

Jeb woke an hour later, the same hum still buzzing on the horizon, maybe a little louder now. He made his way to the porch and looked out over the ocean—still no clouds.

He blew out a breath. So, which job should he start with? In the next week, he could accomplish one of the major renovations or a few of the minor ones.

If it were his own house, he'd start with the most structurally important, but the Lighthouse Board wanted things ticked off a list. He nodded; that sealed it. He'd get the easiest things done first.

At his worktable, Jeb reconnected Samuel's mainspring,

replaced his faceplate, and stood him up. He turned the key at the back of Samuel's neck a few times and watched the automaton move back and forth in the small room. When the spring wound down, and Samuel came to a stop, Jeb wired a paintbrush in his hand and carried him outside and down the porch. It was tricky work with a bum leg and the heavy metal parts of the automaton. It was a good thing Samuel was mostly hollow, and the handrail held. That had been one of the first things Jeb had fixed when he arrived.

Once Samuel was standing on his own, Jeb turned the key again and pointed him in the direction of the lighthouse. Then, he grabbed the whitewash and followed. It took but a few moments to condition the automaton to paint.

Three hours later, Samuel was doing an admirable job whitewashing the lighthouse base. He was slow, and his steps were a bit jerky as he paced from bucket to wall, but he was working. *And isn't that all a man could wish for in this world—a purpose?*

The low hum still came from the direction of the sea. Jeb was no longer convinced that a storm was rolling in. The sound was too constant, too homogenous, to come from nature. He looked to Samuel, who was still plugging along gamely. *Could Samuel's mechanics be echoing across the water?* That didn't make any sense to him either— unless the mainspring was winding itself up so tight it was ready to break—but Jeb hadn't made that kind of mistake since he'd first started building clockwork pieces.

He took out a spyglass and looked out over the water and couldn't believe his eyes. The sound was coming from a ship—but a ship not like any he'd ever seen before. It had a single tremendous sail, and it hovered *over* the undulating waves instead of in them. Further, he couldn't be entirely certain, but it looked like it might be flying— no, floating—if he were any judge of mechanics. The hum was getting

13

louder—so the ship must be getting closer. Jeb glanced at the windsock at the end of the pier. The wind was blowing east—so how the devil was the ship floating west?

"Trudy! Come!" A trilling whistle sounded from the roof of the house, and Trudy flew down to perch on the porch rail. Jeb scribbled a quick note, wired it onto Trudy's leg, then wound her up to full strength. He pointed to the airship. "Deliver to the captain—the uniform," he clarified.

The bird trilled again and flew off. Jeb watched through his glass until she was only a black speck in his sight.

"Intruder! Intruder!"

Jeb looked at the markings on the bird. "Friend or foe, Bess?"

"Uni—"

Bess exploded into a cloud of parts, and then Jeb heard the sound of a gunshot. A piece of metal struck him just under his right eye. He dropped to the porch and crawled into the house, pushing the door closed behind him and locking it. He wiped the blood away from his face and reached for his gun.

It had to be Baird.

Had he meant to destroy Bess, or did his shot go wild? Maybe Baird only meant to destroy the clockwork mechanicals so that Jeb would be forced to leave if he couldn't complete the Lighthouse Board's list.

A bullet struck the wood siding of the house. Then another. Jeb sighed. Since Samuel was in full view of the beach, and Baird hadn't shot at the clockwork man, then it was a safe bet that Baird was after *him*, not the mechanicals.

"Lila!" Jeb called to his remaining seagull. "Bombs away! Uniform!"

Lila whistled her acknowledgment and flew out the window

14

over Jeb's work table.

Jeb crawled to the front window and reached to close the left shutter. A bullet smacked into the hinged wood, slamming it shut. "Dammit, Baird! Shooting me is not going to get you anything!" Baird's reply was another bullet, this one striking the window frame.

Jeb scanned the beach. There were only a few places Baird could hide from Jeb: behind a small patch of scrub pine to the far left of the house, a large rock a dozen or so yards from that, or a cluttered dune on the right, rife with tall, willowy marram grass and oodles of rats—one job he hadn't taken care of yet since the rats were far enough away from the house not to cause him any trouble. Baird had to be in the dune. It offered a more direct shot of the porch, and it was closer to the house.

Lila whistled and flew over the dune, confirming Jeb's assumptions. She held a large sea snail in her feet. "Bombs away! Bombs away!" she called and dropped the snail.

Jeb inched the barrel of his gun out the window.

Crack! Another bullet hit the window frame.

Jeb shrank back, pulling the gun into the house with him. "Bombs away, Lila! Bombs away!"

Lila whistled and swooped over the beach. She snagged another snail and flew over Baird again. "Bombs away! Bombs away!" She dropped the snail.

Jeb heard a muttered oath from the dune and smiled. The second snail must have connected. "Keep it up, Lila! Bombs away!"

Jeb heard her whistle, then heard a second, softer whistle from the window ledge over the table.

"Trudy!" Her eyes were dim. "Come!" Jeb held up his arm, and the bird leaped from the sill. Halfway across the room, her eyes went dark, and she clattered against the wooden floor.

15

"Dammit." Jeb crawled to the bird and picked her up. She'd bent a leg in the fall, but her wings looked fine. Quickly, he opened the case on her back to wind her up and found a piece of paper inside—a note from the airship? He'd look at it later. He wound Trudy up tight and set her down. Her eyes lit up, and Jeb found himself smiling. Trudy always was his favorite. "Bombs away, Trudy! Uniform!"

Trudy whistled, then flew to the window and out. Jeb watched as both birds dropped missiles on Baird's location. One bird had been a nuisance, but two were causing him some aggravation. Jeb couldn't see Baird, but he could only imagine his troubles as the top of the seagrass twitched and swayed as Baird rolled back and forth to avoid the snails.

"Ow!" There was a sudden scream from the dune. "Call off your mechanical rats, Jeb!"

More thrashing. Sand flew in the air, and the grass jerked and disappeared as Baird rolled harder. He screamed again.

"I don't have any mechanical rats!" Jeb studied the dune. Black rats, almost as big as his gulls, poured out of the base of the dune and swarmed over the top. He hadn't realized the colony was so large—or he might have tackled that job first.

Lila and Trudy dropped more snails.

"Call off the birds! They're feeding the rats—and the rats are chewing on *me*!"

"Only if you leave, Baird! And don't come back."

"I'm leaving!" Baird hurried out of the grass and ran down the beach, a stream of rats chasing him as Lila and Trudy followed, dropping more snails.

Jeb called the birds in and watched as Vestal Baird got smaller and smaller, running down the beach. He pulled the shutters closed on the window in case Baird decided to double-back.

16

Finally, he could get to the note. As Lila and Trudy came through the canvas, he opened the brief letter, giving a *whoop!* Trudy flew into the room, dropping something into his lap, which rolled onto the floor. "Bombs away! Bombs away." She whistled and swooped back to the sill.

Jeb smiled and reached for the sea sponge Trudy had dropped. He knew exactly what he was going to do with it. For good measure, he sent the gulls out to retrieve several more. Once he gave the command, he started packing his things.

Jeb had finished packing after breakfast, everything except for his small hand tools, still strewn about the wooden table, and several of the sea sponges the birds had retrieved for him. Samuel and the three other clockwork men were lined up by the door, silent and still, awaiting their next orders.

He finished carving a flat, round section from one of the larger sponges and placed it over the inner workings of the knee joint on his leg, testing the fit. It had taken an hour or so to clean all the sand and hard, crusty sea bits out of the sponge, but he'd been left with a soft, breathable membrane to keep sand out of the joint and protect the knee. Even if sand got onto the front of the sponge, it wouldn't be likely to work its way through all the nooks and crannies and make it into the gears. It might work better than any screen could. He clipped a little more sponge away from one edge.

"Thank you, Trudy. Thanks, Lila," he said as he turned the key to wind the spring. The birds dipped their heads in turn to his remarks, then re-settled on the sill. He'd programmed that response, but it never failed to amuse him. And he *was* thankful.

He hadn't programmed them to find the sponges—and it was a perfect solution to his problem. He tucked the sponge around the key

17

and then closed the knee cap.

"Intruder! Intruder!" Lila sang from the perch above the table. Quickly, Jeb rolled down his pants leg and reached for his handgun, laying on the table beside him. "Friend or foe?"

"Suit and tie! Suit and tie!"

Jeb nodded thoughtfully. He'd been expecting Whitsund's arrival any day now. A moment later, he heard footsteps—quick and heavy—on the planks of the porch. Then, there was a knock on the door, but he was too tired to be polite. "It's open!" Jeb called out, leveling the gun at the door.

A tall, slender man came through the door, doffing his hat. "Mr. Sullivan."

Jeb set the gun down. "Mr. Arnold! I was afraid I'd be meeting with Whitsund again."

"Yes—well, Mr. Whitsund no longer works for the Lighthouse Board."

"I'm sorry to hear that."

"You shouldn't be." Arnold reached inside his coat and pulled out an envelope. He handed it to Jeb. "Did Whitsund tell you he was brother-in-law to Vestal Baird?"

Jeb shook his head. "Why would he?"

Arnold grinned ruefully. "He wouldn't." He nodded at the envelope he'd handed Jeb. "That contains wages for the time you've spent here and reimbursement for when you hired the townsmen to help fix the lens."

"You know what happened?" Arnold nodded. "Even Baird's shooting spree—I take it?"

Arnold tried to keep a straight face and failed. He said, dryly, "Baird lodged a complaint."

"You're joking."

18

Arnold shook his head. "It didn't take long to sort out what happened once he brought up Whitsund. Then, they couldn't blame each other fast enough." He paused. "Whitsund and Baird dreamed up the scheme to ruin you. Baird's wife, Sarah, was Whitsund's sister. Both had reason to see you fail. Whitsund planned to hire Baird as keeper once they'd run you off."

"Or killed me."

Arnold nodded, his face grim.

"So Whitsund was fired. What about Baird?"

"Signed an affidavit that he would cease harassing you and not come within two miles of *any* lighthouse ever again. Whitsun signed the same agreement."

Not what I would have wished for, Jeb thought. "No jail time?"

"Not for Whitsund, since he didn't actually commit a crime. And the Board thought that throwing Baird in jail for a few years might actually make him angrier. They'd have a bigger problem on their hands further down the road. The threat of jail time seemed a better means to keep him in line."

Jeb nodded, running a thumb over the edge of the worn bills inside the envelope Arnold had given him. "Seems there's been a bit of an over-payment here. Even if you'd planned to reimburse me for Samuel—"

"Samuel?"

"One of the clockwork men." Jeb offered Arnold a look of disgust. "Baird shot him in the face. Clipped his mainspring."

"Ah." Arnold looked thoughtful. "No. I hadn't heard about Samuel. We were hoping you'd stay on and complete the lighthouse repairs—no matter how long it takes. Consider it a signing bonus. Though we've one request: you dismantle—or otherwise get rid of—your mechanicals. It's no way to run a lighthouse."

19

"This lighthouse has always been run mechanically." Jeb thought of the weighted chains that he wound to the top of the lighthouse every morning once he extinguished the lamp. He let them drop in the evening—and as they made their slow, twelve-hour descent to the bottom of the weightway, they caused the lens to turn on its axis once every forty seconds.

"Yes—" Arnold agreed, "but the lamp doesn't have *a face.*"

"*That's* the problem?" Jeb could hardly believe it. Where he found comfort, others felt menace.

Arnold nodded.

"You realize that a face is the least of your worries when it comes to mechanics?" Jeb said.

"Automatons and mechanics will soon be putting us all out of work—this kind of work, anyway—probably other kinds, too."

Arnold's lips tightened. His face clouded as though he couldn't believe it. "Not lighthouses. We'll always need keepers: men to light the lamps in the evening and snuff them in the morning. A face—a human face—as a protector of sailors."

"And when there aren't any more boats?"

"That will never happen," Arnold said.

Jeb thought of the airship and whether or not lighthouses would even be relevant in the future. Maybe Arnold was right: there would always be ships, so there would always be a need for lighthouses. But it didn't follow that the keeper needed to be human. If men like him could figure out how to make the lighthouse turn for twelve hours at a time, they could figure out how to turn them indefinitely—and turn on and off its lamp—all without a keeper in residence.

Apparently, men already knew how to make a ship fly—it wouldn't be long before that made keepers obsolete. But airships?

20

What kind of opportunities would that bring? Jeb smiled. He would soon find out.

Jeb peeled several bills away from the envelope and handed the bonus back to Arnold.

"What's this?" Arnold asked.

Jeb started packing up his hand tools. "Consider this my notice."

"You told Whitsund you wanted to stay."

"That was before I'd seen the airship."

"Airship?" Arnold laughed, a look of incredulity on his face. "That's impossible."

Jeb just smiled. The hum he'd heard two days ago was getting louder. It wouldn't be long before the ship arrived. He slipped his hand tools into their case, rolled it up, and then tucked it into his bag.

The hum grew loud enough to shake the small wooden house, then abruptly stopped.

"Ahoy!" came a voice that sounded like it came from the trees. Something dropped past the window. Startled, Arnold swung open the door and stepped onto the porch, Jeb right behind him. A large airship hovered above the rocky cliff. It was held aloft by a bright blue balloon, painted green and gold.

It was the most marvelous thing Jeb had seen in a long time.

A uniformed man was climbing down a rope ladder that had been dropped over the side.

"Mr. Sullivan?" the man asked when he reached the ground. "Builder of magnificent clockwork birds?"

Jeb felt himself grinning. "That would be me."

"Splendid." The man returned Jeb's smile, removed his hat and tucked it under one arm, then held out his hand to shake. "I am Captain Newsome. Your bird is an impeccable reference. I'm happy to offer you

21

a job aboard the *Daedalus*."

Arnold stepped forward. "I'm afraid Mr. Sullivan has a contract with the Lighthouse Board to complete some repairs here, Captain Newsome."

Jeb cocked an eyebrow. "A contract I was unable to fulfill."

Arnold waved his hand. "I told you we are happy to extend that contract—"

"—only if I give up my clockwork men—"

"Clockwork men?" Newsome clapped his hands. "Spectacular."

Jeb turned back to Newsome. "Four of them—and another bird. But I'll need help loading them on board—along with my bag and tools."

Newsome nodded. He took a whistle from his pocket and blew it. Two men in uniform peeked over the gunwales. "Captain?" asked the first.

"Send over the lift."

"Aye, Captain," the second uniformed man responded. A square platform swept over the boat's edge at the end of a boom and lowered swiftly to the ground. Both uniformed men were seated on the platform.

"Just point out your things," Newsome said.

"Inside." Jeb pointed through the open door at two large boxes full of parts and tools and at Samuel and the other clockwork men. The men made quick work of loading them. He retrieved his bag and called to the birds.

"You can't go," Arnold said. "I believe we could find room in the budget for a permanent assistant keeper—and a raise."

Jeb patted him on the shoulder and smiled. "Thank you for the opportunity to get on my feet after the war. Not many men would have done that." He stepped onto the platform beside the uniformed men and the captain and was quickly lifted into the ship. Trudy and Lila swooped upward and landed on the boom arm of the platform.

"Please—stay," Arnold begged.

"I'm sorry, I can't," Jeb said. "I have seen the face of the future, and it's not here."

AUTHOR BIO

Kelly A. Harmon used to write truthful, honest stories about authors and thespians, senators and statesmen, movie stars, and murderers. Now she writes lies, which is infinitely more satisfying, but lacks the convenience of doorstep delivery.

She is an award-winning journalist and author, and a member of the Horror Writers Association and the Science Fiction & Fantasy Writers of America. A Baltimore native, she writes the *Charm City Darkness* series—an urban fantasy adventure set in contemporary Baltimore. Find her short fiction in many magazines and anthologies, including *Occult Detective Quarterly, Terra! Tara! Terror!,* and *Deep Cuts: Mayhem, Menace and Misery.*

For more information, visit her online at KellyAHarmon.com or on Twitter @KellyAHarmon.

INTO THE BLUE

JASON RUSSELL AND A.S. CHARLY

B arlow held his teacup at arm's length to see if any would spill. The old man was right; the rail ship was truly one of the smoothest in the fleet. Fitting, of course, given that it was to serve as the aristocracy's flagship and mobile headquarters.

"You see, Barlow," Withers said, his free hand gently stroking the stubby point of his rusty mustache, "we are trucking along the rails at nearly sixty now, and you can't even tell we're moving."

"A remarkable feat of engineering," Barlow replied. He took a sip of his tea after first blowing away the steam.

"Engineering, yes. Let us not discount the designers' taste for luxury as well. This glorious ship can sleep eighty in addition to its staff and engineering crew. Every bedroom is dressed in the rarest imported linens and silks. Look here..." The rotund man pulled up the corner of the closest drapery, revealing a length of golden embroidery that terminated in a crest.

25

"Very impressive," Barlow said dryly.

"Only the finest, dear boy." Withers spilled a multitude of tea drops on the distention of his generous midsection through no fault of the rail ship. The liquid immediately stained the white fabric brown, a staggered series of circles that looked almost like animal tracks in the snow.

"And the aristocracy is, of course, indebted to your valor. That's why you've been invited upon this inaugural voyage."

"Just doing my job."

"You have my every assurance. I did all I could to have your entire squadron along for this trip to the capital."

"I'm certain that you did."

Withers, oblivious to the weariness of his guest, continued to rattle off details about the rail ship while spilling what remained of his tea upon himself. "The engines are state-of-the-art," he said, leaning in closer from the opposing leather seat. "The steam is enhanced by the very same hydrogen that keeps your dirigibles afloat."

For the first time that day, Barlow was genuinely interested in what the viscount had to say. "This ship burns hydrogen?"

The larger man nodded. "When you burn hydrogen, you get water. The very same water can then be boiled into steam. The range of *The Ara* is unmatched. What's the matter, dear boy? You don't look impressed."

"At these speeds, a tank of charged hydrogen is little more than a bomb."

"Needless to worry," Withers countered with a chuckle. "This has all been taken into consideration. *The Ara's* engines are hardly restricted by the weight considerations of your dirigible fleet. The iron here is thick and reinforced."

A female automaton servant sprang to key-wound life, clumsily approaching them from the corner of the room. "More tea?" she said, getting into position to pour before either man responded. Barlow waved her away, prompting the machine to pivot and begin pouring tea into Withers' cup.

"Oh! Why yes, suppose I will," Withers said, after the liquid was already filling his cup.

Barlow watched as dozens of clockwork intricacies worked harmoniously across her nearly human form, a myriad of interlocking gears, pulleys, and spring tension mimicking the nuances of bone, muscle, and flesh.

"Viscount, do you ever find yourself wondering if the aristocracy cares about people like you and I?"

The larger man looked around the wiry frame of the automaton between them and adjusted his monocle. "What? No, never." Though flustered, he did his best to keep a level hand upon his freshly poured cup of tea. "I don't know how you mean."

"This last bombing mission. We were instructed to take out rebel supply lines."

The automaton clumsily walked away, the key in her back rotating slowly.

"Rightly so. The only way we'll ever put an end to the insurgence is to cut them off at the knees."

"There were women and children in some of those hubs."

"Traitors to the throne," Withers said with newfound resolve. "They are no longer individuals in such instances, old boy. They become little more than rats in need of trapping."

Barlow pursed his lips and turned to watch the scraggly brush of the expanse beyond the rail ship's glass port streak past below a dusky sky.

"Did I mention the finery?" Withers said, the silence clearly causing him discomfort. "Just wait until you experience the bedsheets. The cotton has been imported from the orient. We cut no corners in designing *The Ara*."

A white cloud appeared on the horizon where the train tracks met the gloomy skies. Justine rubbed her tired eyes, careful not to get more dust inside them, and pulled out her rusty telescope.

"Finally," she muttered to herself. "This has to be it!"

Not entirely trusting the coded message box the instructions had been slipped from, she had been camping out in the open by herself for the last two days. She hoped their contact in the capital was trustworthy, as his notes contained valuable information, such as the train schedules, the recommended supplies, and weaknesses of the fleet's machinery. Nothing in the world could make her miss the opportunity to see the aristocracy's fancy toy–and she had made plans with her new companions to have an even closer look than the rail ship's crew would approve.

Her family had given Justine a hard time for leaving during the harvest, but due to the dry heat, it wasn't like there was much to pick. In her opinion, kicking some stuck-up, fat aristocracy asses was way more important anyway. Since the installment of that huge dam near the capital, the once green plains had turned to sand more and more each year.

If the aristocrats can take my people's livelihood, it's only fair to get supplies from the capital's railroad cargo in return, she thought, not feeling like a rebel at all.

With a grim smile, she hung her frayed tool bag around her waist, which was neatly trimmed by her leather corset. She then strapped up the front of her wrinkled skirt to achieve the freedom of movement needed to climb onto her mechanical horse. The sight of the countless scars on her slender legs annoyed her, like always.

She pulled out her pocket watch, swirling it around on its copper chain once, before catching it in her hand and snipping it open. *The Ara* crossed over from the plains into an area of widely scattered rocky hills.

"Right on time."

After letting the watch disappear into her pocket again, she had another look through her telescope. This time, Justine searched for her companions' camp, which was located next to four big rocks. It was hard to spot, even though she knew where it was. To her surprise, she saw Tom waving a red rug: the signal to abort mission.

Irritated, she scanned the surroundings but couldn't find an explanation. Turning her attention to the rails again, she watched *The Ara* draw closer. She had to leave now, or the window of opportunity would pass.

She activated the mechanical horse with a rough kick against its flanks, immediately setting its multiple legs to life. It clumsily teetered down the hill, its feet stretching back and forth in wavelike movements like those of a giant metal millipede. It was a bumpy ride that shook her to the bones.

Justine silently blessed the moment when they finally reached the lowland, and the horse fell into a smoother trot. Using the rocks as cover, she hurried toward the rails. Now and then, she caught sight of *The Ara* through the passing clusters and adjusted her speed accordingly. Then the last rock formations passed. Her friends were nowhere to be seen. Without an alternative, she ventured on by herself, knowing she'd be in plain sight for the last half mile. Fist to her heart, she leaned forward and spurred the mechanical horse to maximum speed, hoping for a miracle.

A few heartbeats later, she heard the rail ship's jarring alarms and the zing of the first barrage of bullets whizzing past. Her heart pounded, memories of the last raid welled up—gunshots and bombs dropping, her little sister bleeding to death in her arms. The sky was alive with war dirigibles, raining violence and carnage down upon her village.

A bullet hit her metallic horse, its tortured screech snapping her back to reality. She adjusted their course parallel to the rails and slid down to the horse's side, balancing her total weight between that one foot in the stirrup and her hand, which still held onto the saddle horn. Not a moment too soon. Several more bullets found their target.

Even if I get close to The Ara now, how could I ever get on with all those eyes on me....

Barlow yawned, making his way down one of the many plush interior corridors of *The Ara*. An evening spent enduring the ramblings of Viscount Withers had done his ability to remain conscious no favors.

For a moment he continued walking toward his suite, convinced he hadn't, in fact, seen a young woman on a metallic horse pacing the rail ship when he absently looked out one of the many glass ports to his side. A second look confirmed his hunch.

Before he could process the oddity of the scene, a series of deafening air alarms sounded. Though he couldn't verify it visually, he felt the vibrations of panic ripple through the massive, mobile complex. No stranger to battle, Barlow knew immediately that the capital ship was under rebel attack. The familiar rush of adrenaline sent him scurrying toward the nearest junction as an eruption of muffled gunfire found his ears.

Locked, as it were, he was forced to cut across a smoky dining room where lower members of the aristocracy looked up from their heaping piles of veal with annoyance.

"I say," one of the portly individuals there said. "So many disruptions."

Another took a long swig of wine, watching as Barlow slipped through the myriad of white-clothed tables.

"For you, I risk my very life," he muttered to himself sardonically. "The gratitude makes it all worthwhile."

A burst of warm evening air took his breath away and rustled his hair once he finally reached an exterior door on the far side of the dining room. He had lost sight of the girl and her steed, but the direction of the rail ship's automated defense guns had him suspecting she was still keeping pace.

Ahead, a rebel party must have been staked out behind a pair of towering rock formations that almost entirely enclosed the rails. It was but a flash to his eyes, but he was sure he saw their airboat lift off from the sandy surface there, kicking up a torrent of thick tan dust in the process.

Barlow barely had a moment to reach for his scarf with leather-gloved hands and wrap it around his mouth before the wall of dust was upon him. It engulfed the entire rail ship in an instant, turning the fading light of the day to immediate night. The automated guns of the ship fell silent.

"Clever girl," he whispered into his scarf.

He stepped to the edge of the ship's exterior rail and looked back. He heard the clopping of metallic hooves on rail gravel before the persistent rebel came into view.

Whether or not she was surprised to find someone standing upon the narrow deck she intended to use to board the vessel, her dark goggles wouldn't say. For a moment, though, they silently regarded one another, scarfs flapping in the dusty wind.

It looked to him like she may have been struggling to remove her revolver from the leather holster that traversed her chest, but he didn't allow it to dictate his decision.

With careful deliberateness, he leaned over the ship's wrought-iron rail and extended a gloved hand to the rebel.

The deafening rumble of spinning gears and her own heart pounding in her ear blocked out every other sound. Justine knew better than to allow herself false security just yet though. Hidden within the gloomy sand-cloud that engulfed them, the crew of *The Ara* was still exchanging fire with her rebel friends. The metal exterior of her mechanical steed grew hotter and hotter, suggesting it was getting close to its limits—not unlike herself.

It was time to act.

Her tired arms almost failed her, but with clenched teeth, she pulled herself upright into the saddle once more and positioned her horse alongside *The Ara*. To her surprise, she found a uniformed man standing on the platform she had selected as the boarding point.

Blast!

Justine tried grabbing for her revolver but froze mid-movement as he extended his hand toward her in a calm, inviting gesture. She looked up at him, her dark googles zooming in on the delicate features of his face.

Long seconds passed, and the wind tousled her hair while she sized him up. To her confusion, there was concern in his eyes. If it was a trap, she decided, it was quite convincing. Hesitantly, she raised her arm to accept his hand.

Their hands nearly touched when another bullet hit her mechanical horse in a sparking ricochet. The steed stumbled, steam bursting out of its fresh wound.

Justine fought for her balance, holding on tight with her arms and legs. She didn't even let go when the steam brushed over her exposed arm, burning the skin. Somehow, the horse managed to sort its many legs and galloped on— noticeably slower now.

Justine needed a moment to adjust herself in the saddle. From the corner of her eye, she saw the man from the platform leaning over the elaborate handrails, shouting at her. Only, to her surprise, he wasn't mad. He seemed genuinely worried.

The distance between them increased, and without much thinking, she knew she could never catch up.

Putting every thought of the stranger aside, Justine pulled on the reins, signaling her horse to line up with the moving train again. They met *The Ara* at a section where its giant, turning wheels were exposed.

Her mechanical horse shook its head, eyes widened in fear. It took Justine a steady hand and all her skill to persuade it to get closer, just right beneath an overhanging service ladder. Her first attempt failed, but the second time she managed to grab it after a wild swing of her arm.

Sweat forming on her temples, she stood up slowly on her horse's back. For a moment, she balanced there, with the wind in her face. Then she let go of the reins.

The shiny horse drew away, falling behind quickly. Justine clung onto the ladder for dear life, the ground below her rushing past faster than anything she'd ever seen. With trembling arms, she pulled herself up until her boots reached the lowest rungs. There she paused, intending to take a few deep breaths to calm her heart, but several uniformed men spotted her.

A rush of adrenaline surged through her aching body and hurried her up a few meters on the metal ladder. There she found a service shaft and disappeared inside *The Ara*.

The cool darkness inside blanketed her, the deafening roar of its operation outside falling into little more than a muffled rumble. If its exterior was a demonstration of might and fortification, the rail ship's interior was that of luxurious refinement.

Justine scrambled through the dimly lit corridors, struggling in vain to try to recall the detailed blueprints her rebel friends had somehow intercepted. Unique to the rail ship was a massive hydrogen induction tank that super-heated the steam. Locating the hydrogen supply was instrumental to her mission. The trouble was that she was now several sections behind where she had planned to enter.

The rail ship's interior was a dizzying maze of passages and junctions, all framed by passenger areas lousy with tea-sipping diplomats. Logic told her that the target must be at the front of this massive machine, but after several turns, Justine was quite unable to tell one direction from another.

She paused, letting her muscles relax enough to sense the tug of momentum upon her body. The ship was undeniably smooth, the only indication of the ship's movement was a slight vibration below her feet.

The gunshot took her by surprise, the bullet finding the wall above her shoulders by the time the report rang in her ears. She turned and ran in the opposite way of the uniformed guard, throwing away any sense of direction her efforts may have yielded in the process.

There were guards coming from both sides of the nearest junction, forcing her to duck into a narrow maintenance shaft. Large rotating gears tugged at the hem of her dress as she stepped around the synchronized chaos.

The guards followed her down the shaft, reluctant to open fire this time on account of the myriad of crucial components surrounding them. Using this to her advantage, Justine slipped through a ventilation grate and wound up smacking into one of the many automaton servants on board.

"Hello," the robot said, springing to life. "Would you like some tea?"

Picking herself up from the floor, Justine dusted herself off. "No," she said to the lifeless request.

"Sure. Let me get that for you," the automaton said, lifting its teapot.

Justine darted through the door and down the nearest hall as the guards emerged through the same grate that she had passed through moments before. The automaton was already pouring tea into small porcelain cups, temporarily blocking their path.

She swung a hard left, then another right, and found herself again in a chamber full of moving componentry. Gears drove large iron levers that rose and fell from an opening in the floor. Knowing the guards would arrive any moment, she contemplated whether the small explosive charges she had packed in her leather satchel would be potent enough to disable the massive rail ship if she set them off in the room. They had been designed specifically to make use of the hydrogen's volatile nature to be effective, but the entire plan had been degenerating before her very eyes and now time was certainly against her.

Before she could reach in to retrieve the first charge, she felt the undeniable tug of one of the gears upon the back of her dress. Its big teeth found the fabric of her garment and brought her down to her knees in one fluid motion. It stopped, thankfully, her dress hopelessly caught between interlocked teeth with the smaller cog above it. Once the lever it was attached to completed its revolution, the gears would turn again, this time crushing her in the process.

Justine struggled wildly to slip out of her clothing, but the tension of the gears was such that it made the gown unbearably tight about the front. In fact, she had trouble moving her arms at all. Panic swept over her, and in an instant, she saw the unmistakable shape of one of the uniformed guards enter the room beside her.

The tension on her dress increased as the gears began to turn once more and, to her surprise, terminated entirely a moment later. A whoosh of air ran down her neck and she was free, the chunk of fabric holding her captive severed cleanly.

The guard's sword gleamed as he returned it to its scabbard. She recognized his gentle face in an instant, too stunned to speak a word. It was the man from earlier, the one who had extended her a hand.

"Go around the next bend and wait for me there," he instructed.

She did as he said and heard as he reported she'd gone up to the level above when his comrades arrived a moment later.

"I believe you are trying to find this," he told her once the remaining guards disappeared up the nearest ladder. He unlocked a heavy door with one of the keys on his ring.

Inside, a massive iron wall marked *Hydrogen: Under Pressure* greeted them.

"Why," she stammered, "why are you helping me? You must know what I'm here to do."

"Do it," he said. "How much time will we have before detonation?"

She pursed her lips. "A minute."

36

"Follow me once you've placed them, and we'll head to the rear of the ship. The blast will be survivable there, and we can step off in the ensuing chaos."

She looked at the stranger, unsure of whether she wanted to wrap her arms around him or surrender to him.

"Go on," he said. "We'll make it off, okay. You have my word."

Barlow turned away from her when their fingers ran out of skin to brush upon, the flickering light of rail ship flames fading to the dawn.

"Where will you go?" Justine asked, stopping him in his tracks.

"There is nothing left for me here," he said, confirming what she already knew.

"There is always room for you with us here. Your knowledge of the aristocracy's military would be invaluable to our strikes. We could really have a chance at evening the playing field."

He shook his head. "There's still so much I would have to consider between here and there. What we did together tonight will buy you time. I suggest you use it wisely. When they return, and they will, expect a well-organized retaliation."

"We'll be ready," Justine said coolly. "You're sure I can't change your mind?"

Barlow sighed after a moment's hesitation, so subtle as to nearly go unnoticed. "It is best that I step away from this conflict for a time. There is an island northeast of Green Harbor with a long-abandoned lighthouse."

"A lighthouse?"

"Yes. A tower containing a chamber of luminiferous ether. It guides wayward ships to shore when the storms become blinding." He could see the wonderment in her eyes. "You've never seen the ocean?"

Justine shook her head.

"I am going to that island. I will restore the ramshackle dwelling there and relight the beacon. The salty mist will do me some good after the years wasted in this unrelenting desert heart."

Justine looked behind her at the flickering carnage. "I want to come with you."

Barlow squinted. "It'll be a hard life," he said earnestly. "The living quarters have been ravaged by decades of inclement weather. I will have to have planks brought in a little at a time by boat."

"Sounds like the kind of place that would benefit by a woman's touch," she said with a wink.

"You mean it? You're serious about leaving this behind?"

"I like to think that together we may be able to come back and turn the tide when you're ready," she admitted. "Until then, it's hard for me to imagine you doing anything other than bringing light to those lost by the storm."

Despite himself, Barlow smiled. He brushed the hair away from her eyes. "Together then."

"Together then," she repeated, slipping her hand into his.

They walked away from the stationary behemoth of metal and flame as the dawn's first light broke the distant horizon.

"What's the ocean like?"

"Like this," Barlow said, sweeping his arm before the twinkling sand. "But blue until it meets the sky."

"If it's blue too, how do you know where it ends and the sky begins?"

"You don't," Barlow said with a smirk. "That's why many think it has no end."

"Does it?" She paused. "Have an end, I mean."

"If it does, I've yet to find it."

She put her face against his shoulder. "To endlessness, then."

"End"

AUTHOR BIO

Jason Russell is a novelist from NY and cofounder of the new science fiction publishing house Starry Eyed Press. Most recently he has edited the space opera anthology Strange Orbits for Black Ink Fiction (available now).

You can learn more about him at:

Goodreads.com/author/show/6564149.Jason_Russell

A.S. Charly is a freelance writer and illustrator from Austria. In addition to having cofounded Starry Eyed Press, her work can be found in a variety of anthologies.

You can learn more about her at: Facebook.com/A.S.Charlydreams

DOWN THE CAT HEAD EAGLE HOLE

MATT MCHUGH

GRESHAM COLLEGE - 1870

"Gentlemen, how long would you say it should take to travel from London to Peking?"

Colonel Julien Laferrière looked up at the elders of The Royal Society for the Advancement of Science. The average member was double his age. Bewhiskered scholars in the lecture hall shifted in their seats and discussed the question amongst themselves. He was amused to see a few members muttering and counting on fingers.

"Better part of a year, I should think," one esteemed fellow replied.

"Twaddle!" objected another. "The *Cutty Sark* did it in half that!"

The susurrus became a rhubarb as spirited indignation—the national sport of Great Britain, so it seemed to Laferrière—took hold of the room. Colonel Laferrière let it run for a while as he adjusted his

41

waistcoat and scratched his smooth-shaven chin before raising his voice above the ballyhoo.

"I can do it in forty-three minutes."

The room went silent before erupting into laughter.

"Shot from what size cannon?" called out a heckler, stirring the bubbling pot of mirth to a full-blown boil.

Laferrière went to the blackboard and drew a circle. He made X's on the circumference at roughly fifty- and forty-degree North antipodes.

"London. Peking. The capitals of two empires that have spread their tendrils across hemispheres. To reach one from the other demands months of sea voyage, but, of course, we all know the shortest distance between two points."

Laferrière slashed a straight line connecting the X's.

"Gentlemen, I give you: the London-Peking Tunnel."

Breathless silence hung in the gallery for a few moments, immediately followed by an explosive collision of indignation and mirth.

"Drill through the Earth's core?" someone shouted. "Hogwash!"

"Not through the core," Laferrière explained, accustomed to the reaction. "Just a dip into the mantle in a long, gentle arc." He scribbled calculations on the blackboard. "Utilizing nothing but gravity, which provides an accelerating force of about ten meters per second squared— oh, that's thirty-two feet for those of you still obsessed with your monarch's shoe size—an object descending into a sloped tunnel will steadily gain speed until it passes the midpoint and begins ascending with a precisely inverse rate of deceleration, arriving at the opposite apex as gently as a ball tossed by a juggler. Total time for transit: forty-three minutes to any two points on the globe, regardless of distance. If you doubt me, consult Sir Isaac Newton."

Disgruntlement transited the room, the occasional articulation of "Balderdash!" or "Podsnappery!" asserting itself.

"Of course, that assumes no loss of velocity from air resistance. The tunnel would need to be sealed and maintained in a state of vacuum, so the walls must be airtight."

Laferrière motioned to a quartet of burly fellows in the hall; they entered carrying between them a block of granite which they set upon a turntable. Laferrière paired mechanical apparatus at opposing sides of the block. Once positioned, he connected copper wires to each then commenced to crank the handle of a dynamo with the fury of a demon.

A whine rose, then a screech, and then a roar like a flock of gulls screaming in a typhoon. Windows rattled in their frames, and the ironmongery holding chairs together twitched. The audience covered their ears and cringed. Mercifully, after only a minute, Laferrière backed off the crank, and the cacophony faded. He removed the apparatus and rotated the turntable, so the block end faced the audience.

A smooth bore, nearly the width of a man's fist and as perfect and polished as a gun barrel, was now lanced clean through the solid stone.

"The dynamo creates a cylindrical field with constant polarity shifts," Laferrière explained. "This temporarily imbues the tiniest particles of matter—*les molécules*, as Descartes once called them—with a charge that oscillates rapidly between positive and negative. This forces the molecules to repel each other along the centerline and attract at the periphery, compacting into a dense ring. I call it the magnetic lathe."

Colonel Laferrière went on to give what he considered a stirring lecture on the logistics of the project, not the least of which was substantial investment in time and funding, concluding with his belief that the tunnel could be completed in as little as fifty years. The audience's attention wandered during the details and utterly bolted at the final figure.

As the crowd departed, a few nodded to Laferrière and said something akin to "Intriguing concept, young man" or "Nearly had me fooled, old boy," but most shuffled out with hunched indifference. Laferrière began to pack his gear, wondering what learned societies or liberal financiers remained in Europe that hadn't yet rejected his appeal, when a portly aristocrat, his girth barely contained behind torturously strained vest buttons, pointed a sausage-thick finger toward the block and said, "Forty-three minutes to the other side of the globe, eh?"

"Were the project completed as specified," replied Laferrière, "that would be a completely accurate figure, sir."

"I know a man who reaches an identical figure with a wholly opposite approach. You lads should meet." He whisked an address card before Laferrière's face. "Two p.m. sharp tomorrow. Catch the Great Western from Victoria Station, no later than nine. Bring your gadgets."

The next day, Laferrière stood holding a bulky valise before St. Aldates gate of Christ Church College in Oxford, listening to the Great Tom Tower bell ring out two p.m. On cue, Lord Hanmarten Steffrith (thus read the sausage-fingered man's card) waddled across the quad and greeted him with a smothering handshake.

"Well done," said Steffrith. "A man determined to bisect the globe should, at the very least, be able to navigate British Rail timetables. First hurdle cleared!"

He led Laferrière through a warren of cloisters and corridors, giving along the way what seemed like the C.V. of every stone ("Mind your step," he said at one point. "Erasmus once took a tumble there," and later, "This was Dr. Johnson's favorite bench!") until at last, they reached a cavernous basement chamber strung like a jungle with wire and cables, and abuzz with neck-prickling static. As they entered, a grey-bearded Chinese don stepped in front of Steffrith and delivered an undeniable threat in musical Mandarin. A young woman stepped beside him. She wore featureless dark attire of long legs and sleeves, appearing wholly androgynous save for her delicate features and intricately braided curls. The woman nodded demurely and translated:

"With respect, sir, Professor Qin says, 'Get ...the devil... out of my laboratory, you... portly fellow'."

"Ah, the exotic charm of the Orient!" gushed Steffrith. "Professor, may I introduce Colonel Laferrière of the… uh… French Science Army, I believe it is. Colonel, this is Master Qin Hui-Shu of Yongzheng Academy, visiting Hooke Professor of Experimental Physics."

Qin ignored the introduction and continued to focus a torrent of wrath upon Lord Steffrith as the translator struggled to keep pace while substituting curses with euphemisms.

"The (confounded) college threatened to remove my equipment! My files… three years of work. The dean said you defaulted on the payments you promised (untruthful) (pouch of leavings). I came to your (wet-smelling) country because you swore to fund my experiments for five years."

"One's circumstances change, old chap. Isn't that the glory of science? Endlessly adaptable with each new discovery? Well, here's a brilliant discovery for you!" Again, he gestured to Laferrière. Again, Qin ignored him and rolled on with his rant.

Laferrière cleared his throat. "Forgive my curiosity, Master Qin, but are you working with induction coils, and, if so, have you read Maxwell's latest theories on vector potential?"

The woman translated. Qin puckered for a moment, then motioned for Laferrière to follow. On a raised platform was a metal bowl wider than a man's arm span and threaded with gleaming braids of copper wire; at the center sat an iron cannonball the size of a man's head. Qin flipped a few sparky switches, and the cannonball gently began to hover. Qin nudged it with a finger, and the massive sphere drifted along the perimeter as lightly as a soap bubble. Once it circled back to its center position, Qin slapped a lever, and the cannonball dropped with a bone-rattling *clank*.

Qin raised an eyebrow at Laferrière. Laferrière opened his valise and positioned his equipment on either side of the ball. Qin folded his hands and watched with cool interest as Laferrière cranked the screaming dynamo for a minute, then stepped back and declared, "Voilà!"

Qin bent forward to peer through the perfect, thumb-thick hole now piercing the cannonball.

"Fascinating," translated the woman. "And you can tunnel through the Earth with this?"

"If we can construct nodes on opposing sides of the globe and supply them with adequate power."

"How much power?"

Laferrière took out a notepad and jotted the formulae with joules per coulomb needed at the distance of a global diameter to deliver the minimal field strength. Qin commandeered the pad and worked out the volts and amperes required. Laferrière sketched alternate distance chords stringing through a proxy-circle globe; Qin worked out the arcs and variables. Back and forth, natives from la République française and

46

the Celestial Empire conversed *sans traductrice* in the tongues of Euclid and Leibniz. Thus, a partnership was born.

After spending the night at the chic Randolph Hotel—where, he discovered, the promissory notes of Lord Steffrith were no longer a welcomed currency—Laferrière again stood in the buzzing basement lab where Professor Qin and his polyglottrix explained a bold proposition, complete with meticulous blackboard graffiti and spellbinding functional maquettes.

"Using high-altitude airships outfitted with magnetic coils, an aero-foil craft is accelerated to sufficient velocity to reach an altitude of fifty miles where it enters the frictionless vacuum of space. From there, the craft maneuvers with rockets to a sub-orbital descent to any point on the globe. Total transit time: about forty minutes."

Laferrière, lost for a moment in fascination with a toy airship levitating a tiny delta-wing rocket car, snapped his attention back to Qin's presentation. "This is amazing, Professor," Laferrière commented. "But, if you don't mind my saying so, it is quite... complex."

Qin clapped chalk dust from his fingers with a sigh. "You have found, as the Greek poets say, the Achilles' heel. Each component has a hundred chances for failure. Across the entire system, the catastrophic potential curves up exponentially toward an asymptotic certainty."

He walked over to a table where Laferrière had placed half a dozen mineral samples, all with a neat hole pierced through by a magnetic lathe.

"Your plan, on the other hand, is exceedingly simple," he continued. "It has few components and requires no energy. Except, of course, what's needed to move billions of tons of rock. And secure a tunnel through unstable magma."

"It is a puzzlement," replied Laferrière.

Qin picked up one of the model airships. "I may have a solution."

Lord Steffrith, his bulk squeezed into a student desk that groaned perilously under the strain, sat in a disused classroom as he listened to Qin and Laferrière unfold their newly hatched scheme. By watching his face, Laferrière could tell the maths were as clear as mud to Steffrith though he did seem utterly captivated by the chalkboard illustrations.

"Never had a doubt you two geniuses would crack the egg!" he said.

"Do you understand your part?" Qin asked.

Steffrith squinted. "It's financing, right? If so, I may be the weakest link."

"Not financing, per se," replied Laferrière. "But fundraising. We need you to exploit your title to meet with government officials to seek investment in a globe-uniting project."

"Right up the alley for an old boffins like me! Is there a travel stipend?"

"No."

"That may put us back to square one, I'm afraid."

"There is a way you can acquire money quickly," said Qin. "Sell your stake in the Millwall Docks."

"What? On the Isle of Dogs?" Steffrith bolted up, his belly snagging on the desk. "That's my inheritance! The rent I receive from shipping companies using that mud pit on the Thames is my only steady income. It's the last bit of land left to my family name!"

"You have an entire estate in Berkshire."

"That doesn't earn a penny!" objected Steffrith. "You two want to dig a bottomless pit? Well, I've already got one in the shape of a mansion into which revenue flows like a drain. If you want to curse someone with a catastrophic gift, the maharaja's white elephants have nothing on an English country manor."

"I have a proposal," said Qin. He led Steffrith away, leaving the translator behind.

Laferrière turned to her and asked, "Shouldn't you go with them?"

"The Professor won't need me for this. We've prepared documents for the occasion."

"I apologize that we have not formally met." He extended a hand. "Julien Laferrière."

She accepted his fingers and gave a hint of a curtsy. "And my name is Eloise. Eloise Meilin Steffrith."

"Steffrith? You're...uh...his...."

"Niece," Eloise replied. "My father was the younger Lord Steffrith, Commodore of the Royal Navy and Foreign Secretary to the Crown colony of Hong Kong."

"That's quite a pedigree. Your father is...?"

"Deceased. Along with my mother, an attendant woman from the imperial Chinese entourage. Both died in a surge of plague on the island when I was thirteen. Professor Qin has sheltered me these ten years since."

"How did you come to know him?"

"Hong Kong's Governor retained Qin to consult on plans for modernization. My father was fascinated by his designs for magnetic trains. He wrote letters of introduction to his alma mater and pledged to help fund Qin's work. His death left my family's fortune in the sole care of my uncle. He's a good man but a poor custodian. After years of delay, Qin was offered an Oxford post, contingent on my uncle's promise to defray the expense of his research. And here we are. I've wondered if my uncle fabricated the promise just to secure my relocation to England."

"Would you prefer to be in the Orient?" asked Laferrière.

"I'd prefer to step between continents like rocks in a stream, hence my enthusiasm for your concept. I'd much rather go tumbling down the rabbit hole than be launched like a tea-tray in the sky." Eloise Steffrith laughed, a pretty ripple of sound. "But come now. I'm bursting to know what my uncle makes of our enticement."

Together, as they proceeded toward the basement laboratory, Lord Steffrith barreled at them, brandishing a stack of certificates with formal calligraphy.

"Look here!" he gushed. "Qin is making me a major stockholder in your newly formed company! And the project is to be re-named 'The Steffrith Tunnel!' Can you fancy that?"

Laferrière met Qin's eyes. Qin gave the most discreet of shrugs.

For the next year, the trio worked in tandem on the endless complications of Laferrière's simple plan. Blackboards of calculations continually scrawled, defaced, and erased, and models constructed and demolished, sometimes in fits of pique. Arguments in such heated language that Eloise refused to referee and sternly banished the combatants to their corners. Any lingering umbrage was dispelled as she hooked the arms of the two men and led them for long strolls along the River Cherwell.

Lord Steffrith sold to the Millwall Freehold Dock Company his landholdings on the Isle of Dogs (with constant reminders of how the property was a gift from no less than Henry the Eighth to his ninth-great grandfather). The lump earnings covered his delinquent grants to the University and secured Qin's resources, with enough left to finance speaking tours to the top academies of England, Scotland, France, Italy, and Prussia—not to mention a few discrete luncheons with select Members of Parliament. Chuffed with a renewed sense of relevance, Steffith proved a surprisingly capable spokesman. His natural gift of gab stoked interest and deflected skepticism about as well as could be realistically hoped.

Their efforts culminated in a packed presentation in the Painted Hall of the Royal Naval College in Greenwich. Qin and Laferrière had prepared their finest demonstration to date. Eloise trained her voice till it rang like a fanfare, and Steffrith shook hands with admirals who still remembered his departed brother. On a scaffolding hung a model of the Earth as tall as a man, its crust and mantle represented by a delicate lattice of wood that exposed a cannonball core. Flags sporting the Union Jack and the Azure Dragon marked the terminal cities, and a dozen miniature airships encircled the globe.

"The premise is simple," trumpeted Eloise as Qin spoke softly. "Using the electromagnetic lathe, a parabolic tunnel—The Steffrith Tunnel—is formed through solid and molten mineral layers. However, to ensure stability, it must be lined with three-meter thick walls of iron, obtained by redirecting the field effect of the lathe. Put simply, we can drill into the core of the Earth and siphon up iron to reinforce the tunnel."

Qin flipped a switch, and a quiet hum filled the hall. Nothing appeared to happen for half a minute, but soon the crowd gasped as a single stalk of iron sprouted from the cannonball like a blade of grass. It split into separate forks that grew toward the opposing capitals as if by magic.

"With coal-fed, steam-powered electrical generators running continuously in each city," said Laferrière, "the tunnel can be completed within nine months. However, these additional nodes are needed to properly direct the flow of rock and iron." He now indicated the tiny airships. "Our plan involves using high-altitude balloons, encircling the globe with high-powered electromagnetic coils. By synchronizing their influence, it will be possible to redirect the force of the lathe from the central juncture to the core. One notable caveat of this plan is that it requires us—temporarily, and in a series of events lasting only a few hours each—to realign the Earth's magnetic field."

Slowly the realization congealed as career officers grasped the implications.

"But won't navigation compasses fail?"

"Ships at sea will be misdirected."

"The entire navy will be rendered impotent!"

"It's a plot! By agents of the Chinese Empire!"

"They're madmen! They must be stopped!"

Men rose from their seats and jabbed condemning fingers with barely contained hostility. Laferrière began to wonder if they'd be given the courtesy of a firing squad or if an improvised public hanging was inevitable when Lord Steffrith interposed his substantial bulk before the mob.

"Shame!" he bellowed like an enraged elephant. "Shame and dishonor to your offices! Were I a younger man, I would knock you senseless and rip the epaulets from your shoulders. Think, gentlemen. Would an enemy warn you of their strategy? Would acolytes of science serve the war lust of one faction? We live in a world where empires snarl at one another across oceans, and when you are shown a glimmer of something with the power to dispel that distrust, you react with outrage?

For shame, gentlemen. For shame. The world is changing—it must change. Will you cling only to your beloved belligerence? Or will you at least hear of another possibility?"

The room was silent as men sat, wary but contrite. Steffrith turned and drew his niece, Laferrière, and Qin into an intimate huddle.

"Alright, that should buy you a few more minutes," he whispered. "But tread carefully because that bollocks will not work twice, and I have no plans to accompany you to the gallows."

After facing two hours of grueling inquisition, Qin and Laferrière were permitted to slink away to a cloakroom while Steffrith and Eloise remained on display to charm the officers over tea and crumpets.

"I thought they might tar-and-feather us," said Laferrière, pacing as Qin stood and breathed himself into a state of calm. "We've accomplished so much, yet the bar just seems to rise higher. The concept is sound, but now there's capital, construction, permission from the Crown—not to mention that everything we manage in this country we have to replicate in yours! Had I thought this through, *mon ami*, I would have torn up Steffrith's card and never sacrificed myself on the altar of this partnership. Ah well. Nowhere to go now but onward."

"Nay, fly to altars; there, they'll talk you dead. For fools rush in where angels fear to tread."

Laferrière snapped around. "What did you just say?"

"From Pope Alexander, I believe it is," replied Qin.

"You know English?"

"I've learned some. Not all. But enough."

"Why the devil haven't you let on?"

"Have you never found it useful to hear others speak when they believe you don't understand?"

Laferrière nodded. "*Oui.*"

Qin stood and gestured to the main room, back to the lions' den where predators waited to pounce on any weakness.

"Onward," he said.

The tunnel that was to be completed in nine months took two years even to begin. As Qin's English improved, Laferrière missed a time when Qin berated him only through the mitigating voice of Eloise. Despite the diminished need for a translator, she remained a frequent collaborator, and even her silent presence was a great comfort to Laferrière.

The science proved the easy part, a string of failures eliminating false paths until only the true one remained. This was not true of politics or commerce or the fickle court of public opinion. Any obstacle there, once cleared, was likely to reposition itself with seemingly no motive but spite.

When the time came to travel to the Orient on board the surprising comfort of a steamship—with the distance halved by the marvel of the Suez Canal—Laferrière began to wonder if the tunnel might not be obsolete before it was even completed. Overwhelmed by an alien culture, he gained a newfound respect for Qin and profound gratitude for Eloise as they navigated a diplomatic labyrinth of paralyzing unfamiliarity. The hurricane-eye stillness of the court of the Empress Dowager was indeed a world apart from blustery English parliaments. The tone was different, but the intent the same: convince an insular empire to make a staggering investment in a previously unimaginable path to openness.

The process and rationale remained opaque to him, but, in the end, the result was the same, and Chinese engineers and laborers were set to build the massive power generators and induction coils at Tianjin Port. The following year, the Tianjin node was activated at precisely the same instant as its mirror at Port Tilbury-on-the-Thames. Nine months later, the Steffrith Tunnel was a scientific fact. Three months later, the ends sealed and the atmosphere extracted, it was ready for the first journey.

The night before their maiden voyage, Qin and Laferrière stood side by side staring at the pair of capsules, one of which on the morrow would carry them to the other side of the world.

"We never gave them names," said Laferrière. "They look like some kind of animal."

The capsules were each about half the size of a train coach, knotted with bulbous tanks and tubes and a set of swept-back delta fins.

"It resembles a crouching cat," said Qin. "But the stabilizers look like wings. Call it 'The Sphinx.'"

"The docking claws are like talons," replied Laferrière. "But the head is wrong. Those two portals in the front look like big, round eyes. It should be *The Owl*. In my language, we'd say *La Chouette*."

"In my language, 'owl' is 'mao toe ying.' *Māotóuyīng*. It means, 'Cat Head Eagle.'"

"Perfect. And the sister ship can be Min-er-va, the goddess of wisdom with the owl symbol. *Māotóuyīng* and *Minerva*. May they unite the world."

Qin began to sing. "The Owl and the Pussy-cat went to sea, in a beautiful pea-green boat. They took some honey and plenty of money wrapped up in a five-pound note. King Lear said that."

"I believe the fellow who wrote that was called Edward Lear," said Laferrière.

"Really? Well, let's hope that's the only mistake I make today."

At eight a.m. sharp, the *Māotóuyīng* was winched nose down into holding clamps just inside the Steffrith Tunnel. The vacuum hatch behind it slid across the ten-meter-wide mouth until a sequence of deadbolts sealed the door with a *clank* that echoed in absolute blackness. A pair of arc lamps in the face of the craft crackled on, and the inner door irised open, revealing a bottomless pit that fell to an infinitesimal vanishing point. Qin and Laferrière were strapped to a pair of chaise lounges—belted over the shoulders and chest—as they dangled face-first above the porthole windows staring into the abyss.

Laferrière tapped their status out in Morse on a telegraph key linked to the control tower. Together, they began the pre-launch checklists, long committed to memory from endless hours of rehearsal.

When all the sequences were completed, Laferrière signaled the tower:

.-. . . .- -.. -.-- *(Ready)*

And the reply chirped back:

--. --- -.. ... .--. . . . -.. *(Godspeed)*

With a pneumatic hiss, the clamps released, and the *Māotóuyīng* fell.

The sensation of dropping lasted only a moment. Soon, there was no feeling of motion, no landmarks to suggest speed. The crush from the harness was gone, and Laferrière felt only airy suspension. The cabin was silent, save for the ticking of a stopwatch Qin triggered at the instant of release.

"We have been falling for two minutes," said Qin. "Can you calculate velocity?"

Laferrière checked a dial that measured the diminishing field strength from the point of origin, then worked the figure on a slide rule. "We're traveling at nearly 1200 kilometers per hour. The speed of sound."

"Sound swiftly flies through silence in the dark."

"Shakespeare?"

"No. Me."

"Bravo," replied Laferrière. "Can you believe we've actually accomplished this?"

"We haven't yet. Your calculation. Do it again, please."

Laferrière computed a new figure. "Now it's 1,850 K.P.H."

"That's too slow. We need to be at exactly 13,931 at the midpoint. We're behind."

"How can that be?"

"The magnetic stabilizers," said Qin. "They keep us aligned in the center of the tunnel, but they must be creating drag. A tiny amount, but enough. We won't make it to the other side."

"Are you sure?" asked Laferrière

"As sure as I was about King Lear. But we have a new problem. Look." Qin pointed to a bank of thermometers, all at different calibrations and creeping up.

"One of the water pumps failed," said Laferrière. He unbuckled his harness and drifted through the cabin in free-fall weightlessness. "I have to restart it, or the coolant will boil in the pipes!" Laferrière found the prime handle and began pumping furiously.

"I'm going to adjust the stabilizing field," said Qin. "Try to eliminate the drag."

"The pump battery failed. I need to get the redundant unit." As Laferrière opened a storage compartment, the *Māotóuyīng* bucked violently.

"*Fils de pute!* What was that?"

"If I reduce stabilizers, we start to shake. But if I can't increase speed, we won't make it to the other side."

"If I can't get coolant flowing, we'll roast."

The *Māotóuyīng* shuddered as Qin kept the field stabilizers teetering on the edge of control. Laferrière wrestled with connecting the backup battery, the cabin sweltering like a Turkish bath.

"We're at the midpoint," yelled Qin.

"Is our velocity good?"

"*Yěxǔ*," Qin replied. "Maybe."

Laferrière heard the pump start. "It's working," he said, gasping oven-hot air. "I'm going to drive the air circulator... try to reduce the cabin temperature." He found the bellows wheel and cranked with all his strength, forcing the tiniest of breezes from a vent. He kept at it, growing faint until he began to feel the forgotten-familiar pull of gravity.

"We're halfway done ascent," rasped Qin's voice. "You need to strap in."

Exhausted, Laferrière crawled into his chair as if he were summiting the Matterhorn. Qin lay with his eyes half closed.

"One minute left," he said.

Laferrière found his sweaty fingers unable to work the buckles, so he simply hugged the straps to his chest as Qin gave the final countdown.

"Wǔ... Sì... Sān... Èr... Yī."

The *Māotóuyīng* stopped. It hung still for an eternal instant—a juggler's ball at its apex—then fell backward.

"We didn't make it," replied Qin. "Two hundred meters short. Quite close, as a percentage, but…." He spread his hands in resignation.

"What now?"

"Now we fall the other way and swing back and forth like a pendulum until we roast. Or suffocate."

"We won't roast," replied Laferrière. "That pump is fine now. Corroded battery terminal. Can't believe I missed it at inspection."

"Then suffocation it will be," said Quin.

"What about the *Minerva*?" asked Laferrière. "Could it give us a push?"

"We do have matching couplers, like train cars," Qin said. "It could latch on and…." Qin's eyes twitched, seeing a new idea. "Rockets!" he shouted. "Remember we tested mounting rockets on a prototype, exactly to add acceleration if needed."

"Didn't we abandon the idea because subterranean heat would make the rocket explode?"

"Not if ignited before reaching depth."

"We can telegraph London, tell them to attach the test rockets to *Minerva*, then drop it just as we reach our apex. But there's one other thing."

"What?"

"Someone has to pilot *Minerva*. Someone who was with us when we designed it."

Qin's face tightened. "She is like a daughter to me," he said softly.

"If we die," replied Laferrière, "she will be very cross. We can't have that."

Laferrière signaled and began to tap out instructions. Time was critical, but he had to be as precise as possible, sending all necessary details and figures, before finally asking the question:

-.-. --- -- . / . .-.. --- .. ..--.. *(Come Eloise?)*

The reply came:

-.-- . ... (*Yes.*)

They had passed the midpoint again, with only twenty minutes for *Minvera* to be loaded and dropped for any hope of rendezvous. Qin counted each second, continually recalculating speed and distance as Laferrière telegraphed updates. Once more, they reached the apex and hung, each man holding his breath as if to stretch the moment—but, inevitably, *Māotóuyīng* once again fell.

They stared at the ticking second hand. Five. Ten. Fifteen seconds.

"Did it work?" asked Laferrière.

No sooner had the words left his lips than a mighty jolt slammed them, a terrific metal *clang* reverberating through the hull. The echoes had barely died when the telegraph announced:

.- - - .- -.-. .... . -.. (*Attached.*)

And then:

.. --. -. .. - .. --- -. (*Ignition.*)

The push was slight, but they felt it. It lasted only a minute, and then Qin worked out their new velocity.

"It's enough," he said. "In fact… it's too much. We're going to crash into the gate. We need to slow down."

"Can you modify the stabilizers?" asked Laferrière.

"No, we need those to—" Again, his face froze, then thawed. "No, we don't. We have two now! If *Minerva* keeps her stabilizers constant, we can manipulate ours. We have magnetic brakes now!"

Constantly adjusting speed and stability, Qin guided *Māotóuyīng* and *Minerva* toward the Peking gate. When the coupled craft reached the apex, it hung in space for an instant—then went *clang* as the front clamps locked into the overhead dock.

60

After a hero's welcome by the Peking crew, complete with a speech from the Empress Dowager's personal attaché, Qin, Laferrière, and Eloise were permitted to change and retire to a private repast. They sat together, sharing roasted duck and a pot of tea—items Qin swore the English never got right, despite ceaseless effort.

"You can have them imported now," said Laferrière. "The planet just got smaller."

"Thanks to the two of you," said Eloise.

"You helped immeasurably."

"I'd like to hope my assistance can be measured," she said. "And merit a footnote or two when the history of this new shrunken world is written."

"O brave new world that has such people in it!" said Qin. "I'm sure that's King Lear."

"Close. Shakespeare, but from *The Tempest*."

"*Wángbā dàn.* I need to read more English things."

Eloise leaned forward. "Oh no."

"What?" asked Laferrière.

"I was reading a book I wanted to finish. I left it in London."

"No problem," said Qin. "We'll pop back after dinner and pick it up."

AUTHOR BIO

Matt McHugh was born in suburban Pennsylvania, attended LaSalle University in Philadelphia, and after a few years as a Manhattanite, currently calls New Jersey home.

To learn more, visit Matt online at MattMchugh.com.

RUMPELSTILTSTEAM

JOHN KISTE

We whirled across the wild spaces of the vast ballroom, spinning like the gears and pinions that danced on innumerable costumes—gears and pinions that had no more true purpose than our waltz. But Danya had agreed to pirouette with me, and that was enough. Her white silk hair leaped behind us, flowing madly from beneath her periwinkle top hat.

I held her impossibly thin waist, made thinner still by her tight violet corset, and spun her like a luscious lavender teetotum atop the shimmering wood tiles. Everyone, man and woman and child, paused in their gambols to watch her exquisite movements. Everyone was infatuated with her mysterious perfection. I alone was not infatuated; I was deeply in love.

At length, Danya pulled me aside to a refreshment table, and the void we made was filled by applauding couples. I offered her raspberry punch in a pewter dip mug and finally pulled my eyes from her purpled lips to survey the great hall. Its unbroken ceiling of steel beams and grilled skylights was supported by massive buttresses on the edges of the wide expanse of open floor. Enormous tables covered with food, beverages, and a myriad of desserts alternated with giant cushioned Victorian chairs, loveseats, and fainting couches along the outskirts of the polished wooden tiles.

All the partygoers and the accouterments of pleasure shimmered in the glow of brass gas lanterns and candelabra within. Above the skylights, dozens of oddly shaped blimps and balloons and cigar-like dirigibles wafted in waiting areas beneath a decidedly lackluster evening sky. Thick clouds crowded into view from the visible horizons, and as I watched, great drops of rain began slapping the stained-glass panes of the fanlights. A peal of thunder startled the musicians, and a violin squeaked in disharmony. The dancers paused, and some of them laughed, but the gaiety of the ball had dissipated in an instant.

Danya touched my arm, and she breathed mint breath into my ear in a tinkling sigh. "That will do it. Everyone will go now. Will you see me to my ship before the mad rush?" I bowed, and we swallowed our punch and decamped.

Far above the ballroom, I watched through the skylights as the party broke up casually beneath us, multicolored players in vests, derbies, bustles, and petticoats gathered velvet coats and leather handbags (and sadly useless parasols) and streamed noisily through the exits.

I held Danya's white-gloved fingers as she buzzed her flying machine to the embarkation dock. The doors slid open, and her chauffeur stood across the two-inch gap, extending a hand from the interior of her lush vessel. The seats and walls of her ride were rich red satin and velvet, but the running lights were dim, and details were unfathomable due to the blackness of the now raging storm.

A bolt of lightning momentarily lit the splendor of the ship as I passed Danya to the goggled and tuxedoed driver, whose nameplate read Fritzweller. Instead of taking that last opportunity to bask in her wonder, I could not help focusing on the gold pocket watch embedded in that chauffeur's black top hat. The thing actually had the correct time. This should not have given me the silly jolt it did. Danya was rich as Croesus; of course, her driver would have the right time.

Still, I had seen watches, clocks, and timepieces used a thousand ways in the outfits and decor of my fellow lovers and cynics, but never had I seen one working properly. Before I had processed this bit of minutiae, Danya had smiled pleasantly and the doors had closed. Other revelers were filling the air dock behind me, so there was nothing for it but to pick my way back to the ground floor and walk home in the icy rain.

I was sick for three days and kept in bed by my landlady, Madame Chrystian. The fine old gal attended to my needs as my mother would never have, but she had stern words for me when I spoke of Danya in my delirium.

"That succubus will be the end of a sweet young simpleton like you. What does she get from you? Don't answer that, you little shite. She a richie; the laddies spin in her orbit like drunken planets. Get yourself a cute bespectacled file clerk, Tobin. D'ya hear?"

I lay miserably amongst the books and papers of my tiny loft. I suffered fever dreams of Danya's violet eyes under heavy smoky lids, of her pouting purple-outlined lips, of her knee-length snow-white hair, and her elfin figure. Always as I turned in my narrow bed, her lithe arms painted in long white gloves reached toward me, but I failed with each try to grasp her tiny hands.

On the third morning, I awoke in a sweat to find Madame

Chrystian holding the oversized receiver of the phone before my eyes. Her stare commingled duty and disgust. I put it to my ear and grunted.

"Tobin, is that you?" It was Danya, speaking breathlessly. "May I see you at once? Please do not refuse me." Stunned, I assured her I would dress and catch a steamcab to her townhouse immediately. "No," she replied, "I am at the country manor. Fritzweller, my chauffeur, will be docking my airship at your roof in ten minutes. Please do not fail me!"

With a finality of urgency, the receiver clicked. I had no idea she even knew where my apartment was. We had only met three times. I did not move as my landlady retreated to the hall. Then I yelled, "Hot water!" and sprang from the covers.

My climb to the roof had been especially perilous for my best suit. All apartment buildings in the city had mooring masts, of course, but our own had not been used in a decade, and the steps to the top were both rickety and filthy.

There was also the matter of dear Madame Chrystian tugging at my cravat and watch fob, begging me not to go. She went so far as to promise me a whole haggis for supper. I shook her off and assured her I would be perfectly fine.

True to her word, Danya's sleek aerostat awaited, and the same pilot with the same tux, goggles, and top hat ushered me aboard. "Strap in," he said matter-of-factly. "It's a good hour to Darwest Manor, even at top speed."

I settled into the velvet lining and, excited though I was, promptly fell asleep. The few times I stirred, it was merely to comment that this was undoubtedly the fleetest dirigible I had ever ridden—the great spires of the city disappeared in seconds, and the trees shifted beneath us like a sheet of kelly baize.

All at once, the gloved hand of my guide touched my shoulder and pointed ahead and below. I had read articles of Darwest Estate and had seen old woodcuts of the grounds, but they had ill-prepared me for its magnificence. I counted four spires, three turrets, and seven dark stone towers, and the walls appeared to stretch for a quarter mile on each side. The forests and the ponds led onto an immaculate lawn, where several dawn age automobiles were parked, both the steam and gasoline-powered hybrid kind.

We sailed beyond them and moored at one of the towers. Before departing, I asked the pilot/chauffeur about that gold timepiece in his hat. "I have seen a thousand watches incorporated into costumes in what our ancestors termed steampunk. Sadly, in this generation, none of them ever work. Even our clocks and pocket watches are rarely accurate. I once saw footage of the Queen wearing her crown with its bejeweled gold timepiece—surprisingly, it sported only a minute hand. But I believe yours is correct."

He smiled wryly and answered in a voice fraught with bygone wisdom that belied his thirty or so years. "We have lost the ways of the artisan, sir. Now the people know frivolity and selfishness and little else. We have long since forsworn the craftsmanship to properly maintain a rapid vessel or rebuild the workings of a chronometer. Yes, my watch is accurate. I keep it so. It would not please Lady Darwest if it were otherwise."

Clearly, he meant Danya. I nodded my understanding. The airship doors opened directly onto a steep circular stone staircase. I thanked the chauffeur, looked around for a lift that was not there, and descended two hundred steps.

Danya awaited me in the Great Hall, a room that climbed to heights on which the nearsighted, like myself, could never focus without goggles. I adjusted mine. She wore a leather and silk hunting outfit, tall jack boots, and a necklace of cogs and pearls. Her hair fanned out behind as she ran wildly into my arms. "I knew you would come, dear Tobin. I knew. Only you can help me now."

I hugged her tightly, for my benefit, and then tried mightily to calm her, for hers. "I pray that I may help, Danya. What can I do? What is it?"

She recovered herself and began leading me toward huge walnut double doors, which opened at a touch. "My parents are waiting to meet you. Come."

I felt a lump rising in my throat. Meet her parents? Yes, I had bathed thoroughly and donned my best suit. And I was no troll. Neither was I a prize to one of Danya Darwest's standing. And as I mentioned, we had met three times, and none of them could be considered true dates, though I had tumbled for her at the very first—a brief chat in an uptown cafe. The ball had been glorious to me, but we had met there by accident. I had no illusions. If I was meeting her parents, something was wrong.

Her mother and father were in full regalia; he wore a military type of getup with ribbons and burst watches (none of them worked), and a bright red bowler; she was decked in brown corset and white petticoats, and somehow her figure made the ensemble work. They sat on chairs that seemed a little less than thrones. A dozen young men of various social strata stood along the vast marble room walls, unmoving and staring at the floor. Before either Danya or I could speak, her mother said, "My daughter tells me you solve puzzles."

I looked at Danya and then back to her mother. "I *design* puzzles. Crosswords, cryptograms, mazes for the rich, escape rooms for entrepreneurs. Yes, I told Danya that."

"Well," her mother replied, "if you can create them, you can solve

68

them. Name your price."

"He doesn't know," said Danya. "I haven't told him of our nightmare."

Her father rose. He was a tall and burly man. Clearly, he was a man used to getting what he desired.

"We haven't much time, young man. Let me explain. Twenty-five years ago, I was an apprentice silversmith with no prospects and little hope. I had once held ideas, but my superiors had dashed them from me. One evening as I walked along the river and considered throwing myself in, a demon creature appeared and offered to sell me a mirror."

"What?" I gasped.

"Please, young man. I do not know what he was. I could not see clearly if he was a troll, a tiny ogre, or an imp. He caused my eyes to blur as if he wished concealed, but he had a cart he dragged behind him, and it contained a silver mirror. He told me if I purchased it from him, I would become wealthy beyond my dreams of avarice and powerful enough to set the paths of other men for good or ill. All I would have to do would be to gaze into it and imagine my desires. I asked him to name his price, and he answered curiously. He said he would claim my first-born daughter on her twenty-first birthday—claim her as his own.

I thought the whole charade was inane but was certain I could get a fine price for the silver. I doubted anyone would ever marry a man as destitute as I, so I saw no possible offspring. I made the deal. The little creature blew some dust, passed the mirror into my hands, and disappeared. I just remember feeling very dizzy."

"You were simply duped—as a young man by a charlatan," I said. "There is no magic, sir. Besides, I read you made your fortune in the manufacture of sailing ships, aerostats, and steamcabs."

He held up a hand imperiously. "I took the mirror to my hovel and stared into it for days. And the idea for the Darwest air brake came to me. It just came to me. You are aware it was an invention that could not be ignored."

"I knew it was the beginning of your empire, sir."

"It was. The next staring match I had with the mirror gave me the formula for helium conservation. I was a billionaire in two years. The year after that, I looked deep into the reflection while reflecting on my loneliness. The next day," he touched his wife, "I met Greta outside my lab. My life was wonderful. I had built an empire. I created factories and labs, and I gave work to thousands. I even hired my servants from the children of my hometown to show that I cared about the poor there. I told my love of my secret treasure. I needed it no longer, and I locked it away, forgotten, like Dorian's portrait. But I ignored the cost that was not yet paid. We had a daughter. She is our world...."

He trailed off. Danya touched my sleeve. "I am twenty-one tomorrow."

Her mother began sobbing and buried her head in her husband's breast. He stroked her hair—hair that was the color of her daughter's.

"Three nights ago, I woke in my study to find the demon, much larger now, wavering in front of me. He was different somehow, but I knew it was him through the blur. He told me he had come to collect his due. I argued with him, but he blew smoke at me and told me I had three days and to look to the mirror. Then he was gone, and I ran to the secluded room. The silver on the frame was horribly rusted and tarnished because of the small copper content, and the glass had clouded over. He appeared again the following night, just for a second, and directed me again to my cursed treasure." Then he addressed me. "Come see it now, young man."

70

Danya and her distraught parents led me to a hallway and entered a cheerless and dismal room. The great mirror on the far wall was not only clouded, long cracks ran its length.

As we stood looking at it, a hushed voice came from nowhere and whispered, "One day remains!" and the pieces of the mirror shattered and fell to the floor. Danya screamed and ran from the room, her parents on her heels. I walked to the wall and picked up a sliver of glass.

When I rejoined the heartbroken family sometime later in the vast marble hall, I asked about the dozen young men lining the walls. They did not look like servants.

"You are most observant." Mr. Darwest nodded to a velvet chair. "So, to the reason you are here. All my riches cannot stop a thing with such power. I admitted that to him. And the demon took pity on my tears when he first came again three nights ago. He agreed to drop his claim against Danya if she could simply say his name when he comes tomorrow to take her from us. She must *speak* his name. I have promised these young men great riches if they could learn the title of this devil. They have been scouring the countryside for three days. Still, others have yet to return. We have received nothing of promise."

Danya held my arm and said, "I learned all this when I returned home after leaving you at the ball. I thought I had gone mad. But you saw the mirror. And now we have heard the voice. I believe my father. And I remembered you had told me of the things you could do: the puzzles and their solutions. I have no desire to be wed to a demon. My father offered these men riches and power. I am willing to offer you more."

My heart skipped a beat—or two. "You would marry me?"

She smiled slightly; she was magnificent. "My parents have agreed. They are not elitists—my father worked for his place—and they have always sworn I could marry the man I wished, class be damned. You are our last hope. I am very fond of you, Tobin. I think you love me."

I mulled this over for a long time, to the surprise of all, including myself. Finally, I took Danya to one side. "You turn twenty-one at midnight?" She nodded. "Then you are safe till then. It is almost seven. I will agree to put forth all my talents to save you on one condition. Come dancing in the city."

She was startled. Her parents, who had overheard, were stunned. Her father protested loudly, and for a moment, I thought he was going to arouse the dozen others to attack me. But suddenly, Danya stepped across and laid her gloved finger on his lips. She turned to me. "I will alert my chauffeur."

A half-hour later, we were making our way back to civilization. The sky was a mix of pink and orange as the sun flirted with the treetops. The chauffeur handled the controls with a finesse I had never seen. I watched the timepiece in his hat tick over 7:25. Danya and I settled into the plush seats. "Where are you going, Miss?" he asked casually.

"Anachrons at Mayfair, thank you." She leaned toward me. "Is there really a plan, or are you taking advantage of me? I know I have used people; those of my ilk always seem to. I never really meant to lead you on, Tobin. Forgive me."

"It's okay." I patted her hand. "I was born to be led on by someone like you. And you are so beautiful. Our generation has forgotten everything but self-gratification." I winked at the pilot; he smiled sadly.

She frowned. "But I will marry you. I promised."

I grinned. "I suppose it beats marrying a demon."

"That's not fair, Tobin." A tear fell from her perfect violet eye.

"Forgive me. My mind is elsewhere." I touched her shaking, slender fingers. "You know, your father was quite a genius in his day, dear

72

Danya. He invented so many wonderful things—all by himself. From his own mind—his own ideas. I am fairly amazed that he also believes in demons."

She sat up. "He saw one. You and I heard his story."

"Of course, our apothecaries can stir up all kinds of powders that a young boy could blow in a man's face, confusing his mind and blurring his eyes. That young man could do the same thing again twenty-five years later to claim his due, long after your father had made him a member of the household from his hometown. But I don't think for a moment he would really try to collect. Not against your will. He's too decent—and methodical for that. Still, he should know, I found his acid etched on the mirror and his microphone hidden in the wainscoting. It's just—I fell in love with you in a week. Imagine how he feels, knowing you your whole life. Think about that."

The airship stopped, and the door opened. Danya looked out, and her purple mouth dropped open when she saw my roof. "Happy Birthday, Danya. When he comes to claim you, you can always refuse. Just whisper, 'Fritzweller.' But think it through first. Think it through very carefully. As for me, Madame Chrystian has a haggis waiting!"

AUTHOR BIO

John Kiste is a horror writer who was previously the president of the Stark County Visitors' Bureau. He is a double-lung transplantee and organ donation ambassador, a McKinley Museum planetarian, and an Edgar Allan Poe impersonator who has been published in Flame Tree Press's Terrifying Ghosts, Third Flatiron, With Painted Words, A Shadow of Autumn, Modern Grimoire, Dark Fire Fiction, Six Guns Straight from Hell 3, Theme of Absence, and The Dark Sire anthologies, as well as Jolly Horror Press's Coffin Blossoms anthology, Unnerving Press's Haunted are These Houses anthology, and Camden Press's Quoth the Raven anthology. He recently won The Dark Sire Award for Best Fiction. You can find him at JohnKiste.wordpress.com.

A TINKER'S DEVIL

VALERIE HUNTER

S tella was the finest medium in the Territories, which probably didn't mean much in the grand scheme of the world, but it paid the bills. She'd built up her clientele to the wealthiest people in Malvern City, and one or another of them had a séance party at least once a fortnight. Between these and the private sessions she held every day but Sunday, she had enough money to live at the Newington Hotel, with plenty more squirreled away in the bank.

None of that would matter, of course, if she became a ghost herself, but she preferred not to dwell on that.

Lately, she'd let her clients come to her to save herself needless exertion. But the lure of the Spiritualists Society's prize money seemed worth the exertion. The competition had been touted all over the Territory. There were two categories—human mediums and spirit-reading machines— and anyone could enter, but only five contestants were chosen on each side for complete analysis: a séance for the committee and two private sessions with different committee members.

Of course, Stella made the short list. She'd expected something official and clinical, but when she arrived, the room was set up like any client looking for a séance, as though Stella needed candlelight and shadows to contact a ghost. Up until then, she'd been planning to play it straight, repeat exactly what the spirits said in a way she rarely did with her usual clients, but she could see now that these so-called experts were no different than her clients. They wanted a show, just like anyone else.

So, she gave them one.

The winner of each side had been invited back today, first for another private reading, and then for a demonstration to the public where Stella was able to observe her competition for the first time.

He was a slight young man with nondescript features, all except his large, doleful eyes. He kept his spirit machine under a blanket while Stella performed first, seeking out the saddest ghost she could find and spinning out his tale of lost love until his sweetheart had to leave the auditorium in hysterics. After that, she did rapid-fire readings, snippets of a dozen different ghosts, imitating their voices, mentioning whatever names they gave her, tweaking their messages for maximum impact.

When she sat down to thunderous applause that drowned out all the ghosts' complaints of her inaccuracies, she smiled like she wasn't exhausted and felt confident in her forthcoming victory.

The young man—he was introduced as Ben Wilshire—got up and revealed his contraption, a simple-looking box with porthole windows on each side and a crank handle. Ben put a lot of muscle into cranking that handle, to the point where Stella felt breathless just watching him. A crackle of sparks could be seen through the portholes, and then a strange hum emanated, a supernatural voice that rose and fell eerily without any discernible words.

It turned out, though, that Ben was also the translator. He talked over the hum in a clear, emotionless voice, and the words spilling from his mouth were verbatim what the loudest ghost in the auditorium was saying. For the first time, Stella believed she might lose.

Of course, no one else could judge the exact accuracy of the ghostly interactions, but Ben's flat recitation, his complete lack of showmanship, gave him credibility. And the machine itself provided a compelling show, all that otherworldly warbling. It was impressive, no doubt.

When he finished, they were both made to wait in a back room while the judges conferred. Stella didn't want to be friendly, but the box was so fascinating that she couldn't help but ask, "How does it work?"

"It filters souls," Ben said in that same flat voice, as though the box wasn't wondrous at all. "Translates their voices to a wavelength anyone can hear."

That didn't tell her much of anything, but then she'd never pretended to understand mechanical things. Still, she enquired, "But how can you make sense of what you hear? I couldn't understand any of it."

He shrugged. "Practice. My master says I have a knack for languages."

She startled and looked at him more closely. An indenture? But why would an indenture be the one to show off such an innovative machine? No, never mind. It was none of her concern.

They were called back to the stage—her, the indenture, and the marvelous machine—and Stella braced herself for bad news and then tried to pretend she never had a doubt when her name was called as the winner. She smiled, ignoring the howls of every ghost in the room proclaiming her a fraud.

77

On her way out of the building, a reporter stopped Stella and asked for an interview. Stella recognized her—Anna Dubrovsky. She'd come for a private session last year, the ghost with her—a young girl—had wanted to tell Miss Dobrovsky her poetry was terrible. Instead, Stella turned it into a loving tribute because surely a client never wanted to hear something cruel. Afterward, Miss Dobrovsky wrote a scathing article, insisting Stella was worse than a fraud. Stella had been horrified, but no one seemed to pay it any heed. Still, it pleased her to refuse Miss Dobrovsky now and head on her way.

She took a carriage back to Newington; it was only a few blocks, but she was too tired to walk. Lynnie looked at her expectantly as she came in. "Well?"

"You could've just come, you know. Seen for yourself." Stella wanted nothing more than to collapse into the armchair, but she changed first, putting on a dressing gown and washing her face. She knew most people thought only fast girls wore paint, but most people found bluish lips and a ghostly pallor alarming, too, so Stella did what she must. A light enough hand and no one could tell she was wearing lipstick and rouge, or that she was on death's doorstep.

"You know I don't like it," Lynnie said, all but shuddering. "But of course, you won."

"Why, of course?" Stella asked, finally sinking into the chair.

"Because you're the darling of the city, and everyone in the Territories distrusts anything mechanical."

"Indeed." She pretended not to notice that Lynnie had said nothing of talent. What did it matter, anyhow? All that mattered was the prize money and the opportunity it could afford.

"And your competitor?" Lynnie asked.

"What of him?"

"Mightn't it have been better to let him win? He'd be more inclined to help you then."

"What kind of help would I need from him?"

"He's a mechanic, isn't he? Surely he has mechanic friends in other fields."

"That seems a long shot." Stella paused. "But if you think that's such a splendid plan, why didn't you mention it before I won?"

Lynnie shrugged. "You wouldn't have listened, anyhow." She disappeared, leaving Stella to contemplate her predicament for the thousandth time.

When the Automatons Act of 1887 was signed into law, there were all sorts of pieces written in the paper. Some lauded it as a beautiful compromise and a kindness towards those mechanical unfortunates whose rights were now protected. Others were outraged that tinkers' devils could be allowed to run around like anyone else, with no requirements to reveal what they were to employers, landlords, or constables.

Nobody called it the death sentence that it was, though. Stella read all the newspapers, but perhaps the reporters never stopped to consider or just didn't care. A few probably realized firsthand how terrible it was but didn't want to risk outing themselves by bringing it up.

Because if you were a tinker's devil, a mech monster, a cog body—any of the derogatory names that had cropped up since the news broke that doctors and mechanics joined forces during the war and successfully replaced various human organs with mechanical parts—you wanted to *stay* hidden. There were witch hunts for several years, till it got to the point that even those with mechanized limbs, prostheses that had been around for decades, stopped wearing them for fear of being mistaken for something else.

The truth was, most mechs weren't readily apparent. Wind-up keys and crank handles could easily be hidden underneath clothing. And few people realized not all mechs were war veterans. The bio-mechanics had honed their skills on anyone they could get their hands on both during and after the war, setting up laboratories at orphanages, workhouses, and prisons throughout the west. And while it might seem like a good thing that the new laws stopped these bio-mechanics from performing such operations, it also prevented them from caring for the thousands of former patients who needed maintenance to continue living.

Stella was good at keeping quiet about what she was, but she didn't plan on dying quietly. She knew a valve pump generally lasted twelve years, and hers was on year fourteen. She also knew there must be bio-mechanics who would still do the work for a price, and with her winnings today, she felt confident she had that price covered. Now she just needed to find a willing bio-mechanic.

Stella was exhausted the following day. After several failed attempts to get up by a quarter to eleven, she decided that the premier medium in the Territories deserved a day in bed.

She had no sooner turned back over when she heard knocking. She groaned and buried her head in the pillows. Whoever it was would just have to be disappointed.

Lynnie appeared. "It's a boy."

"I don't care," Stella mumbled into the pillow.

"He looks quite anxious."

"Well, I feel quite tired."

"It's the boy from yesterday. The one with the ghost-reading machine."

Now Stella raised her head. "I thought you didn't come."

Lynnie looked away. "I just went for a little. To see what he could do." She paused. "I found him rather impressive."

Stella let her head drop back on the pillow. She was tempted to tell Lynnie that she should entertain him, but that seemed overly cruel.

"I think you should see what he wants," Lynnie said.

"He's probably already left," Stella said, just as they heard another knock.

Sighing, she got up and threw on her dressing gown, then tied back her hair and put on a bit of rouge despite Lynnie telling her to hurry.

She opened the door to see Ben retreating down the hallway. He turned, eyes widening at the sight of her dressing gown. "Miss Abbott. I...that is, Dr. Egerton..."

The hallway was no place to stand around, waiting for him to stutter out his message. "Come in," Stella said, retreating to the sofa without bothering to see if he followed.

By the time she sat down, he was hovering in the doorway, still looking anxious. "Shut the door," she said. "Have a seat. I don't bite."

Beside her, Lynnie snorted.

Ben did as he was told, though judging by his perch on the edge of the chair, he was ready to jump up at any moment. "Dr. Egerton would like you to pay him a visit tomorrow," he said.

"That's your master?"

He nodded.

"What does he want with me?"

"To congratulate you on your victory."

81

"He could've just sent a note," she muttered, then tried to be more polite. "I'm afraid I'm rather indisposed at the moment. Such a big display takes a lot out of me. Please send your boss my regrets and say perhaps another time."

"You should meet with him," Lynnie hissed. "See if he knows anyone who could help you. Or at least ask Ben. And offer him some refreshments. You're a terrible hostess."

Stella rolled her eyes but asked, "Shall I ring for tea?"

"No…no…" Stella waited for him to take his leave, but he continued to sit there, eyes on his lap.

"Ask him," Lynnie hissed.

"She doesn't listen. Might as well come to terms with that," Ben said, looking directly at Lynnie.

Stella stared at him, the truth dawning on her in stages. "That box wasn't doing anything at all. You're a medium, same as me."

He just sat there, but he'd already confirmed it, hadn't he? Lynnie stared at him, open-mouthed.

"My goodness, and I thought I was the one with guile," Stella said because it was easier to talk than think. "You had us all hoodwinked."

"Except I was supposed to win. And I didn't."

"A little more practice is all you need. You have to learn to tell people what they want to hear."

"Even if it's a lie?"

"Sometimes people want to be lied to."

He looked at her like she was plumb crazy.

"What's your Dr. Egerton playing at, anyhow? Is he truly a mechanic?"

"He is."

"So why the ruse? Why not build a working machine, or stay out

82

of such things altogether?"

Ben seemed to shrink into himself, as though realizing he'd led her to the wrong question.

Well? she wanted to demand. She was used to ghosts, always so eager to blab everything, always so excited to be heard. Sometimes it was hard to remember that flesh-and-blood humans were different.

Trust. That was what she had to build. "Never mind. I was wondering if you might be able to help me, though," she said.

Ben's shoulders relaxed a smidge, and Lynnie lifted her eyes skyward as if to say, *Finally.*

"I was hoping you—or Dr. Egerton— might know of a bio-mechanic."

Ben tensed again. "What do you need with a bio-mechanic?"

She hesitated, then said, "My sister. She had a pump valve installed before the new legislature, but now it's failing. She needs fixing."

Ben regarded her with a rather penetrating stare. Stella stared right back. "Well? Do you know of anyone?"

"And if I did? Why trust me?"

It seemed an odd question. "Should I not trust you?"

"Why did your sister get a pump valve?"

"Because she had a weak heart, why else?"

Ben exhaled forcefully. "And who did it? Do you know the name of the doctor?"

"No. I was just a child myself. We were at a foundlings' home."

"You have to be careful. You don't just need to find a bio-mechanic. You need to find a *trustworthy* bio-mechanic." He said this like it was some grand pronouncement.

"Are there many untrustworthy ones?" she asked.

He nodded emphatically.

"Untrustworthy, how?"

But Ben was on his feet now. "Never mind…I'll ask around for you, shall I? See if I can find…."

How was this bumbler ever going to find anything? No, it was up to her. "Don't go yet," she said, giving him a charming smile she reserved for clients. "I'll write my regrets to Dr. Egerton, so you don't have to convey them yourself."

He looked relieved. Stella went to the desk and wrote a note requesting that the doctor call on her tomorrow afternoon. If Ben knew something about bio-mechanics, surely his master knew more.

Stella didn't tell Lynnie what she'd done until the next day, as she awaited Dr. Egerton's arrival.

"Are you sure that's wise?" Lynnie said.

"You're the one who wanted me to meet with him."

"That was before I saw how terrified Ben seems of him."

"He never said that."

"He didn't have to! Every time he mentioned him, he seemed to shrink in on himself."

Stella flicked a dismissive hand. "That boy was scared of his own shadow. I don't trust him or his cryptic warnings."

"But—"

Whatever Lynnie was going to stay was cut off by a knock at the door. Stella let in Dr. Egerton, a thin man with bright blue eyes who accepted her offer of tea. He congratulated her on her victory, and they made polite small talk. She tried to get him to talk about his work, but he was vague on his mechanical background, so she finally asked outright,

84

"Might you know any bio-mechanics?"

His expression was impassive. "No such thing as bio-mechanics anymore. The law has seen to that."

She gave what she hoped was her most winsome smile. "But I'm not the law."

"I have no way of knowing that. It's a dangerous thing, admitting to being a bio-mechanic."

She tried to hide her shock at his phrasing. Admitting to *being*, not admitting to *knowing*. Well, then. "Yes," she agreed. "About as dangerous as admitting to *being* a tinker's devil."

He looked at her shrewdly now, as though she had his full attention. "Show me," he said finally.

"Excuse me?"

"If you want my help—and mind you, I'm not saying I can give it— then show me whatever part of you in need of repair."

"It's my heart. A valve pump."

"Show me," he repeated.

"Don't," Lyddie gasped.

Stella ignored her, unbuttoning her shirtwaist. She took off her shirt and then her chemise, bracing herself for his gaze. But he had eyes only for the metal key, as though her flesh—her womanhood—didn't matter at all.

"Fine workmanship," he murmured. "You want an upgrade?"

"I *need* an upgrade," she corrected. "My heart is failing."

"And can you pay?"

She nodded. "I have my winnings from—"

"No," he cut her off. "I'll need more than that."

She bit her lip and waited for him to quote a price, willing it to be within the realm of her savings.

"I need *you*, Miss Abbot," he said with a wolfish smile. "I'd like you to take over the helm of my spirit machine."

"Me?"

"You know everything about reading ghosts."

She decided not to let on that she knew Ben was a medium. "But surely you don't need such subterfuge. Your assistant did a most impressive job."

"Yet he still lost to you and your superior showmanship."

"But I'm famous in Malvern City. People will realize...."

"So, we'll go to a different city. Dye your hair, pad your cheeks. It's easy enough to make someone unrecognizable. Will you agree? My services for yours?"

"Don't," Lynnie said sharply.

"How long would you like my services for?"

"A year should do. Shall I draw up a contract?"

It sounded fair enough. Stella didn't like or entirely trust him, but she needed his skills more than he needed hers. "Certainly," she said and redressed herself.

After the doctor left, Stella felt stronger than she had in months, as though just the promise of help was a balm to her heart.

"How could you agree to this?" Lynnie demanded.

"How could I not? He can fix my heart."

"But Ben's warning—"

"Oh, Ben...He was sore that I beat him and didn't want to help me."

"Or he knows full well that his boss is nefarious and tried to warn you off."

"Then he should have warned me outright. He could have just

said, 'Don't trust Dr. Egerton.' He didn't. Besides, the doctor needs me. He's hardly going to do anything awful to me when I'm the one who can bring him fame for his machine."

"Why does a bio-mechanic care about ghosts, anyhow?"

Stella ignored her because what did it matter? Everyone had their eccentricities, after all.

Her eccentricity was Lynnie. She'd been with Stella since the foundlings' home, like an older sister of sorts. Though lately, Stella had felt like the eldest, the one who always had to take care of everything. Perhaps Lynnie had forgotten just how hard a person would fight to stay alive, the lengths they'd go. Perhaps there was no explaining to a ghost.

The knock at the door the next morning came before Stella had even finished breakfast. It was Ben, his eyes wild with fury. "You've entered into a contract with him?"

"What business is it of yours?" she asked. She was tempted to slam the door in his face, but she couldn't have him making a scene in the hallway, possibly revealing what she was, so she moved aside.

He paced the sitting room. "Why would you...I tried to tell you...."

"You didn't tell me anything specifically. You never said not to trust Dr. Egerton."

Ben just looked at her with those wild eyes. Not fury, she realized. Something else.

Desperation.

"What's so terrible about him?" she asked outright.

Ben looked away, worrying the cuff of his sleeve between his fingers. "He cares more about the science than the person. We're just bodies for him to tinker with."

Stella waved impatiently. "Yes, yes. I know all about the experimentation during the war. Terrible, of course, but it allowed the bio-mechanics to perfect their techniques, and—"

"We," Lynnie interrupted.

"What?" Stella asked, though her eyes were on Ben. His face had gone red.

"He said, '*We're* just bodies for them to tinker with.' He's like you, Stell."

"Are you?" she asked Ben, but all she could think was she should have picked up on that *we* herself.

Ben turned his back to her. For a moment, she thought he was going to walk out, but he didn't, and then she realized he was unbuttoning his shirt.

He pulled it off, and she looked at the patchwork of his back. Thick scars on either side of his spine. Strange bulges in his flesh. A right arm that was entirely metal from shoulder to elbow, skin folded over in seams.

He turned to face her again, and she could see the familiar crank in his left breast, but there were others, too, including a metal panel in his stomach with a switch where his navel should be and a particularly scarred area on the right side of his chest with another, larger crank handle.

"I'll let you decide if I'm like you," he said quietly.

She could feel herself gawping and made an effort to purse her lips together, though they soon parted again as she stammered, "Did...how can...was...."

She swallowed and tried again. "Did Egerton do all that?"

"He did."

She kept staring.

"Ask me why," he said.

"Why?" she parroted.

"Because he could." Ben put his shirt back on, buttoned it up until everything was hidden, then looked her full in the eyes. "To sign a contract with him...."

"I haven't indentured myself," she said, keeping herself from adding, *I'm not that stupid.* "It's only a year. A specific job."

Ben shook his head. "It doesn't matter. Once he has you, he can do whatever he likes. Your life is in his hands."

"How much longer is your contract, anyhow?"

"Five years."

She looked at him with surprise. An indenture contract was always fifteen years, and he didn't look more than twenty.

"Your parents signed the contract," Lynnie said. Always so quick on the uptake.

Ben nodded. "Too many children. They were going to indenture my oldest brother—he was thirteen then and big for his age, sure to bring a good price as a hired boy—but Dr. Egerton asked for me instead. My parents couldn't believe their luck. Someone willing to pay top dollar for their scrawny nine-year-old."

"You needed a valve?" Stella asked.

He shrugged. "He said I did. Said he was saving my life. I idolized him that first year. But after the next surgery, and the next... I'm just his toy, Miss Abbott, and now I'm all used up. He's looking forward to a new plaything."

"You," Lynnie said to Stella, as though she was too stupid to realize.

Stella said nothing. What was there to say?

Of course, she was horrified by Ben, by the sight of all his modifications. He was more machine than man now, forced to rely on Egerton for his upkeep and maintenance.

Still, he was living.

This last thought came unbidden, but it couldn't be batted away. Which was worse, a life of metal parts or death that could be avoided?

Farther back niggled the thought that the first operation might not have been necessary for both Ben and herself. That they had no way of knowing. But there was no sense in *what-ifs*. She needed Egerton's skills, and so, she would sign his contract.

"What's a bio-mechanic wasting his time on ghost amplifiers for anyhow?" she asked because she couldn't voice any of the rest of it.

"Could you always see ghosts?"

"Yes."

"When did you get your upgrade?"

It took her a moment to realize he meant the pump. "I was five."

"And are you certain that you could see ghosts before that?"

She tried to think back, but her early childhood was hazy, slippery. "You're saying they're related?"

"They were for me. There's a moment during the operation when you cross to the other side. Dead. And then you're pulled back again. Maybe something else came with us." He shrugged. "Anyhow, Egerton's trying to prove a point. He doesn't care about the ghosts, but it's as good a way as any to draw attention."

"Attention to what?"

"If I had won, he meant to reveal what I was to the Spiritualists and the reporters. That instead of building a box that could talk to ghosts, someone had built a person."

"He'd be arrested!"

90

"He wasn't going to take the credit. He had a whole story ready to spin, that I was a war orphan and some talented bio-mechanic had saved my life after a grievous accident, but that my parts would break down soon unless the laws were changed."

Would it have worked? Stella tried to imagine the article that might be in the newspaper right now if Ben had won, how much she would have enjoyed reading it.

"So, he'll do it with me instead," she said.

Ben nodded.

She tried to imagine that, too. She'd be a martyr, a human face to make the mechs less reviled. Things wouldn't change overnight, but perhaps it could be a step in the right direction. Surely sacrifices had to be made for the hope of progress.

She didn't say any of this aloud. Instead, she said, "You've given me a lot to consider," and ignored the desperation in Ben's eyes as she shooed him out the door.

Lynnie gave her a disgusted look and went with him.

Lynnie didn't return until the afternoon. Stella tried to explain herself, but it sounded all wrong, too many hopes and maybes.

"Do you care about anybody else?" Lynnie asked. "Deep down, I think this is just about you trying to stay alive."

"Is that such a terrible thing?" Stella blurted.

Lynnie frowned. "It depends on the cost."

"Maybe it's not such a steep price, being Egerton's toy. I stay alive and get to help with vital medical research…."

Lynnie chuckled mirthlessly. "Is that what it is? I suppose I was vital medical research to the doctor at the foundlings' home. Should I be

91

grateful I gave my life, so he did better with his next patient? Which might very well have been you, actually."

Stella stared at her. She'd asked Lynnie about her death many times when she was a child, but Lynnie had never answered. Stella figured she'd died of illness, as so many of the foundlings had. "You had an operation?"

Lynnie looked away. "Not everyone was as lucky as you, Stella."

She had never once considered herself lucky, but she couldn't say that, not to Lynnie.

"You didn't ask where I was just now," Lynnie said.

"Where were you?" she asked.

"I followed Ben home."

"And?"

"Egerton treats him worse than a dog. He was furious with him for going out. Ben wouldn't say where he'd been, even when the doctor hit him. Then Egerton locked him in the cellar."

"Did Ben see you?"

Lynnie nodded.

"And did he ask you to tell me all this?"

"No! He looked ashamed when he saw me. He didn't say anything. And I'm not a messenger service, you know. I'm perfectly capable of deciding to tell you things on my own. Even if you never listen."

"I listen," Stella mumbled. She couldn't remember ever hearing Lynnie so incensed.

"You don't listen! You don't *think*! What do you suppose will happen to Ben now that Egerton has you?" Lynnie gave her a sharp look, and when Stella didn't immediately answer, she barreled on. "He's done all he can to Ben. He's not worthwhile to Egerton anymore, but Egerton can't let Ben go. There's too much risk he might talk. He's going to kill him, Stell."

"You don't know that!"

"I do. I saw the diagrams spread across his workbench. Dissections, to see how Ben's remaining organs held up. Vital medical research, I'm sure." She spat out this last sentence.

Stella felt queasy. She tried to tell herself it wasn't her fault, that she wasn't responsible for anyone's potential death, but it sounded wispy, hollow.

"What am I supposed to do?" she asked, and these words sounded hollow, too.

"Find a way to set it right," Lynnie said, as though this was both obvious and easy.

"Sometimes, I think you forget that being alive doesn't grant a person unlimited abilities," she blurted out.

Lynnie glared at her so hard that Stella braced herself for a slap, almost forgetting it was impossible. Instead, Lynnie disappeared, leaving behind silence as sharp as a stab.

When Stella was young, Lynnie had always been there, ready to tell her things. Not in an overbearing way, just in a supportive, friendly manner. Answers she couldn't quite remember during school recitations. Gentle suggestions about how best to approach various adults at the foundlings' home. Reminders of when the rent was due and recommendations of how much to charge a new client.

It was true that as Stella got older, she didn't always follow what Lynnie said—she chose to settle in Malvern City rather than give in to Lynnie's pleas that they have grand adventures farther west— but that didn't mean she wasn't listening. She always heard her.

And now, all she could hear was the terrible silence muffling against her ears, a reminder that she was truly alone with her problems.

She shook her head. She didn't need Lynnie for this. She was perfectly capable of coming up with a plan on her own.

She ignored the fact that her last plan hadn't gone so well and focused on the problem at hand. She had to save Ben, had to get herself out of the deal, had to expose Dr. Egerton.

It could work, couldn't it? Egerton wanted to expose her, let the world see that mechs weren't monsters, didn't deserve to die. Suppose she beat him to it, but in addition to exposing herself, she exposed him and how he played God in the name of experimentation?

She reached for her make-up, then decided to let the world see her for who she was. She headed for the lobby and had the doorman hail a carriage for her.

It was a ten-minute drive to the *Malvern Herald* building, a bustling, noisy place that made her head ache as soon as she entered. Miss Dobrovsky didn't have her own office, but she took one look at Stella and led her out of the building and to a quiet café down the street.

She had her ghost with her, the same dark-haired girl from their session at the hotel. Most ghosts didn't stick around so long, but Stella got the feeling that this one, despite her youthful appearance, was quite old.

"You see ghosts, too, don't you?" Stella quietly asked once they were seated with their tea.

Miss Dobrovsky shook her head. "Not generally, no. Just the one."

Stella looked the ghostly girl straight in the eyes. "I'm sorry I didn't give your message properly."

The girl shrugged. "Didn't matter since Anna can hear me anyway. She knows I hate her poetry."

94

Miss Dobrovsky chuckled.

"Pretty terrible for everyone else you should be helping, though," the ghost added.

Stella nodded, turning from the ghost to the reporter and recognizing that they had the same eyes. "Your sister?" she asked.

"Cousin. We were best friends. We went skating on the river one day, and the ice cracked beneath me. Jenny died saving me. I nearly died myself. But she stayed with me."

Stella wanted to tell her about Lynnie, wished Lynnie was here right now so they could all have a proper chat. But this wasn't the time.

"I have a story for you," Stella said.

Miss Dobrovsky nodded. "Go on."

So, she did. Stella spilled the whole thing, with a few exceptions. She didn't mention Ben because his secrets weren't for her to share. She said she'd seen terribly unnecessary handiwork from Dr. Egerton and left it at that.

"It sounds like some lurid penny dreadful," Miss Dobrovsky said once she wound down.

Stella wanted to cry. She'd just bared her soul only for Miss Dobrovsky to not believe her story. Stella knew she must prove she had told the truth, but she couldn't very well strip down in the middle of the café. So, she grabbed Miss Dobrovsky's hand and pushed it against her bosom and its metal key.

"It's not."

Miss Dobrovsky shook herself gently from Stella's grip. "I believe you, Miss Abbott. I know all about the evils of bio-mechanics. My sweetheart served in the war and was injured at Charlestown. A bio-mechanic took him on like he was a project, did all sorts to him…." She looked murderous.

"He didn't survive," Stella guessed.

"He did not. I was working on an exposé years ago, but the Automations Act pardoned the bio-mechanics so long as they promised not to practice their trade again. But now you've given me proof that Egerton hasn't stopped."

"You'll run the story?"

"Just try and stop me!" She paused. "Are you willing to be named as my source? It'll have more weight with your name attached, but of course, I understand if…."

"You can use my name."

"Thank you. Now let's go back to the office. I've something for you in return."

"For me?"

"A contact in Dakota. There are some bio-mechanics out there working with the resistance movement to fix their colleagues' wrongs. They should be able to replace your valve for you, no strings attached."

Stella stared, unable to believe her luck.

Miss Dobrovsky looked at her with concern. "Are you alright? Can you afford a train ticket? You're not afraid to go, are you?"

She nodded mutely. She could more than afford two train tickets to Dakota, and though there were all sorts of stories about the wilds of Dakota, they didn't scare her. "It sounds like a miracle."

Miss Dobrovsky laughed. "A well-connected journalist always has a miracle or two up her sleeve. Come along now."

They returned to the office, got the precious information, went over a few more details. It was dusk by the time Stella left, and she felt exhausted. Her good fortune glowed around her, and she imagined a dozen bright futures in Dakota. Were they as wild for ghosts out there as they were here? Perhaps she could reinvent herself, be a truthful medium instead of hiding behind what she thought her clients wanted. Or maybe she could be something else altogether once her heart was working properly, a journalist, or a rancher, or a revolutionist.

But she knew she wasn't in the clear yet. At the hotel, she ran down the hallway despite how it made her heart race and fumbled with the key.

The suite was empty. Lynnie hadn't returned.

Stella forced herself to pack, but her head was a muddle. She sank onto the bed, exhaustion overcoming her. Maybe her heart was going to give out right now. Wouldn't that be ironic? She attempted to laugh, but it came out as a sob. She couldn't do this without Lynnie. She couldn't—

"Feeling sorry for yourself?"

Lynnie's tone was disapproving, but her eyes were full of concern. Stella wanted to hug her, but of course, that was impossible.

"Missing you," she said. "We're going to Dakota, but I need your help.

"Dakota?"

"Yes. Do you think it'll be hard to smuggle Ben out of that cellar?"

Lynnie shook her head. "I just came from there. Egerton's gone out to the saloon. It would be easy enough to break into the house, and there's only a deadbolt on the cellar. But what—"

Stella was already halfway to the door, suitcase in hand. Of course, she wasn't dying tonight; she had Lynnie by her side, and together they could do anything.

"We're going on a wondrous adventure," she said. "Come on. I'll explain on the way."

AUTHOR BIO

Valerie Hunter teaches high school English and has an MFA from Vermont College of Fine Arts in Writing for Children and Young Adults. Her stories have appeared in magazines such as *Cicada*, *Colp*, and *Storyteller*, as well as anthologies such as What Remains (Inked in Gray), Water: Selkies, Sirens, and Sea Monsters (Tyche Books), and Because That's Where Your Heart Is (Sans Press).

THE LAST FLIGHTS OF THE BLACKBIRD

JOSEPH S. WALKER

Alexandria Oberon shook her head, trying to clear her mental fog. She felt like she'd just woken up, though the morning was well advanced. An odd bout of disorientation, something she rarely experienced.

The thinness of the air, no doubt, Oberon thought, looking out the window. A mile below, the massive shadow of the *Abigail Adams* slid across the jumbled peaks and pines of the upper Rockies.

At almost two miles long, the airship was one of the largest manmade things in the world and easily the largest that actually moved. Oberon often imagined how it must look from the ground: the emerald green envelope blotting out the sun; the name of the third American president in red letters four stories high; the two enormous gondolas, like ocean liners slung under the superstructure; the lightning rods and ley line detectors and antennae bristling out in every direction; the steam-powered propellers at the rear, blades sweeping long circles through the

99

air. If anyone down there had never seen an airship, they must think the gods were descending to the earth.

As Oberon's head cleared, memory returned. She'd boarded five days ago in New York. This morning, she learned that the Scribe she requested had joined the ship during an overnight stop in Denver. She sent a message suggesting they meet in the lounge, otherwise empty at this hour, and it was immediately after sitting down across the table from him that she had her moment of confusion.

"I'm sorry," she said. "Could you repeat your name?"

"Jedidiah Janus," the young man said. "People call me JJ. It's quite all right. To tell the truth, I had an odd moment myself just then."

By a wide measure, JJ was the youngest Scribe Oberon had ever met. The beard he was attempting to grow, in accordance with the fashion of the day, was barely more than peach fuzz on his soft cheeks. The insignia on his purple tunic was authentic, though, as was his Autosten, the black box strapped to his chest. A spool of impossibly thin wire inside recorded electrical impulses from JJ's fingers, each of which was backed with a thin, articulated metal sensor.

It may have looked as though the hands he rested on the table were simply shaking, but each twitch of each finger sent the code for a specific letter to the Autosten. Later, the wire could be fed into another machine that would spit out pages of finished prose, to become the basis of news stories or, if things went well, one of the lucrative pulp novels about Oberon's investigations. Good Scribes could keep up with the normal conversation pace, capturing every word as it was spoken, even as they also described the settings and events they encountered.

"Welcome aboard, JJ," she said. "My card." She slid the small, black card with embossed gold lettering across the table.

ALEXANDRIA OBERON

INVESTIGATIONS & INQUIRIES

Specializing in Extranormal Affairs

JJ barely glanced at the card. "You hardly need to introduce yourself, Miss Oberon. Even if I hadn't seen your photograph many times, your coiffure is unique, is it not?"

The hair above Oberon's left ear was the color of refined gold, in stark contrast to the ebony tresses on the rest of her head. "Very inconvenient for undercover work," she said. "It's impossible to dye or color."

"It's truly a souvenir of your encounter with the New Jersey Terror?"

"It is." She was accustomed to the somewhat stilted manner of speech favored by Scribes, designed to elicit substance and detail for the stories they were perpetually composing. She was happy to play along if mentioning a previous case ended up selling a few more copies of *Alexandria Oberon and the Thing From the Woods*. "Though I've always found it odd to refer to the basilisk that way since it was in its lair centuries before New Jersey existed."

"Whatever its name, the important thing is that you prevented it from killing Colonel Lindbergh's child." JJ's fingers danced. "Do you consider defeating it to be the greatest triumph of your career?"

Oberon made a noncommittal gesture. "Surely that's not for me to judge. I prefer to look to the future. To focus on the case at hand."

"Of course. Before you tell me about that, though, may I ask you to describe your attire and equipment? It's good to have that on the record, in case it becomes important later."

101

Oberon stood and turned slowly in place. "As you can see, my clothing has been chosen for comfort and ease of movement. Underneath a floor-length leather duster, I wear loose trousers and a man's work shirt. All with hidden pockets, of course, carrying various small items of potential use."

"The boots?"

Oberon sat back down and propped a leg on the table. "Fashioned from a hide no scientist has been able to identify. Incredibly comfortable and strong, but lightweight. I acquired them in 1931, in Brazil, when I broke up a smuggling ring dealing in rare plants and animals."

"*Alexandria Oberon and the Zoo of Death.*"

"You've prepared for this assignment well, JJ."

Scribes were trained not to show emotion, but JJ blushed. "I must confess that I have been a fan of your exploits for some time, Miss Oberon."

"Just make it, Oberon, please. That's what almost everyone calls me."

"Oberon," JJ said with evident pleasure. "And your weapons? Is that the famous Spectral Bane?"

"It is." Oberon drew the gun from the holster slung on her hip, spun it skillfully, and set it on the table. "Originally a Colt Peacemaker, but I've made some special modifications. Loaded with alternating silver and ectoplasmic bullets."

"And are you also carrying the Tooth of the Nile?"

Oberon smiled. "You *are* a fan." She shot out her right hand, and a dagger sprang from the rig strapped to her forearm, settling into her palm. The blade, only a few inches long, was jet black. Oberon picked up one of the linen napkins from the table and let it fall onto the edge, which sliced it neatly in two. "Forged some five hundred years ago, we believe from a meteorite. Never needs sharpening."

"Marvelous. Anything else readers should know?"

Oberon chuckled. "If I were to list everything on my person, we'd be at it all day. I'll give you a sample, perhaps. One of the things I'm wearing around my neck is an amulet of silence, which prevents anyone from eavesdropping on my conversations by mystical means. Then there's this ring." She gestured, and a series of rods with various hooks and indentations arose from the purple stone adorning her right ring finger. "The shape can be altered to fit any lock. A gift from a friend, the most skilled magical artisan in Rome."

JJ nodded. "Perhaps now you should tell me about your current case. Is Seattle your final destination?"

"For the moment," Oberon said. She took a photograph from an inner pocket and put it on the table in front of him. "I've been hired to retrieve this stolen artifact."

JJ leaned over the picture, his fingers twitching faster than ever as he recorded his impressions. "A circular black medallion, appearing roughly six inches in diameter. It takes the form of a blackbird with spread wings, which curve to meet at the top, completing the circle. Other than the red stone forming the bird's eye, the piece is entirely black and seems to be carved from a single piece of—." He looked up. "Metal?"

"Rock," Oberon said. "A particularly dense form of volcanic basalt, as far as can be determined."

"Its origins?"

Oberon pursed her lips. "Most of this is not publicly known. Can you assure me that I'll have an opportunity to review your work prior to publication?"

"Of course."

She nodded. "Two years ago, a series of magnetic and electrical abnormalities led to the discovery of an ancient city buried in the Australian desert, a few miles from Ayers Rock. It seems to predate known human occupation of the continent, and the architecture is completely unfamiliar. This was found on what seemed to be an altar in one of the structures."

"I'm surprised it was allowed to leave the country," JJ said. The nation of Interior Australia was fiercely protective of its heritage and territory, resisting most interaction with the rest of the world. Clashes with the smaller countries that claimed various parts of the Australian coast were frequent.

"Here's where we get to the secret stuff," Oberon said. "Within the last five years, similar cities have been found in Siberia, South Africa, Alaska, and Peru." She tapped the picture. "In every one of them, a piece identical to this has been found, except each is carved from rock of a different color. The Siberian one is red, the Alaskan blue, and so on. They are bizarre artifacts. A watch placed near one, for example, runs either much slower or much faster than it should, or sometimes stops working completely."

"Why?"

Oberon shrugged. "Nobody has any idea. However, it was thought that something might be learned by bringing them together in one place. The last year has been spent in fierce negotiations. Ultimately it was agreed that a carefully screened team led by Professor Einstein would be allowed to study the five pieces for a period of two weeks in New York City."

"I assume this is where things went wrong."

"Very perceptive. Last week the Australian artifact, the blackbird, was the first to arrive in the US. Within a day, it had been stolen."

104

JJ raised an eyebrow. "I imagine that caused a commotion."

"Oh, very much so. The Aussies are up in arms, and their governments have withdrawn the other four artifacts. Every law enforcement agency in the world is hunting for this little trinket."

"As are you."

"The transport company hired me. They're going to be on the hook for a staggering sum if the blackbird isn't recovered."

"So why Seattle?"

"I have consulted my oracles and scried myself, using certain tools and rituals that must remain secret. The results were somewhat confusing but consistent." Oberon leaned forward. "I got this message over and over again: *the blackbird will be in Seattle in two weeks. The blackbird will never arrive in Seattle.*"

JJ frowned. "That appears self-contradictory."

"It does. I can only assume that it has something to do with the bird's odd relationship with time. In my experience, such riddles resolve themselves with patience."

"What will be your first step when we arrive?"

"I have also consulted more conventional sources in the underworld." Oberon's mouth twitched in a brief smile. "The *human* underworld, that is. They tell me that the actual crime was probably carried out by Aleister Hawke, an English art thief. Our paths have crossed before, and I know something of his methods. I will begin by searching for him."

"Can you provide a description?" JJ's fingers hovered, briefly still.

"I can do better," Oberon said. She picked up the picture of the blackbird and put it back in her pocket, withdrawing another. "Here's his picture."

The man in the photograph was wearing a tuxedo and holding a glass of champagne, chatting with someone who had been cropped from the image. The impression he created was dominated by hair. A thick blond mane fell to his shoulders, and his eyebrows were nearly as bushy as his full mustache. Heavy sideburns completed the picture of someone in the early stages of lycanthropy.

JJ's fingers started to move, then froze again as he looked at the picture. "But this man is on board."

Oberon's eyes widened. "On the *Abigail Adams*?"

"Yes. I could hardly mistake him. He and I were both in the group that boarded overnight."

Oberon leaped to her feet. "There's the answer to the riddle," she exclaimed. "The blackbird will never arrive in Seattle because I will find it first!"

"But Seattle is the next stop," JJ said. "Won't it still arrive in your possession?"

He was talking to himself. Oberon was halfway across the room, heading for a group of stewards setting up a buffet in the corner. JJ followed as quickly as possible, but Oberon had long legs and a determined stride. By the time he got to the group, Oberon was moving among the stewards, showing the picture of Hawke. Most of them glanced briefly and shrugged, but one nodded immediately. "Yes, ma'am. I saw this gentleman not ten minutes ago on the observation deck."

Oberon clenched her fist triumphantly. "An open space with few entrances," she said. "It appears you'll have some action to describe sooner than I anticipated, JJ. Follow me."

The *Abigail Adams* had two colossal gondolas, the front dedicated to crew quarters and cargo, the rear to passenger cabins and services. On the top level of the passenger gondola, the observation deck was said to offer the most stunning views in the world, with windows canted outward so that it was possible to look almost straight down. It was two stories above the lounge. JJ followed Oberon as she hurried to the nearest staircase.

At the entrance to the observation deck, she held up a cautious hand. "Hawke is always armed," she said. "I'll understand if you want to wait here."

"I'm a Scribe," JJ said. "I would be denying my role if I did not follow you."

Oberon nodded and drew the Spectral Bane. "I knew you would say that, of course. Try to stay out of the line of fire." She opened the door and moved quickly into the room, her leather coat flapping behind her. JJ followed, his fingers flying.

The observation deck stretched to the front of the gondola, a long, open space with benches and chairs scattered around. A few dozen people were looking out the windows, moving from view to view. JJ saw Hawke immediately. He was near the front of the deck, looking at the vista unfolding as the *Abigail Adams* advanced. Even from behind, his sideburns and prominent eyebrows gave his head a kind of fuzzy halo. A brown satchel was slung over his shoulder.

Oberon moved quickly toward him, her weapon held low by her side to avoid arousing excitement. She was about twenty yards behind him, just passing a small refreshment stand, when Hawke suddenly spun toward her, alerted, perhaps, by a reflection in the glass. He had a gun, and he and Oberon began firing simultaneously. Screams erupted from the other passengers, who ran frantically in every direction. Oberon dove behind the refreshment stand, pulling JJ with her.

"Bad luck," she said, reloading. "But we've got him cornered."

JJ peered cautiously around the corner of the stand. "I'm afraid not," he said. "He seems to have vanished."

Oberon frowned. "That's not possible," she said. "There's no way a stealth garment would have fit in that bag, certainly not with its power source." She snapped the Bane's cylinder into place. "He's mine," she said and charged around the corner.

Hawke wasn't there, but he hadn't gotten past her, either. She saw at once what JJ had been unable to see from his low vantage point: the access hatch in the floor, its lock snapped off and cover shoved aside. Cursing, she ran forward. The cover was emblazoned with big red letters: *EMERGENCY CREW ACCESS ONLY*. A short ladder dropped to a small deck below, open to the elements. Without hesitation, Oberon dropped through.

JJ followed her out into what seemed like a different world. Outside the gondola's sophisticated climate control, the air was thin and cold. He willed himself not to shiver, knowing that it would send an incomprehensible mass of letters to the Autosten. The deck led to a catwalk, a narrow metal pathway with waist-high railings on either side, that ran out through empty space to the cargo gondola, far ahead. Hawke was on it, running for all he was worth, while Oberon followed. JJ thought he heard her yell something—a warning? —but the sound died in the yawning void around them.

JJ went after them. Almost unconsciously, his fingers twitched with the effort to describe the clutching terror of the nothingness around them. The *Abigail Adams* was a mile above a rough, jumbled landscape of cliffs and crevices. To fall from here would mean a long torture of suspension before the final, crushing end.

Hawke was almost halfway to the cargo gondola. If he reached it, he would be able to take cover and pick Oberon off at his leisure. Perhaps the same thought had occurred to the renowned detective. She dropped to one knee, took careful aim, and fired.

An ectoplasmic bullet traced a blue path through the air and hit Hawke in the back of his left thigh. Oberon fired again, a silver bullet that went over Hawke's head as he stumbled and fell, skidding across the corrugated steel. JJ saw his gun fly off to the side and begin a lazy arc that would end on the rocks below. He caught up with Oberon as she rose and began walking toward her fallen foe, the Spectral Bane still aimed at him. Hawke was clawing his way forward, the satchel in his left hand. Feeling the vibration of their steps, he rolled to his back, glowering.

Oberon stopped eight feet away, JJ immediately behind her. "I'll take the blackbird now, Hawke."

The thief sneered. "Maybe I'll drop it," he said.

"Then you go after it," Oberon said.

He grunted. "We seem to be at an impasse, detective," he said. "Not unlike Zurich five years ago, eh?"

"As I recall, that ended up with you in prison, and the da Vinci device returned."

"Temporarily," Hawke said. He and Oberon were both speaking loudly to be heard over the rush of the thin breeze. "Perhaps we can barter."

"What could you possibly have to bargain with, Hawke?"

"Just this."

Oberon was taller than JJ, but she was partly crouched and close to the righthand railing, while JJ was standing straight and slightly to her left. He had a perfect view as, with lightning speed, Hawke's right arm abruptly jerked forward, and a knife appeared in his hand. Evidently, the thief and the detective had similar tricks up their sleeves. JJ saw the blade

109

leave Hawke's hand. He saw it embed itself in Oberon's shoulder as she fired. He saw the blue line of the bullet dart toward Hawke and hit the satchel he had instinctively jerked up to serve as a shield.

A pulse of light erupted from the satchel, an explosion without sound, a pure white sphere of nothing that grew outward and swallowed them with astonishing speed. JJ thought he heard someone scream. It might have been him. The last words his fingers encoded, before the world erased itself in front of him, were *not again*.

JJ blinked.

The woman sitting across the table from him shook her head, blinking her eyes as though something had fogged her vision. She seemed familiar, though he was sure they'd never met before.

"I'm sorry," she said. "Could you repeat your name?"

AUTHOR BIO

Joseph S. Walker lives in Indiana and teaches college literature and composition courses. His short fiction has appeared in Alfred Hitchcock's Mystery Magazine, Ellery Queen's Mystery Magazine, Mystery Weekly, Tough, and a number of other magazines and anthologies. He has been nominated for the Edgar Award and the Derringer Award and has won the Bill Crider Prize for Short Fiction. He also won the Al Blanchard Award in 2019 and 2021. Follow him on Twitter @JSWalkerAuthor and visit his website at https://jsw47408.wixsite.com/website.

BRASS COBBLED

RIV RAINS

"Bloody thing!" Sunny Hallin kicked at the seized bearing three times with her brass cobbled boots for good measure. The hub of the air purification turbine only moaned at her in reproach; winds whistling in accusation around the massive, stationary one-hundred-and-fifty-foot blades.

"Yeah, well. I'm not happy about it either." She plunked down on the steel, staring out over the sooted sewer that was her city, four-hundred feet down. It should have been a beautiful sight, fresh skies, green parks, sun and moon upon leaf and limb.

It wasn't. Likely never would be again.

Angry, she tore her copper and leather ventilator mask free and rammed it down her cleavage for safekeeping. It was all hopeless. She, and the machinery she fixed for a living, worked to death in a futile attempt at cleaning a society that had no intention of recovering.

Sunny drove her head into her hands, then regretted it. Her fingers were a mucky map. No way could she scrub up well enough to attend the SkyBell Ball! Nope! She wasn't built for frocks and follies. Mags could take her fancy white invitation, her arrogant brother, and shove them up her finely polished arse!

The defiance burned out swiftly, leaving charred scraps of hope. The truth hurt. No matter how nicely she was trussed up, they'd take one look, then order her to grease some ventilation shaft. Mags would be wildly offended, her brother, affronted. All of it would end terribly.

Surely Mags knew that?

She scrubbed her offensive hands down work-stained pants and vest. Could she hide? His arsed-ness certainly wasn't going to dent his polished toes clambering up there to get her. She frowned around at the vast, rusting assembly dwarfing her, then squinted back out into the smog, trying to make out the elegant lines of the evening's destination.

SkyBell Manor was an exquisitely dressed Victorian estate, surrounded by rutted cobbles from the last progressive century. The shining jewel of what had been, it was cinched at the sides by river and rail, boasted acres of rare flora and fauna, and remained one of the only surviving electric exhibits in the country. Beneath government control, the whole lot was preserved in a shimmering, gauzy oasis of man-made purified air, and from her vantage, thousands of its brass roof tiles gleamed through the haze like a personal challenge.

She really should stop breathing the smog.

Cramming the mask back onto her face, she hauled to her feet and turned to the bearing. There was no servicing it. The components had collapsed beneath demand, much like she longed to. Sunny sighed. On days like these, the future seemed dull and cowled.

Pollution was winning, and she was supposed to dance?

"Oh! Sun-sun! You look positively divine!"

Maggie Lloydton circled the red-faced Sunny and carried right on gushing. "The color is rather dark, of course, but that suits you, don't you think?'

Her dainty painted nails plucked and fluffed at Sunny's backside in a way she wasn't going to become accustomed to.

"Mags! Would you stop?!" She turned, causing her dress to spin, hands wringing in front of her russet bodice, still too anxious to touch a single thread despite hours of nail scrubbing. "You think I can pull this off? I feel utterly ridiculous!"

"Don't you dare!" Mags jerked Sunny's arm to her own lacy, mint-green bosom. "You're going through with this because you promised me!" The fierceness of her utter offset the pastel pink of her lips. "Besides, we're going to prove you're more than a set of wrenches."

"I happen to like my wrenches." Sunny regained her arm and heaved an indignant breath that was far too restricted for her tastes. Damn corsets! She winced, her hands gingerly passing over the brass-boning at her stomach.

Mags tut-tutted and floated off to her robe, voice singsong in her wake. "I have booties for you! Crocodile ones, over on my bed!"

That couldn't be good. Sunny balled up her skirts and began to clamor over mountains of petticoats and drowned velvet lounges. The bed—mechanically canopied in dusty silvers—had been rebuilt by Sunny so many times, she'd lost count. Occasionally, she'd rerigged it after the drapes were replaced, but most times, it needed repairs after one of Maggie's high society bed partners became a little too enamored with its silken ropes.

114

Rolling a heap of finery unceremoniously to the carpet, Sunny groaned. Oh *no*. She held the 'bootie' up to a gently smoking lamp.

Shiny, pinchy, pointy, heeled, *and* scaled? Could it get any worse?

"Did you find them?" Maggie's call was obscured by what had to be another layer of lipstick.

"Yes!" With a strategic flip, the booties landed atop the bed canopy with a gear-hitting twang. Sunny winced, awkwardly sneak-hopping across the room to ferret through her own decrepit pile of belongings. Faithful, sagging, tan leather work boots would come to the rescue. They might be perfectly useless for dancing, but she wouldn't be doing that anyway, would she?

Sunny was examining her work in the full-length mirrors—brass-capped toes hidden sufficiently—when Maggie appeared, brandishing dangerous implements.

"And now, for my second miracle." Her hand waved suggestively at Sunny's head.

Ah. Apparently, it *could* get worse.

"Stop fussing!"

Maggie swatted Sunny's hand from her primped curls for the hundredth time. Being fussed over just felt so...unnatural.

The carriage bumped over a rut and set her mousy ringlets, and the plum plush seats—geared and sprung for supposed comfort—to a haphazard bouncing. Blowing a huff past her nose, Sunny failed to control even the curls.

"Don't make faces. You'll ruin your makeup." Mags's hands were folded neatly in her lap, unperturbed despite the seats.

It ground her gears.

Sunny could run on a turbine fin or climb endless ladders with full tool harness, but with all the finery impeding her, she felt useless as a stripped-out socket. Pre-fuel crisis, the two girls had lived parallel lives. Their days of braids and frog-catching had been before the world plummeted into recession, when Maggie's family prospered and Sunny's folded.

"Do you ever wonder, Mags, what it would've been like if electricity hadn't failed?" Sunny was murmuring to the window, shop fronts wheedling by with smoking lanterns over discolored glass. The fancy Lloydton steam carriage had its own air purifier, so her painted, maskless face seemed too sharp and bare in reflection.

"I try not to." Maggie's hands smoothed her skirts. "It's difficult to consider." She bit a lip, nearly destroying her liner. "You know I sometimes envy you. Up there, in the clouds, free."

"Poisoned by smog..."

"That's not the point! I would be too if I weren't so..." Mags fluttered a hand, hunting for the word.

"Precious?" Sunny supplied with a devilish grin.

Mags swatted her knee.

"I was going for *privileged*." Her nose lifted as she spoke the term, but a spark of amusement found her eye.

Initially, it had been hard watching Maggie dress up and parade about. She'd had better food, education, house, clothes, suitors, parties, future, dreams—but as it started to change her—to erode her best parts, Sunny began to envy her less and less.

If the privileged side of the fuel recession meant turning your heart into a polished, brittle bauble on a shelf, Mags could keep it. Sunny's parents mightn't have been able to support her, but Mags was right; she had freedom and choices. She wasn't a puppet towing a wealthy family line.

"You're brooding again." Mags wasn't wrong.

The man they were about to pick up was a bad piece of work.

For the Lloydtons, business was business, and influential people had to be wooed—no matter how revolting—but Maggie's first encounter with the forthcoming shareholder had resulted in both girls crashed across her canopy bed, drowning sorrows in a cheap bootlegged bottle. Mags had poured the woes, Sunny the rum.

"How long until we get to Sir Touch-a-lot's house?"

Their derogatory name made Maggie smirk. They might be almost nineteen, but hopefully, stupid names for those they loathed would never go out of style.

Despite the jest, Maggie's face paled beneath her powder. "Two more streets."

Sunny leaned over to squeeze her hand.

Mag's dove grey eyes clouded with worry. "You'll be nice, right? Civil at least? Even after...after..." She swallowed.

"After that arrogant bastard mauled my best friend in a lift car?" Sunny's eyes weren't cloudy; they were fire-bright hazel. "Oh, I'll be on my best behavior. Brother's orders."

Maggie's brother, not hers. Did that count?

Her best friend shook herself, then patted gently at her reflection in the darkening window. "We need this deal. It's complicated but necessary."

"I know, but I don't have to like how it's done." Sunny checked her window but looked away from her own scowl. "Does Tevan realize what a scumbag this guy is?"

Tevan was two years older, and while growing up, he'd often amounted to an arrogant prig. Since taking over as figurehead of the family business, he'd seemed to enjoy the wheeling, dealing—or drinking and canoodling—a little too much.

Maggie nodded. "He wasn't going to make me do this again, but we're out of options."

"He was insane to agree to that *and* me."

"No choice." Her chin came up in an undeniable show of defiance. "We have to stay ahead of this deal. Touch-a-lotis powerful. They swarm him. Just wait and see. Try not to vomit on that new dress."

"You told me this was an old one!"

Her eyes glittered. "I might have lied. None of mine suited your coloring."

Shit.

As they jerked and bounced to a stop, the boots tucked beneath her skirts seemed a terrible slight on Maggie's generosity.

"You need better friends."

Mags peered through the glass at Touch-a-lot's ostentatious bronze staircase. "No, just better dates."

If you asked the male passengers, conversation within the carriage peaked during Tevan's rendition of how he'd once been caught by the manor guards fornicating with a ball belle beneath a topiary of a flamingo. Touch-a-lot roared in delight, Maggie pulled painfully tight to his side.

Sunny fantasized about tearing both men's nails out with her teeth.

No, too bloody; the dress had to at least *arrive* unscathed.

"I do so enjoy stories from another lady's man!" Touch-a-lot—whose actual name was something like Olsen Derink—wiped the hysterical tears from his eyes on Maggie's lace handkerchief before tossing it back at her chest. He was a short-built, middle-aged jerk, round in chin and dark of eye. He lowered his voice to Tevan. "I hope we can coin a few more this evening. Lord knows it's been a rough month in the trenches!"

He winked at Maggie.

Did Sunny imagine a cringe as Tevan glanced at his own date?

"May opportunities abound!" Mag's brother wallowed in Sunny's revulsion. "I'm often partial to getting amongst the hedges."

Yuck.

Even the attractive crinkles at the corners of Tevan's perfect eyes couldn't hide the waste he'd made of his soul. As raven-haired as Maggie, but taller and broader, Tevan carried a suit in a way that made mincemeat of most women and probably enough men. Unlucky for him, his date that evening agreed with neither.

Relieved to turn through the gates, Sunny shifted her attention out her window lest she put him through his. If he was trying to piss her off early, he was doing spectacularly.

Beyond the glass, the haze rippled as they pierced the purification bubble. Sunny felt the rush of air, then a lightness as they swept into the protected atmosphere. Even though their windows didn't open, she felt the need to take a long, deep breath.

Rows of electric lanterns glowed along the drive, clean as diamonds against the night. Ruining that effect, an assortment of soot spewing transportation like their own chittered and hummocked down the time-rutted cobbles.

Sunny's heart beat faster. She wanted to pretend it wasn't exciting for her; wanted to appear as bored and resentful towards the event as she was with her escort, but as her nose squeaked against the glass, Sunny found herself giddy with oxygen-soaked anticipation.

SkyBell Manor, not often open to droves of inventors and investors, was teeming with folks eager to glorify their prowess. A couple in their later years descended from a purple and brass carriage with a matching clockwork horse. Two men in silver brocade and ostentatious top hats leaped from the backs of steam-billowing elephants. To the right, the track siding was lit with faceted lamps on chains, and rows of private locomotives stretched beyond her window scope. On the left, the river bumped polished, ornate vessels tight against the gaudy brass railings. Among it all, attendants dashed to and fro, pressed neatly into sky-blue livery, the color paying homage to their fallen sky.

Sunny breathed the spectacle in awe—certain she'd inhaled everything—only to relinquish her jaw to a burst of floating fire dazzling across the brassy roof. Floating fire? Floating balloons! Airships! Plus, winged creations that weren't certain what they were. They idled and anchored above, some with flame, some scudding steam or soot against the clouds, but all dropping fantastically clad guests off on airy bell tower platforms.

Magnificent! What Sunny would give for an airship to run away in. "I bloody want one." She hadn't realized she'd spoken aloud until the preceding silence.

Whoops.

Sunny glanced at Maggie, who was studiously smoothing her skirts once more, then at Tevan, who wore a pained expression that might have spelled hemorrhoids on anyone else. Finally, she spied Touch-a-lot. His beady black eyes hooked into Sunny.

"Well, well. She does speak, and with a vocabulary to match the rest of her." The smile he offered was not one of humor.

He must have seen the venom slide through Sunny's eye, for in lazy, deliberate movements, he moved one heavily signeted hand to squeeze Maggie's thigh, eliciting a startled jump poor Mags couldn't quite cover.

The air in the cabin grew thick and tense despite the filters. Just as Sunny was about to articulate what he could do with his evening, the carriage jolted to a vacant curb, and their faithful coachman bounded down to throw open the door.

Noah Sterling—strangely maskless, turned out in gray and brass, all freckled and grinning—bowed graciously for the third time that day. Another friend from childhood, Noah was impeccably clever, had won his spot on the Lloydton payroll admirably, and also happened to be completely gorgeous.

Unfortunately, his lopsided grin was short-lived due to the decaying atmosphere wafting from the cabin. "Have a good evening?"

The sarcasm made Sunny snort.

That, perhaps, was another mistake.

In surly succession, Touch-a-lot lumbered down, snatched out Maggie, then stomped up the stairs, leaving the three alone.

"She made me do this, you know." Tevan stared out the door, watching his business target manhandle his sister. Every word was bitten and chewed. "I knew you couldn't do it."

He pinned Sunny to the sprung seat with a piercing blue look until she swore the thing adjusted beneath the weight.

"Don't fuck this up for us." With that, he pushed past her skirts, swung from the carriage, and breezed up the stairs without a backward glance.

Well.

A sandy flop of hair peeked sheepishly around the door. "Did I make that worse?"

Sunny sighed, grateful for a comfortable conversation. "Nah. I managed that all on my own."

Could she just go home?

Blinking what couldn't be tears, she gritted down on the image of Touch-a-lot's hand on Maggie's thigh. That *bastard!* In angry yanks, she gathered her skirts and bumped into Noah, attempting to help.

He faltered, tugging awkwardly at the high collar of an elaborately buttoned jacket, and cleared his throat. "Look, if you're still goin', let me help?"

Dammit, he was so sweet! Sunny's frustration melted beneath his uncovered grin. Too bad Noah always had eyes for Maggie.

"I have to go." The truth tripped off her painted lips. "I'm meant to keep that pawsy slime ball off her." She threw her hands up. "I'm leach patrol."

"Well then, Miss DeLeach." He bowed and offered her his hand, long lashes dipping shyly.

Somehow, Sunny laughed. What were the chances that her working-class driver would be the first and last gentleman she'd encounter that evening? She took his hand—only blushing a little—and together they righted her hems and sanity.

She was just about to climb down, when Noah slammed himself across the doorway, hastily glancing over his shoulder.

What now?

He gleefully let out a long, low whistle aimed at her boots.

Oh. *That.*

Instead of embarrassment, she felt a deeper laugh hit her corset. "Never seen practical footwear before?" She craned her neck. "Don't see you wearing ridiculous heeled nightmares." Sunny collapsed back into the seat with a springing flop. "I couldn't stand being even more uncomfortable *all night*."

He shook his head. "Never said it wasn't smart. Never thought it, neither." He looked back over his shoulder, waiting until two manor attendants skipped by. "Just makin' sure they let you in. You gotta do what you gotta do. Anyway, that guy's the arse that completes the hole—and that's just her brother." He grinned, dimples forming in the carriage lamps.

Perhaps losing composure with *him* wouldn't be so terrible...

Noah half closed one eye, sizing her up, face falling serious. "As for the other, I've heard of him." Slipping a hand under his jacket, he alarmingly—or perhaps interestingly—covertly palmed something into her boot top.

The cold press of metal settled against her ankle. He winked, then in one fluid motion, scooped her skirts over her boots, whipped her off the seat, and deposited her on the cobbles in front of him.

Safe and steady, he hunted her eyes, worry clouding their coppery depths. "Just be careful, alright? There's perilous paths about." He frowned. "Even for those boots."

Sunny wished he'd meant the cobbles. She nodded mutely and stepped out towards the staircase, feeling uncertain all over again.

His voice followed her up, strong and reassuring, just as his grip had been. "You know where I'll be!"

Only one thought escaped the trap of her pulse unscathed: was Noah sure he wanted Maggie?

"You still came!"

Not far over the threshold, Maggie grabbed Sunny's arm and began to steer her through the boisterous, richly clad throng.

It was…staggering. Everything seemed gilded or bejeweled within an inch of its life. Clockwork contraptions and steam-driven marvels rattled and spun among the guests, operating as the waiters, coat racks, jugglers, and dealers. Their brass smiles twitched, geared eyes rotated, and seemingly everyone watched and applauded: how many mouths could be fed with the sum of their parts?

"I was worried! I turned at the top of the stairs, and Tevan was right behind us, face like thunder—"

Sunny cut her tirade short. "—where are they?"

Maggie cringed and wordlessly nudged her on. A few moments later, she pushed Sunny into a curtained alcove, tucked off a relatively quiet lounge. She turned to face her with a grave expression. "Why don't you start with what happened in that carriage?"

For a heart-stopping moment, Sunny believed she was asking about Noah, but as Mags prattled on, her stomach eased.

"…I know he didn't appreciate my ultimatum, but I didn't expect such open hostility." Maggie began picking and preening Sunny's outfit, then her own, as if the motions helped her gather loose thoughts. "Some of the things they were saying…ugh! Father taught us better than that! How could he have turned into such abysmal dross?"

Sunny made a face. "He seems to think I'm going to ruin this for you."

Mags stopped her picking and gawked. "Ruin it? You? *He'll* do that!" She threw her hands in the air and shifted to snatch the curtain open a crack, eyeing the room.

"The moment we walked in, Touch-a-lot's original deal-dalliance walked over—practically bare-chested—and flounced away with both of them!" Her dove eye looked sharp as a hawk's, cut by the sliver of light from the curtains.

Needing movement for calm, Sunny began pacing in the small alcove, her boots familiar and strong as they wore at her problems. "Okay, so, how do we salvage this?"

Maggie considered—black manicured brows pulled together. She started a slow nod like she shifted each piece of the dilemma into place with the tip of her nose. "We need to force a contract from Touch-a-lot. Tonight. If the others get hold of his electricity shares, they'll dominate the pricing, and then we'll be stuck using coal for decades."

Sunny blinked. "That's what we're doing here? That's what you're angling for?" She was stunned. Not that Maggie had a good heart, but that her brother was also trying to help.

"Why did you think we were here? To make us richer? So Tevan could fuck some blonde in the potpourri? We all need this!" She dropped her shoulders. "Trouble is, I don't know how to get it without losing myself." She looked up at Sunny with tears on her lashes. "I should've gone through with it the first time—I could've persuaded him. I should've been able to...to..." Maggie swayed and pressed her fingers to her mouth, forsaking lipstick.

Protective fury sawed through Sunny's middle, roughing her words. "To *what*? No! Damn you for thinking it! Damn Tevan, for considering it! While I'm at it, damn that ex-tramp who's probably doing that right now!" Sunny crossed to the woman she'd grown up with and squeezed her shoulders, dragging in a calming breath for both of them. "You don't want to be that, even to save us from the smog."

Fat tears welled in Maggie's eyes, swiftly followed by alarm. Tipping her head back, she started waving frantically at her face, swatting

125

at Sunny. "Get something! I threw my hanky! I can't run! Not here!" Her fanning continued, eyes pinned wide, lest a blink send those damp boulders crashing.

Sunny panicked. Hankies? She wasn't refined enough to carry hankies! A napkin? Maybe the curtain? What a spectacle that would be—

"Quick! Anything!"

Sunny looked left, right, then down. With a triumphant flourish, she handed Mags the edge of a petticoat still attached to the wearer. At the look on Mag's face, Sunny shrugged, a grin hitched across her cheeks.

"You did say anything."

"Maybe through here..."

Their hunt was taking some time. The place was enormous! They'd navigated room after room: courtyards, dance floors, parlors, even libraries. Once again, Mags tried to slide them around the edge of a vast hall, but the surge of sound and the press of eager bodies swept them inwards. Teeth gritted behind a salvaged, painted smile, Maggie abruptly looped her arm through Sunny's, threw her head back, and manufactured a torrent of fake laughter.

Between batches, Mags nodded pointedly ahead. "Blend in."

Oh.

A sea of rapt faces surrounded Tevan and Touch-a-lot, including a gaggle of well-bosomed corsets for each hip. It appeared they had commandeered an elaborate mechanical bar wagon—kicked out the bartender—and were romping it about the room to uproarious laughter from their audience.

The pointless contraption was constructed like a horseshoe; polished timber countertops on three sides and an elaborate iron gate enclosing the back. Above their heads, various bar regalia swung and sloshed alarmingly in hanging ornate racks. Tevan—somehow already inebriated—swatted at a set of controls supposedly intended to walk the thing smoothly through the crowd. It certainly wasn't smooth anymore. A multitude of glittering, hinged, brass legs tried to clatter across the marble beneath it, but Tevan's haphazard directions resulted in the whole thing resembling a rollicking octopus.

Mags met Sunny's expression with a pained grimace of her own. "Care for a drink?"

Sunny sighed. "Would hate one."

By the time they'd cut their way to the shambling, leaping party, the thing had crashed into an interior pillar, knocked a chunk of gilding to the floor, and nearly rendered three folks unconscious.

Did it matter? Judging by the surrounding gaiety, apparently not. However, it presented the exact moment they needed.

Two swift steps, and Sunny caught the first rail that came to hand. She swung both herself and her voluminous skirts up over the bar, flung her curls back indignantly, and kicked open the gate. She passed a more demure hand down for Mags, but failed to notice that every beat of her boarding had been accompanied by delighted applause.

Shit. She blushed.

Mags leaned in. "Smile. Curtsy, do something." Her elbow connected with Sunny's ribs. "Then later, we'll talk about those boots."

"Lil' sis!" Saved by Tevan?

The unfocused sway of his gaze somewhat ruined his welcome.

"Grease girl, get off my bar-ship!" On the other side of the gathering, he pulled two separate handfuls of female to his shirt front and kissed both of their necks, one after the other.

Sunny shuddered. Mags *had* said she couldn't vomit on the dress?

Distracted, she didn't see Touch-a-lot snake out an arm. In rough succession, he snagged her hips, dragged her to his chest, and nearly drowned her in the sour stench of his breath.

Shit, shit, shit!

"That was some display, you delicious, salacious creature. I might have saddled the wrong filly." Ignoring her protests, he wrenched her closer and ran the tip of his tongue along the curve of her ear.

Revulsion clattered her spine. The filthy, slimy son of a bitch! Sunny would give no warnings. Grimly, she swung a boot, embedding her knee so hard into his favorite accessories that his fancy suit folded into her arms. For onlookers, she locked him in the most passionate, bosomy parody of a headlock she could muster and lowered his wheezing arse to the floor.

Noah's tiny, screwed, and brass-plated revolver met her palm, sheltered by her skirts. "Feel that?"

Touch-a-lot's unfocused eyes widened as she pressed the pistol to the inside of his thigh. She smiled wickedly.

His alarm culminated in a sputter. "What do you want?"

Sunny twisted the barrel, sliding it a mite higher for his—ah—pleasure. "Oh, nothing. We simply request control of a certain influential market and the displeasure of your company."

Still smiling, she reached out and towed Mags down by the back of her skirts. The revolver changed hands, disappearing into the folds of Maggie's fabrics, yet never shifted from their target. Dresses might be useful after all.

"Now, you stay put and don't think she won't use that. I recall a little incident some weeks ago in a lift car that cut her trigger a little fine."

In response, Maggie parted her lips, showing far too many teeth.

Sunny turned to her ear. "Your brother?"

Mags shook her head, tossing her chin in the direction of a black shock of hair splashed over the chest of a very giggly corset.

Ah. Wonderful.

The cluttered, lopsided bar required some wading, but eventually, Sunny tapped on Tevan's shoulder.

"Go away, Mags!"

"Oh, barkeep?"

"Even better. Go away, Sun-sun."

Grinding her teeth, she tapped again, harder. Not only was he irritating, but he'd used her childhood nickname to thicken it.

"Surely you can see I'm *busy*."

She clicked her tongue in annoyance. Things were about to go badly.

Smiling sarcastically at the canoodling blonde, Sunny stepped in close behind the older Lloydton, hiked up her skirts, and used one brass boot heel to rip his feet out from under him.

The girl squealed, he screeched, Sunny laughed. Everyone else who could, fled.

"Do you bloody mind?!" Tevan rubbed the back of his head.

"Not at all. Finished?"

"I intended to be later, if you hadn't run everyone off." He was slurring and trying to cross his arms indignantly, but instead, he only managed an awkward hug of her ankle, possibly because he was being stood on. He frowned at her brass cobbled boot. "What are you wearing?"

"Liberation, for women. Did you even know her name?"

"Who trades names anymore?" He blinked several times, attempting to focus. "That's a currency well left behind."

Sunny snorted. "You've turned from prig to pig, Tevan Lloydton, and I'm almost sorry we need you for this."

She checked over her shoulder, where Maggie was eagle-eyed, and Touch-a-lot was resolutely upending a brown liquor bottle.

"Dammit! Don't let him pass out!"

Tevan craned his neck, but the mountain of her russet skirts rendered his seeing impossible. "What's goin' on? Who's passing out?" His head dropped back with a thunk, eyes squeezing shut in a fledgling attempt to regain his addled wits. "What have you done?"

"Well. Let's recap." Sunny shifted her weight, making him wheeze beautifully.

"This morning, I worked on a purification turbine but didn't have the parts, then lunch—bread and salami, perhaps a little too much gherkin. I scrubbed my nails for half an hour each to help *your* family. Let my hair suffer at the hands of your sister, then the steam carriage...oh, yes, and being threatened by you." Sunny tapped her chin thoughtfully. "That pretty much wraps it up. Except, your darling sister has Olsen Derink at gunpoint, and we're about to procure a contract for the good of humanity." She shrugged.

The color drained from Tevan's face.

Sunny leaned over to place the tip of one finger on the end of his nose.

"And naturally, you're going to write it."

Apparently, galloping a liberated bar-ship through an arched patio window—festoons of coppery-gossamer drapes billowing behind—left enough chaos in its wake for a borrowed airship to rise demurely from the manor topiary gardens.

"That way?" Noah pointed over the helm, the city a smudge below his finger.

She nodded, then realized the only lights on her face were the same dull amber gauges that hugged the slope of his jaw.

Focus.

"Pull in nice and close on the lee side. Try to get that gangway on the center."

Behind her, the cabin—all timber paneling and leather benches—creaked with Noah's adjustments. She glanced back; Maggie stood with the revolver trained on Touch-a-lot, who sat propped up with a terrific case of injured arrogance. Nearby, Tevan sat with a feeble lantern at one elbow and a pot of stale coffee at the other, feverishly scribbling out legal terms like a man possessed.

Sunny's brow hitched with doubt. They were a bunch. Could they truly succeed? Her arms and chin dropped to the back of the pilot's chair, her heart squeezing out through the faceted windshield. Bathed in light from the blighted moon, the city almost looked clean. She couldn't help but curse the world's quota of Touch-a-lots: for the corruption, for taking her sky, and now for pushing her to violence.

Picking up her wavelength, Noah turned his warm lips in against her ear for privacy. "You sure you wanna do this?" He glanced pointedly behind and then lifted one shoulder. "Not sayin' there's another way—and I'm stayin' with you no matter—but there'll be repercussions. Sure you wanna go down for *this*?"

"Please don't say 'go down' while we're up here."

She turned, expecting his amused smile, but instead found herself falling into an earnest gaze—open, trusting—and not just soft from the ambers. In any other light, he might have blushed. Noah cleared his throat.

"Stop it, Sun-sun."

"Nup and no."

Fast as that, they were back in the forest as kids, throwing jibes, laughing, hanging upside down from every tree, stealing moments of sky—fearless, tireless dreamers. The trees were gone, killed by the fuel war, the skies lost, yet the people who loved them, weren't. Dreams could be rekindled, right?

"Will you dance with me?" The words popped out of her mouth unbidden. She ducked her head, embarrassed, then felt her chin lift on the back of his knuckle.

Was he pleased? Repulsed?

Noah's words came carefully. "Will you wait for me to return this ship? 'Cos, I don't intend to be condemned as a thief for the rest of my life." He shrugged. "A vigilante, sure, but not a thief. I have a reputation, ya' know."

Sunny opened her mouth, wanting to reassure him—maybe kiss him—but a different, nervous twist of her gut stole her away.

Rising out of the gloom was their target.

Regretfully, she pulled away from Noah's shoulder, and instead turned to their unwilling passenger. "Well, Derink. This is your stop."

"You'll pay for this! I'll have you fed to a furnace!"

Touch-a-lot was being a little screechy for Sunny's taste. With exaggerated care, she examined a nail, leaning one hip on the bobbing airship gangway rail.

"We know your threats," she turned to regard her partners in crime framed by the airship hatch, "and we're just not bothered by

132

them." She flipped a hand upside down to illustrate the lightweight of his point. "The Lloydtons have their own protections, and as for me…" She shrugged at him, "I have little to lose."

Touch-a-lot huffed and heaved at the night air, so much thicker up on the turbine than down on the ground. He clung like a limpet to the curved, rusting, steel hub; heavy beads of sweat drowning his brow and upper lip. Beneath her vent mask, Sunny's nose wrinkled. Not so powerful anymore.

"Derink," Maggie's clear reasoning rang through the clotted dark, "perhaps now is the time to reconsider your position on that market share?"

Touch-a-lot glared at her, fury contorting his filthy mouth. "You won't break me with your underhanded ways, you bitch!"

Maggie threw a hand to her breast, feigning offense, before she marched straight out that gangway, snatched the mask from her face, and stabbed a finger towards his chest.

"*I'm* underhanded?" She snarled at him. "Tell me, is rucking up a woman's skirts and smothering her cries considered *underhanded* too?" She was bristling—the injustice crackling off her skin—every pebble of her hate trodden to sand, ready to fling in his face. "I know what you are! *We* know. Don't think for one second we wouldn't let you meet an untimely death if it suited our needs!"

A fresh wave of vindication raced through him. "I'll never sign! Women lie, and men need not believe them! I'll do what I like with who I like, and they'll be grateful!" He looked past Mags to the shadowy doorway where Tevan stood. "You understand me, don't you? Stop this! We don't have to answer to them!"

It seemed that's where he crossed the line.

133

Tevan took a measured step from the hatch. The man not entirely on board until that moment, looked colder than the coffee he'd been sculling. "*Never* presume I'm one of you." He shot Touch-a-lot a look that would have bared blades anywhere else. "And *never* speak about another living thing with such dismissal again."

Everyone's gaze swung back to Touch-a-lot.

His jaw gaped, then recovered into a clench. "I thought you were better than this!" He scoffed. "Think of your family name, man!"

"She *is* my family!" Tevan's roar cracked like thunder. He strode out, planting himself sideways between the two women's skirts. "You vile, pathetic bastard! You'll be measured for what you've done to her and your other boasts!" He flung a hand over the city below. "Business has daughters and sisters, too! We've marked you, coward. We're coming for you. Enjoy *that*!"

Sunny and Mags stared at Tevan, stunned.

"What?" Tevan stuck his hands in his pockets and shrugged at the smoggy horizon. "You really thought I was all that?"

Mags leaned forward, tucked her head into his chest, and hugged him fiercely. Touch-a-lot, however, spat uselessly towards the nose of the turbine, not even mustering enough gusto to make the distance.

"Should we tell him he's got about an hour until the smog taints his lungs?" Sunny shifted to the very end of the gangway. "Mind you, if the wind comes first, the blades will turn, and he'll plummet to the ground." She leaned out on a rope, looking down. "He'd make a nasty crack, but I'm willing to make the sacrifice, aren't you?" Lifting her mask to lick a finger, she pretended to test the wind. "I think I feel a breeze coming on." She turned to the others. "Mags, is that a breeze?"

Maggie's face lifted from her brother's jacket, tearful but lit with zeal. "Brr!" She finished clipping her mask back into place and rubbed her arms for warmth. "Sure seems that way, I wonder"—she turned to Derink— "do you feel that?"

As if on cue, a breeze tousled Sunny's freed waves back off her face.

Touch-a-lot began to panic.

With a flourish, Mags produced a sheaf of papers clipped with Sunny's hairpins, and waved them across the divide, "Options are on offer." Her single raised eyebrow spoke the smirk.

He grimaced. "Girly, I'd rather die than set pen to that." But his resignation hovered, seeping into the edges of his voice, his hands twitching in rhythmic terror against the sloping steel.

"That can be arranged." Sunny beamed at him. "This weather!" She fanned at her face. "So unpredictable. Mags, let's ask Noah to kick in the side thrusters. They're ever so refreshing."

Their target froze, on all fours, like a dog on a carriage roof. Chest heaving, he scuttled back to cling between two—unknowingly—seized fan blades, looking hounded. His eyes caught the edge of the formidable ladders Sunny knew all too well.

"Four-hundred rungs. Think you'll make it?" She grinned beneath her mask, then feigned calling to the pilothouse. "Oh, Noah?!"

Mags nudged her arm. "I think Noah likes you."

Sunny rolled her eyes. "Agh, don't start! He's always liked you!"

Her best friend reeled back, eyes like saucers. "Oh, please! He's not my type! He's cute and sweet and not brooding or irritating at all!" She swooped in to shake Sunny's arm, half crushing the contract in her grip. "He likes *you*. I know it." Her eyes sparkled with mischief. "Even better, I know you like him, too."

"I do not!"

Mags set her fists to her hips. "Sun-sun, don't you dare. We've known each other too long. You like him, and that's that."

Sunny chewed her lip beneath the safety of her mask and glanced around Mags to the pilothouse window. Her whisper spilled out onto the wind. "I asked him to dance."

A squeal fell out of Maggie, spiraling away to the city below. "What did he say?!"

"Well, it was a sort of 'yes'—"

"—if you don't mind?!"

Both girls stopped their chatter and turned to blink at the man not ten feet away, clinging to a four-hundred-foot-high piece of machinery, contemplating his mortality.

It was Sunny who recovered first. "I do believe we're having a private conversation, but by all means, what can we do for *you*?"

He cleared his throat, not managing to dislodge its quiver. "It seems I'd like to make you an offer for my electric market share."

Sunny turned to the others with feigned surprise. "Did you hear that? How generous!"

"A true humanitarian."

"Absolutely."

"Shut up, you pathetic wenches!" Touch-a-lot curled his lip. "You've made an enemy tonight! One who doesn't care about any besides himself! You'll get what you want, but not before you get me off of here!" His fist rang on a turbine fin.

"He does have a temper, doesn't he?" Sunny made a face. "I hardly think you're in any position to make demands, but it seems *we* are. So,"—she retrieved a landing hook with a sack affixed and waggled it suggestively at Touch-a-lot— "be a good boy, and you'll make it safely to

136

the ground." Sunny winked at the others. "One way or another. But first, I think we'll get that in writing."

"You know he'll come after us, don't you?"

Noah slid his hand around Sunny's waist and dipped the ends of her tangled curls to the marble floor. Rakish in his loosened coachman's jacket, Noah truly was a rather adept dancer.

"Yeah, but by then, the dancing will be over." She swept up into his embrace, her lashes clinging—blinking—at disheveled strands of her hair.

Mischief on his lips, Noah steadied her chin, blowing softly across her nose until each one yielded to him. "So, what then?"

Damn! Did he know he'd rendered her knees useless for any ladder? Did he also know it was her turn? Sunny stretched up with a shrug, sliding her arms around his turned-up collar, the rows of unfastened brass buttons deliciously cold on her skin. She relished the hitch of his chest, her lips brushing the line of his jaw.

But, what indeed? The airship was tethered overhead once more, the ball was brimming with the rumor of their exploits, and the contract was nestled safely in the cleavage of Maggie Lloydton—dancing and chatting with her brother—beyond Noah's shoulder.

Sunny tilted back, gazing at him slyly. "Oh, I dunno. We make a reasonable team. Perhaps we should keep fixing things."

Noah nodded, shifting her effortlessly under the gilded domes, around a circle of gawking onlookers. "What kind of things?"

She smiled, feeling rogue. "Hmm. Does it matter? I need a pilot. Let's just start with the sky and work from there." Her fingertips chased the nape of his neck, drawing him close, her lips stealing the breath from his. *Could* the sky be their limit?

Noah whistled against her, then caught the tease as a truer kiss. His voice was ragged when he finally spoke. "Deal. But first," he dropped a hand to sweep up her hopeless hems, furling them with a flourish, "those boots must dance."

Flying out on his sure hand, skirts hiked up, laughing alongside Maggie, she soared; her sky already breaking open, brighter and higher.

Besides, who knew?

Brass cobbled boots could dance, after all.

AUTHOR BIO

Riv Rains is a collection of rusting gears lubricated exclusively by chocolate. Book-geek, author, and conjurer of creative daemons, she'd have a lot more time if she wasn't also captain and chief to two kids, four boats, and one husband. Born amid the sticks of rural Australia, she finds words in the magic of sunsets and river swells, chassis and unsuspecting rib cages. Riv welcomes you to seek out the spawn of her tumultuous mind at RivRains.com or @rivrains, and hopes to reach for you through the gaps of many more heartfelt pages.

Irregular Constructions

Richard M. Ankers

My mother understood. My sister did not.

Those I considered my closest friends deserted me in increments of disrespect. Their venomous words came as a verbal flood, and there was me without a dam. There was a continual barrage of back without a retorted forth; my replies melted on lips too dry to speak.

"I knew him when he had potential."

I still have.

"He was once such a good man, so like his father."

I am good.

"He always had a touch of the mad scientist about him, though. Too much poor lighting, if you ask me."

I'm not.

In any number of weasel-faced jibes, they took me apart, piece by tiny piece. It could have been worse, though. It could have been so much worse.

In truth, I counted myself lucky. The university wing was named after my deceased father, and to dump his son on the proverbial scrapheap was to taint their name by association. However, when expulsion failed, seclusion took prominence. The alumni, ever resourceful, relegated my work to the darkest, dingiest corner of the building where even the rats went round in pairs, and the equipment was, at best, antique, at worst, useless. There in the basement, surrounded by filaments and copper thread, brass cogs, and tin plate, I watched the mildewed walls grow damper, the rain outside pooling far above my subterranean lab's single doorway. There wasn't a window, and I was glad of it. I had no desire to gaze upon a world that hated me. An outcast who didn't give a damn, I patrolled those stygian depths where others sought only angelic heights.

My father had exuded magnificence. A marvelous creator of curios and more wondrous paraphernalia, word of his knack for contraptions soon spread amongst Europe's societal elite. You were not somebody until you owned one of Gustav Schmidt's marvelous, mechanical figurines. They were the pinnacle of clockwork creation, and nobody could match my father's work. What Mozart was to music, my father was to the creative sciences.

Of course, there were innate problems with being in demand. Where most eligible men mingled with high-class women hoping to find a bride, he gathered clientele hoping to further his reputation. From humble beginnings working out of a small workshop in a side street of Nuremberg, my father crossed the English Channel in a boat stuffed full of dreams and found residence in the hallowed halls of Oxford, his skills

141

a welcome addition to the establishment. He became an English citizen when the opportunity arose and took a wife soon after. How remained a mystery to many when he spent both day and night secreted in the complexities of the university's facilities. I supposed it was his charisma that drew her. *Another trait I lacked!*

My father was an old man by the time I was born and died within two years of making me his sole student, much to the chagrin of my younger sister Alberta. His loss devastated my mother, whilst I was inconvenienced. Alberta seemed inexpressive about the whole event and remained so throughout her years. Her coolness towards father's demise tore at our familial bonds, her tearless expression at his funeral, more so. Regardless of her emotionless persona, a trait shared with my mother on all subjects but father's death, I loved them both very much. The pair were all I had, and I vowed to never lose them, not even to time itself.

I traded on my father's name for several years and even attempted to branch out into the brave new world of technological sciences. I failed miserably. My inability to comprehend such advancements was a blow to my self-esteem, one from which I never quite recovered. A consequence of my abject failure was a return to my first love, clockwork. That was when Alberta first took ill, and I realized my sister would do well to see out another year. She decayed by the day, and my mother fell apart.

I used all my savings taking Alberta to the best specialists, the crème de la crème of Harley Street, the finest physicians and surgeons money could buy. Herbal medicines and near voodoo fared no better, and I was left a broken shell of a man. The shock of it almost killed my mother.

"She has a tick-tock heart," the last of them had ventured. He'd shrugged and turned back to his notes.

"Haven't we all?" I'd replied.

142

So, I took it upon myself to cure my ailing sister and submerged myself in the study of human anatomy. I strived to create something artificial to replace Alberta's failing organ, a pneumatic pump of sorts. But despite making the greatest efforts to assemble such a device, I could not. I did not possess my father's abilities; I never had. My fingers were too fat and the parts too small. The whale oil, spermaceti, my father had used to lubricate his creations cost too much, and no other oil possessed the necessary qualities for the task. I lost confidence by the day, grew nauseous at the slightest setback, and developed a permanent grinding in the gut. In short, I struggled, but doesn't everyone at some point in their lives?

For the longest time, all hope was lost, my misery compounded by my abject attempts to help Alberta or ease the suffering upon my dear mother. One day, however, everything changed. Whilst hurling my father's written notes about my office in a fit of volcanic temper, I stumbled upon a miracle.

Three solid months I spent in that direst of workplaces. Not once did I feel the sun upon my skin, nor the rain upon my face. A virtual recluse, more mole than man, I pushed the boundaries of human endurance.

Others noticed the inevitable changes: the pallid skin, bloodshot eyes...the smell. My closest associate, Professor Klaus Mortenson, a fine fellow of Danish heritage, entered my lair of gears and springs to speak on behalf of my betters.

"Albert," he began formally, "this cannot go on."

"What cannot go on?" A snapped retort.

"You cannot do anything for your sister if you are dead yourself."

"How did you know about my sister? That is a secret I have not shared."

"Give me some credit, man. This may be an establishment for scholars, but we intermingle with the outside world on occasion. When we must, anyway," he added, with the kind smile that was his calling card.

"Well, I am quite capable, thank you."

"You are one of the most capable men I know, but that is not the issue."

"Then, pray, tell, what is?"

"Your health, Albert. You are hardly a bull of a man, never have been. You can ill afford to spend so many hours secreted down here. No one could!" Klaus gave my basement workplace a furrowed once over and returned his attention to me. "I would aid you if you would but let me."

I smiled at that. Friendship was not something I valued because I had no friends to share it with, or so I had thought.

"Will you not, at least, allow me to assist you? I could refuse to budge, after all. I am much larger than you."

"But I have the assumed power of a crazy man," I replied, waving my hands in the air.

"You've always had that, my friend. I'm quite used to it by now." Klaus chuckled like a naughty schoolboy, and I wondered if he'd always been this way. "But seriously," he continued, "you know how high a regard I hold for you and your family."

"I do, and I am very grateful for it."

"Then, let me help. Please. If not for you, then for Alberta's sake. Don't make me beg."

How could I refuse?

We set about the task with renewed vigor, Klaus suggesting this and that, and I attempting to build it. A surgeon of some repute, he had an

144

innermost knowledge of human anatomy that I would never have, and his words made constant sense. He pointed, prodded, and commented, as I twiddled, tightened, and replied. This was our way, a constant him to me. Klaus possessed an infectious enthusiasm in his belief that mechanical support might aid the organic, which revitalized my confidence in the same. Well, not quite the same, but a conjunction was due. It had to be! We ate together, toiled together, and then one day, quite out of the blue, he said, "Should I examine her?" It was like he'd just thought it, when it ought to have been the first thing on both our lips and certainly mine. Perhaps I was mad, after all?

Klaus's words, as always, held an unerring logic. I immediately acquiesced to his wishes. We dropped everything, and I escorted him to our family home that very evening. I had to because Alberta was far too unwell to be brought to him. It rained all the way there.

"Good day, Missus Schmidt," I heard my friend say from the front door. "You don't look a day older than when last I saw you." He always did have a way with the ladies.

Mother had given a polite nod and then led Klaus into the living room, where having rushed ahead like a demented rabbit, I already attended to my sister's needs.

Klaus eased me aside and knelt before Albert. He looked at her askance and placed a reassuring hand upon her knee. It was a simple gesture but one of unwavering faith. He smiled, and I knew in my heart all would be well.

She huddled within the depths of our comfiest chair as though it were the Arctic. The fire blazed in the hearth as always. Still, my sister's slight frame shivered to such a degree one could have heard her teeth chattering from the kitchen.

Klaus manipulated his instruments like a musician might the strings of his guitar, with a gentle panache and delicate reassurance that seemed to ease Alberta's strife.

I watched on as the ruby flames flickered across the walls, almost spellbound by the way in which my friend administered his trade. His findings were less reassuring.

I will never forget the look Klaus cast as he placed his stethoscope on Alberta's bared chest. I could never be sure if it were disappointment or astonishment in his big, brown eyes. My own heart lurched, and I gulped. Everyone heard.

Klaus patted Alberta upon the knee, an act of symmetry with his arrival, and told her not to worry. Beckoning me to follow, I strode from the room in his wake. Mother observed everything from her seat in the hallway, straight-backed and alert.

"Were you never going to tell me? Did you think I would not notice?" Klaus breathed the words so silent as to have gone unheard, yet his diction was unmistakable in its intent. He suppressed his anger only from former respect.

"I am unaware as to what you allude?"

"There's no allude about it."

"Really."

"Really!" Klaus bit his lip, managed his anger in a way I was incapable. "Then let me say this: tick-tock, tick-tock, tick-tock." Klaus gave me a hard stare and an almost imperceptible shake of the head.

"I'm sorry, my friend, but I am still quite clueless."

"She is abnormal, by which I mean inhuman. Your sister is of an irregular construction. To be blunt, your sister has no heart. What is more, having frequented your workshop for the time I have, I imagine you

146

must be well aware of such a fact."

I believe Klaus would have walked out on us then, stormed away in protest, but he did not. Instead, always a good man, he offered a handkerchief, for I could contain my emotions no longer.

He led me to the kitchen, sat me down, and soon returned to my side bearing a scowl and a glass of water.

"You seek to build her a clockwork heart. Am I correct? Not to supplement, but to replace."

I nodded.

"Your sister is an… automaton. I am sorry, but I can think of no polite way to put it."

"Yes," I whispered. "And she is still my dear sister."

"I know," Klaus replied. "I know, Albert. But I think the greater question should be, how?"

"My father and mother were too old for children, or so I have surmised from his notes. I believe he built her before my own miraculous conception and could not bear to part with her. He must have waited the appropriate number of months before giving life to her as my sister. I cannot tell you more, for this is all I know."

Klaus considered my words as he paced about the kitchen, the tip-tap of his brogues mimicking that which he'd heard from within. He thought long and hard before saying, "So what are we to do?"

"I cannot replicate her workings. I am not the machinist my father was. It is beyond my capabilities. Perhaps, I held out some freak hope you might aid her where I could not, some desperate last chance."

"I cannot, my friend, though I would try. The problem is, I wouldn't know where to start."

"With this," my mother said, walking into the room with

something clutched in her small hands. The thing ticked, and hope returned.

"From where?" Klaus began.

"Just know it is mine to give, Doctor Klaus Mortenson, the man I entrust with my daughter's life."

We operated on Alberta that very evening. My sister was too far removed from reality to care what we did to her. Where others would have writhed in anguish, screaming bloody murder, she remained motionless as the scalpel sliced her in twain.

"Oh, my!" gasped Klaus.

I could only nod for words deserted me.

The intricacies of Alberta's form were a marvel to behold. In place of blood, she had oil; instead of organs, she had automata; she was my father's most incredible creation. How could anything have compared? She was unparalleled in her perfection.

"Over to you, old boy," Klaus announced and backed away from the stiffened form before him.

I took the heart of brass from the silver salver on which it rested; it beat a rhythm all its own. The thing echoed in its displaced mechanics like a miniature Big Ben housed in the confines of our own living room. I had never held, nor seen, anything of such exquisite craftsmanship. The tiny, metallic organ gleamed in the firelight like a star clasped in my palm. Part pocket watch, part far more, I marveled at the delicacy of the thing, at what my father had created. Yet, despite the fear of breaking it, I knew just what to do with undeniable certainty. A silent prayer to my father, a clenching and unclenching of trembling fingers, and I set to work.

It was many hours later when I sat back upon the sofa, Klaus at my side, both of us exhausted. Yet seeing Alberta lift from our makeshift operating table and step across the room towards us was worth more than all the gold in the world. I could never thank Klaus enough for his help. The joy of taking Alberta in my arms and hearing the ticking of her new heart was matched only by the sorrow of seeing my mother lay prone in the kitchen doorway. A gaping hole in her revealed chest, the former home of Alberta's second coming. Mother had died in silence, concern etched across her placid features.

When Alberta spied her, she flew into a fury. She tore at herself with a rage that neither of us men could calm. She flung Klaus out into the hallway, me following close behind, the two of us collapsing in a shared heap beneath the coat stand. By the time we picked ourselves up, two female automata were lying on the kitchen floor, each bearing cavernous openings to the chest. Klaus was shattered. I was inconsolable.

We remained the best of friends, closer because of our shared experience. I gave up my position at Oxford. Nobody cared. I sold our house, a mansion by most standards, and moved into a small flat. Klaus would, on occasion, visit and regale me with tales of my old colleagues. We laughed at this nonsense, chuckling at the various rumors, but we never spoke of our own past.

And so it was that many years later, when time had caught up with me, it already having seen off Klaus, I found myself sitting in my favorite chair by the fire. This was what old people did in place of living: sit and reminisce. A sudden silence fell upon my home, even the flames extinguishing as though blown out by God himself. All was silent. All was still. Then...

A strange tick-tock sound emanated from somewhere like the

counting of an irregular clock, a sound I had always known but only now truly heard. The noise was everywhere and nowhere, both within and without. A hand placed on my chest told me all I needed to know.

I could not say if Klaus had suspected and remained silent from respect. One can never be sure of such things. How could one tell another that one's best friend was not a man but a monster, and if he had, would it have mattered? The time for such concerns had long since gone.

As I sat there, the beating slowed, and I, in turn, felt the toll of the years upon me. The fire's golden embers dimmed, or my eyes did. England darkened, and the world stalled like an unwound clock. Time warped into something other, something else.

I was the last of my father's creations, the last of a family made but no less loved. I waited for that final tick without a tock. I waited and waited and waited.

Silence marked my death, my ceasing to work.

AUTHOR BIO

Richard M. Ankers is the English author of The Eternals dark fantasy series. Richard has featured in Expanded Field Journal, Love Letters To Poe, After The Pause and feels privileged to have appeared in many more. Richard lives to write. Visit Richard online at RichardAnkers.com.

151

MEISNER THE MAGNIFICENT

KELLY ZIMMER

"A magician? The old king's assassin is a magician?"

King Victor considered his private secretary with puzzled skepticism, but Gerard remained composed as though announcing breakfast rather than providing the resume of a killer. "He performs for children, Excellency. Rabbits from hats, escape stunts, card tricks, that sort of thing."

The king's features creased in disbelief. "Uncle Richard entrusted a clown with dispatching his enemies?"

"I'm told Meisner never failed the late king."

Victor scowled at his aide, his trusted right hand. "You stood by me during my struggle to secure the crown, put your life and your family's safety at risk but, I swear Gerard, if you're joking, you'll spend the night in a cell."

"I'm told your uncle trusted him with his life," Gerard said with an uneasy smile.

"Very well, get him up here. Let's meet this Meisner the Magnificent."

Though the black-and-gold clad figure had held two dozen eight-year-olds spellbound for an hour, a fresh wave of breathless excitement rippled through the party as the act reached its climax. Mothers and nannies lined the walls and gaped at the impossible: a room of quiet children.

The conjurer deposited his top hat on the fringed shawl covering a grand piano. From the hat, he pulled a long-stemmed rose. He inhaled its perfume, then extended it toward his audience.

"Behold this common red rose," he commanded. Flourishing the stem in a figure-eight, he returned it, bloom first, into the black hat. Nimble fingers waggled before dipping inside and retrieving a new treasure. "Behold the tiger," he said in a voice hoarse with reverence.

The diminutive heirs and heiresses gasped in unison at the ginger kitten in Meisner's outstretched palms. He presented the manifestation to the birthday girl with a shallow bow. The starched and ruffled duchess-to-be accepted the trembling ball of orange fluff with a squeal of delight. High-pitched chatter and laughter filled the room, and even the sourest nanny applauded.

A solemn man wearing an austere black swallow-tail jacket and satin waistcoat watched Meisner distribute sweets as he passed through the sea of waist-high heads. Gerard found Meisner ridiculous and winced at the thought of introducing the magician to King Victor. What if the legends were merely rumors? Would Victor really throw him into a cell?

Meisner reached the back of the room to receive his hosts' accolades. He agreed his skills were unsurpassed with a dismissive wave and inquired about his fee.

153

Once the magician settled his finances, Gerard extended his hand. "A moment, sir?" he said and led Meisner away to talk business.

Leo Meisner appeared in the king's study the following day wearing a crimson-lined cape over a heavily embroidered, velvet-trimmed frock coat in an unnatural shade of green. As Gerard presented him to the king, Meisner doffed his hat, revealing a head of untamed black curls flecked with white. The magician bowed deeply, and with a lightening-swift flick of his wrist, reached behind His Majesty's head.

"You have pulled a coin from my ear," Victor said with regal dignity.

The magician bowed again. "An honor, Your Majesty."

Gerard hoped that, given his status in court, he'd be permitted an extra blanket. The cells were notoriously dank.

Victor clasped his hands behind his back and considered his guest with narrowed eyes. "I understand you performed special services for my late uncle."

"A sideline, sir. Entertaining the children of your realm is my true calling."

"But you removed Uncle Richard's enemies?"

"I had that privilege."

"Right," Victor said. "Richard died before producing an heir and, though he'd publicly acknowledged me as his successor, he left no will. You've heard that my cousin Phillip inspired a feeble opposition to my ascent to the throne."

"I'm sure the duke was merely misguided, sir."

"Misguided or not, he's still making trouble. He has to go, and the deed cannot come back to me."

"Understood. It must appear an unfortunate accident."

"You can do that?" Victor asked. He ran his gaze over the ill-favored assassin's flamboyant attire. "Discretely?"

"I will be as a wraith." Meisner kissed his fingertips and blew the kiss to heaven.

His patience with Meisner's buffoonery already at its end, Victor turned his back to the clown and studied the misty afternoon outside his study window. "Gerard will see to your payment."

When Gerard returned to Victor's study, the king continued to ponder the plan's wisdom.

"Is it possible Uncle Richard lost his reason at the end?"

"The king fell from his horse. Your uncle suffered no illness, mental or otherwise."

"The witnesses say the fall was just an unfortunate accident," Victor mused aloud. The gray afternoon and the possibility that Richard's accident had been arranged made him crave the comfort of brandy and a fire—luxuries the demands of his new office seldom permitted.

"If you have concerns about the man's loyalty," Gerard said, echoing the king's thoughts, "perhaps we should assign someone to watch him."

Victor turned to face his confidante. "Who?"

"Lady Genesa."

"The one you hired to keep an eye on my wife's lover?"

"The queen's," Gerard paused to gather an inoffensive word, "companion has been called from the capital on business, so Genesa is at liberty for the moment."

"If that fool is captured, we can't have him bleating to Phillip that I hired him. Is she capable of silencing the man?"

"Lady Genesa is capable of almost anything," Gerard said and stepped silently from the study to make the arrangements.

The bay window of Leo Meisner's modest flat jutted over the capital's main street. On a clear day, he enjoyed views of the hectic shops below, the dreary castle towers to the north, and billowing steam puffing from ships gliding along the river to the south. Watching the capital at work passed the time waiting for his train to Gorde, where Archduke Phillip had prudently decamped after his failed coup.

Leo used the time to plot his next move. Taking the man in his home would be impossible. However, a garrulous publican who entertained many travelers from Gorde confided Phillip spent his nights gambling and drinking in town. And while not as populous as the capital, Gorde was still a fair-sized city, a good hunting ground. A stranger wouldn't stand out, but an archduke would, making his target easy to track while Leo remained anonymous. A day and a half should be enough to familiarize himself with the place, locate Phillip's preferred haunts, and devise an unhappy accident.

Leo consulted his gold pocket watch, a gift from his mentor, Eduard. Leo learned both his trades from the impish illusionist, who commissioned the watch to commemorate Leo's first royal assignment, the dispatch of an inconvenient bureaucrat. Eduard retired soon after. These days he performed without charge at His Majesty's Asylum for Orphans. He also eliminated pests such as blackmailers and rapists at reduced rates for clients of modest means, leaving the nobility's problems to Leo.

Though Eduard was proud of his student, Leo's lack of modesty remained a source of profound embarrassment. This brash arrogance, Leo explained, was necessary to inspire the confidence of a king. Or, Eduard countered, provoke one, but Leo was soon Richard's preferred henchman. Victor, however, lacked Richard's patience. Failure meant an end to royal commissions—or worse.

Leo returned his watch to his waistcoat pocket and hefted his two bags. The smaller held clothing and toiletries; the larger, his costumes and equipment. Both were heavy, but the walk allowed him time to consider schemes to wash Archduke Phillip out of Victor's hair.

The clack of the rails sent Leo into a doze. He woke as Gorde Station was announced. Compared to the capital, the place was bucolic. Horses were more common than steam cycles on the narrow, cobbled streets and the air clearer. Spring blooms blossomed in pots and, despite the lingering chill, citizens lounged outside every restaurant and public house.

He registered as Paul Martin at the hotel and requested a room overlooking the street. While enjoying a long-delayed lunch at a café, he listened to the surrounding speech, mentally adopting its cadence and accent. Afterward, he walked the boulevards, lanes, and alleys in every direction, noting landmarks, hiding places, and constables' routes. By dark, he could draw the city from memory.

Back in his rooms, Leo donned the simple frock coat he'd worn on the train, adding a silk cravat for the evening. It wouldn't do to be seen asking about the duke's favorite gaming parlor, at least not as himself, so he slicked his hair back and affixed a false beard to his clean-shaven jaw. Wearing his top hat and swinging his retractable cane, he joined the night-time crowd on the streets.

The first public house he encountered was frequented by honest working people: seamstresses, clerks, shopkeepers, and housemaids. Diligent eavesdropping provided no clues to Phillip's current whereabouts but plenty of gossip. Phillip's failed coup left him bitter, and his behavior grew increasingly erratic. The duchess had taken their children via airship to visit family and was not expected to return. Ever. Whether this was because of her husband's treason or violent temperament was a topic of vigorous debate.

Traffic grew as Leo ambled toward the town center where Phillip's favorite haunt, The Briar House, occupied half a block in a district filled with courts, legal offices, and banks. He studied the entry from across a wide boulevard. The men entering The Briar House dressed much like himself, and no constables were about.

This, Leo determined, could work.

Dodging steam messenger cycles, vendors hawking wares from atop clockwork carts, and horse-drawn carriages, he dashed across the street to the elegant but lively establishment.

Inside, he milled about with a pint, picking up bits of conversation. As he passed a trio near the fire, the words "cards" and "dealer" drifted his way. Leo settled in an upholstered chair near the group as a supercilious voice related an event that had happened that very evening.

"Everyone dropped out until it was just Old Louie and his nibs. One raised, then the other, then don't you know the duke is shy, not enough funds to call Louie!" The amused voice allowed his audience a raucous chuckle before continuing. "So, the duke asks his two men if he might have a loan!"

The laughter turned to guffaws.

"The duke gets his loan and calls. There's Old Louie, grinning from ear to ear, laying down his cards one by one and reaching for the pile. The duke, he says nothing but fans his cards on the table. Louie goes pale as a corpse." The storyteller continued in a cheerful tone. "The duke gathers up his winnings and pays back his man. With interest, mind you. Then he buys a round for the table and goes upstairs to visit the girls."

After murmurings of "poor Old Louie" and "uncanny luck," the conversation turned to the quality of female companionship at The Briar House compared to other establishments.

Leo abandoned his pint and returned to his room. He'd learned a great deal. Phillip went about with two guards, visited the tables early in the evening and the brothel afterward. The man telling the story hadn't said whether the duke had dealt the hand that ruined Old Louie's evening, but Leo suspected he had. If so, Phillip was an accomplished player and a cheat. This created possibilities.

The next day, Leo spent the daylight hours memorizing the routes to and from The Briar House, perfecting his disguise, and practicing. After an early supper, he strode into the gaming house. A keen observer might have noted that he did not hand his hat and cane to the hostess, but perhaps he wasn't staying. Gorde's most notable citizens frequented The Briar House, so curious onlookers were not uncommon.

Leo joined a game in the public room and fleeced a good-natured banker before moving on to a smaller, more private chamber. If the duke played, it would be in this room. Leo assumed Phillip's two men would guard the door, one watching the entrance, the other the windows. Their attention would be on the access points, not the table.

Leo didn't expect Phillip that night and used the time to familiarize himself with the players and their style of play. He bet prudently and won and lost small sums while absorbing the conversation at and around the table. After an hour, he cashed out and returned to the lounge, where he nursed a brandy and thought.

"That cravat brings out the gold flecks in your eyes."

Leo wheeled his head toward a woman with black hair and a creamy, coppery complexion. Peering through an eyeglass suspended from a ribbon around her neck, she studied the silk at his throat, which was of a similar golden hue as her gown.

"Did you buy it here in Gorde?" she asked.

Leo approved of bold women. In his experience, their candor saved time, but this one's stealthy approach unnerved him.

"No, madame, it was a gift from a friend." Leo refocused his attention on his drink.

"I'm Genesa LePage."

"My heartiest congratulations."

"This is my first visit to Gorde."

"I can recommend the museum. They have a fine portrait of his late Majesty."

"Richard?"

Leo's brow furrowed. The woman could be a danger if she recognized him from home.

"You were acquainted with our late monarch?"

"Intimately," Genesa lied.

"Then you're from the capital. You don't, by chance, have children?"

"Sadly, my husband died mere weeks after our honeymoon."

Leo determined it was unlikely they'd ever met, but though she presented no danger, the company of a lovely woman might attract unwelcome attention. "How tragic."

"Do you also come from the capital?

He dodged the question by offering to buy her a brandy.

Lady Genesa could think of nothing she wanted less. Still, Gerard's assignments were her only income, so she smiled an acceptance, a move Genesa soon regretted. Her mind slowly numbed as Leo prevaricated wildly about imaginary success in international trade. Gerard said the magician was arrogant but didn't mention he was a bore. Having identified her target, Genesa finished her brandy, said a quick goodnight, and dashed back to her hotel room to avoid the possibility of running into the lout later. She'd resume her surveillance in the morning but from a distance.

The following evening, Leo returned to The Briar House and enjoyed a delightful dinner, free of unexpected female companionship. When excited chatter filtered from the public room, Leo set his cutlery aside to observe Archduke Phillip's slow advance through the dining room. The guards at his side scanned the crowd with wary eyes, and their hands clenched when onlookers approached the duke. Both were tall and broad-shouldered, but Leo doubted they were agile.

After settling his bill, Leo strode into the card room, where he watched the play and waited. The first seat vacated was too far from his target, so he let another late arrival take it. When the chair to Phillip's left opened up, Leo pounced. He bought into the game and let the cards unfold, making no effort to improve his luck. Gain was not his objective.

Leo's opportunity arose when an attendant freshened the duke's drink. With his right hand, Phillip scooped up his cards. With his left, he raised his glass and, after a long swallow, set it aside inches from Leo's right hand.

Leo wore a gold ring with a black stone on the fourth finger of that hand. A depression beneath the gem concealed a deadly, but slow-acting, powder. Leo angled the ring toward Phillip's glass with a fluttering heart but steady hands.

While awaiting the right moment, he envisioned how events might unfold. With luck, Phillip's heart would give out after a strenuous session with his favorite hostess. Not wanting their charge to be found dead in such undignified circumstances, Phillip's men would sneak him off somewhere. Then, to avoid blame, they would claim he was overtaken by drink and fell, or perhaps they'd tuck him in his bed and let his valet find him in the morning. However it played out, Leo would be long forgotten and awaiting the next train home.

When the player to Phillip's right diverted the table's attention by mulling over his bet too long, Leo joined in the banter, leaning toward the man to screen a deft turn of his wrist. The ring's hinge flipped open, and its contents dissolved in the duke's brandy.

As Leo withdrew his hand, a flash of gold silk caught his eye, disrupting his timing. His ring clinked against the rim of Phillip's glass. Both guards fixed their eyes on the glass, then Leo.

Phillip scowled. "What's this?"

"I've bumped your glass, Your Grace. Let me get you a fresh one," Leo said and rose. Three steps put him at the window, but he needed a moment to collect his hat and cane, and the guards were already advancing.

As Leo twisted the window's latch, Genesa surged forward and clutched each guard by a wrist. "I know that man. Empress Pathei employs him." Her voice was shrill and her grip on the duke's men formidable.

Leo pushed through the open window. He slipped into the crowd, but, to his horror, a surly growl carried over the midnight throng, "There he is."

Hoping to put ten seconds between himself and his pursuers, Leo ran, not toward his hotel but toward a clandestine mist-shrouded alley he'd identified on his first day in Gorde. His chance came when a carriage

162

paused outside a public house to disgorge a tipsy couple. Leo dropped to the ground, rolled beneath it, and dashed into the shadows. While the guards wasted time searching the carriage, Leo slipped into the crowd and strode off at a dignified pace, swinging his cane and keeping his face turned from the streetlamp's flickering gaslight.

The hidden alley wasn't far. There, in the gloom of a recessed doorway, Leo Meisner removed his false beard and ruffled his slicked-back hair into damp curls. He collapsed his cane and shoved it into an inside pocket of his frock coat. His gold cravat went into another. After watching the mouth of the alley for thirty minutes, he ambled back to his hotel.

Leo spent the walk damn and blasting the infernal LePage woman. What was she doing there, and why had she mentioned Empress Pathei? The empress was ninety and had wielded no actual power in decades. Not that it mattered. He'd never get close to Phillip now, not at the tables. He needed a new plan and a fresh disguise.

Leo removed the cane from his jacket pocket at his hotel room door and extended it to its full length before inserting his key into the lock. He tensed, raised the cane over his shoulder, then unlocked the door with his free hand, leaping back to give potential lurkers time to show themselves.

"If you strike me, I will stab you in your sleep."

Genesa LePage lounged on his bed. "Where have you been? I've been waiting for hours."

"Watching for followers, Madame. You haven't led them to my door, have you?"

She swung her feet to the floor and stood, hands on hips. "I'm supposed to keep you out of trouble, not get you arrested."

"They sent you to spy on me?" Leo closed the door behind him.

"Entrusting this job to a clown didn't sit well with Victor. It appears his instincts are correct. Your sleight of hand leaves much to be desired."

"You distracted me."

"If you fall into Phillip's clutches, I'm to ensure you don't talk under torture."

"And how would you do that?"

Genesa flopped her hands at her sides, rustling the gold silk of her skirt. "By helping you escape."

"So you did. What was all that about the empress?"

"It was obvious you were poisoning Phillip. Given recent events, everyone would assume Victor hired you, so I gave them another candidate. The empress imagines plots and routinely orders her enemies killed. It would be like her to send a bumbling clown to do the job."

Leo drew himself erect. "Madame, I'm the finest illusionist in the kingdom and was within seconds of accomplishing my task when you interrupted."

"I was observing."

"You rustled."

"I what?"

"Your skirt rustled."

Genesa folded her arms over the bodice of the offending gown. "Many skirts rustled. Shoes scuffed and clocks ticked. Did they distract you?"

Rather than answer, Leo slumped into the chair beside the writing desk. "The question is, how now to proceed?"

"You can't try the card thing again."

"Quite. I'll have to arrange an accident from a distance. Tricky but not impossible."

"Can I help?"

A shudder rippled along Leo's spine. "It would help if you stayed out of my way. Go home."

"I can't. Gerard's already paid me, and I need the money."

"The story about your husband's death is true?"

Genesa lowered herself to the foot of the bed and rested her elbows on her knees. "He died three months after our wedding, leaving me with a title and debts. Gerard pays me to spy on the queen's lovers."

Leo arched a brow. "You're a busy girl then."

"I hate it, and it's so unfair. Her Majesty doesn't complain about the king having a mistress."

"Her Majesty no doubt considers Victor's mistress a friend and ally."

"I'd hoped this job would get me out of the domestic surveillance business, but this will never work."

"It will if you stay out of my way."

"You're an idiot."

"And you're a distraction."

Genesa brightened. "You'll need a distraction if you hope to get close to Phillip again."

Leo pushed to his feet. "This commission is at an end. I will return home in disgrace and return my fee. In the future, I shall stick to performing magic acts for fresh-faced tykes."

"You're trying to trick me into thinking you're giving up, so I'll go home."

Perhaps, Leo thought, the pest had a brain. He sat. "Show me how clever you are. Devise a way to kill Phillip without getting near him. And remember, it must appear to be an accident or death from some natural cause."

Genesa huffed, flopped back on the bed, and stared at the ceiling. Hours later, when she woke, Leo Meisner snored at her side. She studied his features in the weak spring dawn. His best quality, expressive gold-brown eyes were shut. His nose was too sharp, and his lips too thin. Though he lacked the noble gentility of court, Meisner wasn't a bad-looking man, and Genesa was sick to tears of the court and its intrigues. Still, there had to be a middle ground between false civility and arrogant buffoonery.

She slipped from the bed to her own room on the floor above. No one waited, and it didn't appear the place had been searched. She hadn't expected to be followed. The guards had chased Leo, not her. Still, the elegant lady of the evening before needed to disappear, so she arranged her hair in a braided bun and applied cosmetics to give her complexion a ruddy, outdoor look. Glasses with smoked lenses obscured her eyes, and a fitted vest over trim trousers accentuated the curves her gown had obscured.

When she returned to Leo's room, Genesa found he had also transformed. The white flecks in his curls were gone, hidden with boot polish. He wore rough slacks under a tattered jacket with leather trim at the collar and cuffs.

Leo appraised Genesa's attire with an approving nod. "We'll get close to Phillip's house by posing as a couple enjoying a picnic."

Genesa blinked in surprise. "You want my help?"

Leo pulled a battered straw hat from his case and patted it on his head. "Let's hire a couple of horses and put your powers of observation to the test."

Archduke Phillip's villa lay in a valley to the west of town, its ancient stone glowing gold in the noontime sun. Genesa and Leo studied the wide two-story entrance from their damp, grassy hillock. No one was about. Genesa rotated the bezel on her glass to increase the power, bringing the windows into better focus. "Does he even live here? Gossip says the duchess and the children are gone, probably for good."

"He mentioned the villa over cards last night." Leo unscrewed the brass handle of his cane and twisted caps from both ends, revealing a short telescope which he trained on the sprawling house. "He damned Victor's tax policies, saying they may cost him the family estate."

"Easier than admitting you've gambled your fortune away," Genesa said.

"Don't forget the pockets he lined in his ill-advised bid for the throne." Leo lowered the glass. "No signs of life. Let's enjoy our lunch and hope he returns before dark."

They'd barely dug into the fruit and cheese when their horses shuffled and whinnied. Leo's head snapped up, and he raised the telescope toward a cloud of dust rising in the distance.

"Men on horseback." He reassembled his cane and slid it under their blanket.

Genesa grabbed her straw hat, purchased that morning from a street vendor, and adjusted it to shadow her features. She arranged the ribbon holding her glass under her shirt, then stood and grasped Leo's arm, as a wife or lover would.

The riders paused ten feet from the picnickers. Phillip and his guards glared down at them.

"You're trespassing," a guard barked.

"Oh dear," Leo responded in a nasal whine. "Our innkeeper recommended this spot for a quiet picnic."

Phillip grunted a false laugh. "I don't doubt that. I'm always chasing townspeople off my land."

Leo brought a hand to his chest and waved the other toward the villa. "My apologies, sir. Is that your fine home?"

"This is Archduke Phillip of Gorde, the king's cousin," the guard replied. "Get off of his land."

Phillip had noticed Genesa and liked what he saw. "Don't rush the lady, Harry. Please finish your lunch, but tell your innkeeper to stop sending guests to camp on my estate."

"Thank you, and good luck on your hunt," Leo said, but the duke and his men had already turned their horses.

Leo and Genesa dropped onto the blanket.

"What did you observe?" Leo asked.

"They're hunting with crossbows. We could hide in the trees and shoot Phillip through the heart unobserved."

Leo cocked a brow. "Really? In early spring with the trees denuded of leaves?"

Genesa raised her gaze to the budding branches above her.

"Nor would his death look like an accident."

"It would if Phillip was shot with his own arrow," Genesa said.

Leo blinked in surprise. "A daring notion. How do we arrange it?"

"Steal one from his house." Genesa nodded toward the villa. "I don't see any servants about."

Leo retrieved his cane and disengaged the telescope again. He studied the grounds for a full five minutes. "Arrows will be in an outbuilding, a workshop."

They rode further up the hillside to get a better view of Phillip's estate. Near the main house, they spotted a stable surrounded by a cluster of huts. Leo pointed out a squat gray stone building set near the stables in the distance. "That door's been left ajar. Someone has saved themselves the trouble of unlocking it when the duke returns. I'll approach from the far side."

"What about me?"

Leo pointed further up the hill. "Hide the horses behind those thorn bushes and watch for Phillip and his men. The game bags were empty when they accosted us, so they may have just begun their hunt, but they'll return soon if they're successful. If you spot them, sound a warning. Can you mimic the song of the rainbow-throated carol jay?"

"I've never heard of a rainbow-throated carol jay."

Leo tapped his ear then screeched, "Eeee," before letting the note rise to an "Ah," then falling to a rather musical "Ooo." He tapped his ear again and repeated the call. "You try."

"Eee-ah-Oh," Genesa said in a wobbly tremolo.

"Ooo, not Oh," Leo said.

She tried again.

"Better. Now louder. I have to hear you from inside a stone shack."

Genesa warbled louder.

"It'll have to do." Leo scampered down the line of thorny brown hedges toward the stables.

Genesa watched, convinced of the plan's inevitable failure. Even if Leo managed to steal an arrow, how did he shoot Phillip undetected? What if Leo were captured? Would she have to kill him to keep him from talking? What if *she* was captured? Rather than consider torture, Genesa scanned the horizon for riders.

Below, inside the stone hut, Leo struggled to recall the duke's fletchings. He was certain he'd seen one cock feather and two hens, but were the hens' feathers brown or russet? The arrows must be a perfect match to convince Phillip's men he'd met with an accident. At last, Leo spotted a single arrow wedged in a vice under a clutter of leather wraps, feathers, and glue pots.

Leo pocketed his find and searched for a bow. In a corner filled with scrap wood, he uncovered a longbow with a cracked grip, hopefully long forgotten. As Leo slung the bow over a shoulder, the call of a sick or wounded rainbow-throated carol jay reached him. He scurried from the hut, not pausing when he reached Genesa but continuing his dash to the horses. Genesa fell in behind him, launching questions that Leo ignored.

"Which direction are they coming from?" he asked.

"The north."

"They'll head straight for the stables. We need to get closer. Bring the horses and stay silent."

Grabbing the reins, she led the horses down the hill. This is real, Genesa thought. Leo's going to assassinate the duke. Her heart pounded in time with the horses' hooves, and she wished herself back home, gossiping with the queen's ladies in the garden.

They tied the horses behind the thorny hedge that bordered Phillip's property. When Leo spotted a broad trunk halfway between them and the stables, he turned to Genesa. "If anything goes wrong, ride into town and be on the next train home. Whatever Gerard is paying you isn't worth your life."

Though she had no intention of abandoning Leo, at least not alive, Genesa nodded.

Leo edged down the embankment, crouched at the tree's thick base, and waited while the three horses strode into the yard.

As the hunting party dismounted, two young men appeared from inside the stable. Phillip passed his game bag to Harry, and then both guards strode off toward the house with that evening's dinner. The duke spoke to the grooms, who then disappeared inside the stable with the horses, leaving Phillip alone, his crossbow at his side.

Leo straightened and notched the arrow. He raised the longbow, drew the string back, and waited.

Phillip shouted into the stable, drank deeply from a flask, then took one step toward his villa.

Leo released the arrow. The bow's string still hummed when Phillip fell backward.

Leo lowered the bow and waited, his breath shallow puffs in the silent afternoon. The guards continued their march toward the house, their backs to the stable and their fallen master. Keeping his eyes forward, Leo backed up the hill to where Genesa waited with wide eyes.

"You did it," she said.

"Lead the horses. If they suspect foul play, the guards will look for someone rushing away. We'll take our time."

Genesa focused on leading her horse, her eyes trained on Meisner's battered straw hat ahead of her. They hadn't gone a hundred yards when shouting rose from below, calling for help. From the pitch of the voices, it was the stable boys. Genesa kept her eyes forward but pictured the scene in her mind. The boys would kneel beside the duke's body while the guards rushed back from the villa. Together, they'd examine the arrow lodged in the duke's chest and ask each other if it could be Phillip's.

Puzzled, they'd notice the bow was still in the duke's hand. Had he shot an arrow into the air then watched its descent? The duke was subject to fits of exuberance, especially after drinking, which they'd done all afternoon. The guards would study the surroundings, searching for someone or something out of place. Would they remember the couple in the field?

When they finally reached the main road, Leo snapped the longbow into three pieces. The coiled string went into a pocket, and he dropped the bits of the bow into the river as they crossed the bridge back into town.

After returning the horses, the co-conspirators walked to the hotel, packed, and were at Gorde Station ahead of the news of Duke Phillip's tragic accident.

The next train to the capital didn't leave for two hours. Bags at their feet, Leo and Genesa settled onto an iron bench facing the station's ornate glass and steel entrance. They didn't have long to wait. Phillip's guard, the one called Harry, burst through the door, his head swiveling, his eyes wild.

Leo and Genesa crouched low, but they'd been spotted. Leo grasped Genesa's hand and dragged her from the bench, pulling her outside to the platform. An arrow whizzed past Leo's ear and thunked into a post.

Screaming citizens streamed from the arrow's path, leaving Leo and Genesa as exposed as two trees in the desert. They jumped from the

172

platform as another arrow split the air between them. They ran north, under the raised platform. No footsteps crunched the gravel behind them, so Leo slowed, got his bearings, and led them into the alley running between the station and a public house catering to travelers.

Three steps from the street and freedom, Harry's menacing form filled the gap between the buildings.

"Why do you chase us, sir?" Leo blustered.

"I said it was you two." Harry reloaded his crossbow. "The others said it was an accident, but I said, even drunk, Phillip isn't stupid enough to shoot himself."

Genesa brought a hand to her heart. "The duke is shot?"

Harry leveled the bow at Genesa. "You're the woman from the card room who held us back to let him escape."

Genesa opened her mouth to reply, but the oaf said, "Don't spin tales about Empress Pathei. Victor sent you, didn't he?"

Leo stepped between his terrified companion and Harry, putting his chest directly in front of the arrow. "What are you saying, sir?"

"That the king hired you and this lady to kill the archduke."

"Preposterous! We're on holiday, and this lady has certainly never been in any card room."

"Then there's no harm in you coming along to answer a few questions though the questioning might get rather," he dropped his head to one side, "intense. We'll start with the lady. Ladies do like to chat, especially when in danger of losing their tongues. Now move!"

A moan escaped Genesa, but Leo chuckled at the man's suggestion. "You can't march us through the streets with a loaded crossbow at our backs. You'll frighten the populace, and you can only shoot one of us at a time."

"I'll catch up with the one that gets away," Harry assured him.

"Why should we run off?" Leo asked. "We've done nothing wrong."

"We'll find out soon enough," Harry said.

Leo pulled the bowstring from his pocket. "Restrain me with this and hold the lady close. Keep the crossbow loaded at your side if you wish, but I believe if the duke were alive, he'd prefer you not create a public spectacle."

Though Harry saw the wisdom of the stranger's suggestion, he distrusted him on principle. "I won't lower my weapon to tie you up."

"Of course not," Leo said. "That would be foolish. Have the woman do it."

Harry's eyes narrowed to slits, but it was that or make a scene, and, with the duke dead, his future was uncertain enough. He nodded.

Leo handed the bowstring to Genesa, then turned his back to her, his hands crossed at the wrists. "Pretend you're tying your horse to a post, dear. Get it good and tight, then let the gentleman test it."

Genesa's expression grew uncertain, but she did as she was told. After she gave the knot a final yank, Leo turned his back to their captor. Harry pulled at the string with a thick forefinger. He grunted, lowered his bow, and pulled Genesa close enough for her to smell sour wine on his breath.

"Walk to the end of the street," he ordered. "I have a carriage waiting."

Leo shot the man a lopsided grin and stepped into the busy street from the alley. He spotted the duke's carriage and made for it at such a brisk pace, Harry had to drag Genesa to keep up.

The carriage driver remained silent and motionless as Leo and Genesa climbed into the plush coach. They sat side-by-side facing Harry, who lay his bow across his lap. His eyes leveled on his prisoners, the guard pounded the roof twice, and the carriage lurched forward.

They rolled over the cobblestones with a rumbling Genesa found unnerving. Leo, however, commented on the smooth ride. "The duke's coach has good springs. I haven't introduced myself. Paul Martin, from Pathei."

Harry snorted. "And what do you do in Pathei, liar?"

"Card tricks," Leo said.

The guard's belly jiggled with laughter. "Card tricks?"

"Would you like to see one?"

"You do card tricks with your hands tied behind your back?" Harry asked.

"You'll have to help. Reach into my inside pocket. Left side, I think. You'll find a deck of cards." Leo angled toward their captor to make the reach easier and distract Harry from Leo's attempts to free himself from Genesa's impressive knots.

Harry pulled the deck from Leo's pocket.

"Shuffle the deck," Leo commanded in his magician's voice, "then remove a card, memorize it, and return it to the deck."

Harry did so.

"Now," Leo said, "close your eyes and concentrate on your card. Hold a picture in your head, and I will attempt to read your mind."

A puff of false laughter escaped Harry's full lips, but he squeezed his eyes tight.

Leo pulled unbound hands from behind his back, clamped them together above his head, and asked, "Got it?"

"Yeah," Harry said.

Leo brought his clubbed fists down on the base of the man's skull. Harry fell forward, stunned, and another blow ensured he'd remain unconscious for some time.

"His mind is such a small place," Leo said. "I'm surprised it had room for a card."

Leo tied Harry's hands with the bowstring while Genesa gagged their victim with his own scarf. Stretching his cane to its full length, Leo tapped the roof twice. The carriage slowed to a stop. The driver took no notice of them as they descended. Leo thumped the door twice with his fist, and the coach rolled off. He doubted Harry would wake before it reached the villa.

They returned arm-in-arm to the station. Other than a nick from Harry's arrow on a post, there were no signs of the earlier excitement. They collected their luggage, waited unmolested under the abandoned bench, boarded the train, and located their private car. An extravagant expense, but Victor could afford it.

When the porter left, a still-flushed Genesa said, "You're such a clown. You could have gotten us killed."

"I?"

"Card tricks? That man was going to torture us and see us hanged."

"When Harry wakes, he'll have Phillip's people looking for a mythical Paul from Pathei." Leo shrugged one shoulder. "Assuming anyone listens to him. I doubt he'll admit he ran down the duke's killers then let them escape. My guess is, he'll keep his mouth shut and agree with the others that Phillip's death was a tragic accident."

"Nobody will believe Phillip shot himself!"

"The next logical suspect is one of the guards, but the grooms will swear to their innocence, and the arrow was Phillip's. The widow won't press for an investigation, and Victor certainly won't. What is your fee, by the way?"

"My fee?"

"What did Gerard pay you to keep me from implicating the king? I'll match it."

Her fear-fired anger spent, Genesa said, "Thank you. I could use the money."

"There are conditions."

Genesa rolled her glistening brown eyes to the elaborate ceiling. "What conditions?"

"If you're to be my assistant, you'll have to polish my brass and keep my equipment organized, including the doves and rabbits."

"Your assistant?" Genesa's voice rose to a wail.

"If you prefer peeking through Her Majesty's bed curtains, I understand, but I believe you show promise."

"As an assassin or a clown?"

Leo stretched his arms across the crimson velvet seatback. "At making others believe what you want them to see. You've been playing make-believe for a long time, Genesa LePage. Join me and make it profitable."

Genesa turned her face to the window and watched the farmland roll by. She imagined telling the queen's ladies she'd helped assassinate Archduke Phillip. They'd laugh at her, but she suspected the queen wouldn't. Would Her Majesty be horrified or consider Genesa with more respect?

Genesa dozed and dreamed. She was the favored lady in her dream, no longer a bedroom spy hovering at the fringes. When the screech of the train's whistle disturbed her nap, she blinked herself awake and raised her head to ask Meisner if his offer was sincere, but, like a wraith, he was gone.

AUTHOR BIO

Kelly Zimmer read her first Agatha Christie mystery at age thirteen. She quickly moved on and has lived on a steady diet of murder, thrillers, horror, and suspense novels while laboring in a stifling corporate atmosphere in the wonderfully bizarre and diverse landscape of Florida, USA.

She now crafts cozy mysteries and fantasies set in those environments. Her work always includes unlikely protagonists and a touch of humor. Kelly's stories have been featured online and in anthologies.

Visit Kelly online at KellyZimmerAuthor.com where you'll find her Emi Watson magical realism/chick-lit/adventure novels and short stories.

179

INSPECTOR MCWILLIAMS OF THE
AERIAL CORPS!

J. F. BENEDETTO

Her Majesty's Spiralifter ALACRITY

Shantung Peninsula, China, 1895

"I know exactly where we are," declared Lord Percy Titsworth Hobart. The RPC Inspector, dressed in the uniform and leather shoulder pauldron of an army lieutenant, authoritatively stabbed a finger against the chart of the Shantung Peninsula on the wall of the spiralifter's wheelhouse. "Right there. Nowhere near the German Neutral Zone. Does that satisfy you, McWilliams?"

Inspector McWilliams of the Aerial Corps of the Royal Peninsular Constabulary, who also wore the same uniform, pushed his wind goggles up onto his pith helmet and sighed. "Your lordship has his finger on the Chinese coast," the Canadian-bred Englishman said. "That would place the entire Yellow Sea on the left." He waved his hand out the wheelhouse window at the green expanse of land beneath the aeroship. "Do you see a sea, Yellow or any other color?"

Lord Hobart frowned, glanced at the map, then looked out at the ground below. "Harrumph! These Chinese charts are notoriously unreliable."

Inspector McWilliams ignored him. He went to the wheelhouse phoneter on the wall and cranked the handle. A moment later, an electric voice came out of the dome above it. "Lookout here."

"We are trying to fix our position," McWilliams said into the phoneter. "Keep a sharp lookout to the south and west." He replaced the unit and turned to Lord Hobart. "I would remind you my lord that our orders are to apprehend the pirate, Wing Ho, determine the whereabouts of the female bandit, Shih Yang, and most important of all, to intercept smugglers operating inside the—"

"I know full well what our orders are!"

"I rather doubt that," McWilliams said. "You've spent the whole patrol in your cabin, counting the money from your latest sale of scrap to the natives. That hardly suggests you remember what our orders are."

Lord Hobart's eyes narrowed. "Just because our commissions were both signed on the same day, that does not make you my equal, McWilliams! Nor does it give you license to treat me as though I were—"

The voice from the dome on the wall interrupted them. "Are we looking only for landmarks, sir?"

McWilliams activated the phoneter. "Anything, lookout."

"Well, sir, there is something aloft, abeam of us, away to the south. Could be another aeroship."

McWilliams stepped out of the wheelhouse onto the walkway mounted atop Alacrity's hull, bracing himself in the downwind of the overhead screws. Each of the eight masts bore two horizontal screws driven at a prodigious speed, the upper ones rotating counter to the direction of the lower ones to retain their equilibrium by their horizontal resistance. It was these helical screws that kept Alacrity in the air, although their constant downwind made walking the catwalk difficult.

McWilliams scanned the horizon. Yes, there was something aloft in the air to the south, but it did not look like another spiralifter; it had no upright masts for lifting screws. "Aerostat, I think," he said, squinting at it. He lowered his goggles and activated the crystal lenses to enlarge the object in sight.

Yes, it was an aerostat. The gasbag—cigar-shaped, with a sharply pointed nose—bore a flared German cross on its side, announcing its ownership. The long metal hull hanging below the gasbag had a sharply pointed front to act as a ram, similar in function to the large steel spike that jutted out from the bow of Alacrity.

But the German's wheelhouse was an armored barbette. Where the British ship had a full-length casemate, the German aerostat had the center portion of her hull cut back, providing a large fighting deck, upon which stood several sailors in blue naval uniforms. Further aft sat a flying bridge with steerage vanes jutting out from the sides and, at her rear, a vertical propeller spinning fast enough to be a blur.

McWilliams examined her flag: a black, white, and blue Prussian tricolor with a large white circle in the center bearing an imperial crown above a fouled yellow anchor. It was the flag of Germany's Kiao-Chau Bay Territory.

So much for Lord Hobart's navigation skills.

"German gunfloat," he announced. "Falke class, I think."

The sound of rifle fire came to them on the wind, and Lord Hobart clutched the railing. "They're shooting at us!"

"No gun flashes," McWilliams noted. "Her crew must be firing away from us, at something to their south. I doubt that they've even spotted us yet."

"Good!" Lord Hobart declared. "We can leave undetected." He turned to the wheelhouse.

McWilliams stopped him. "Do you have any idea of what the Germans are firing on?"

"I do not know, and I do not care!" Lord Hobart said. "We are obviously over the German colony. We must depart at once!"

McWilliams returned to his binoculars. "We are not yet within the German Neutral Zone surrounding Tsingtao. As we are outside of the Deutsches neutrales Gebiet, we will stay and investigate this matter."

"Are you questioning my order to depart?" Lord Hobart demanded.

McWilliams glanced at the baron from Kent with a stare that made his unspoken answer quite evident.

"Sir!" the lookout yelled down. "Second craft to the south of the gunfloat."

The German aerostat blocked McWilliams' view. "Can you make him out?"

"Spiralifter," came the surprising reply. The British were the only force in China that used them. "Short hull," the lookout continued. "Looks rather like a Chinese junk, sir. Six masts, six sets of screws. One propeller and a single rudder aft. No colors showing." A pause. "She appears to be fleeing, sir. It looks like the Germans are trying to stop her."

A small spiralifter with just six lifting screws that looked like a junk? Chinese, obviously. But the Chinese had no spiralifters whatsoever!

"Accelerate to intercept the German ship. And ring for the

183

signalman," McWilliams ordered.

Pulling ahead allowed them to see the spiralifter the German aerostat was chasing. It indeed looked like a Chinese junk with six masts mounting lifting screws, pushed by a propeller astern. The German gunfloat was now turning straight toward the fleeing spiralifter. Preparing to ram? Most likely, since the gunfloat appeared to have no cannon pointing straight ahead.

McWilliams spoke up, "Bring us in between—"

He stopped. The bottom section of the airship's pointed nose dropped down, like an enormous jaw opening up, revealing within its "mouth" a gun of such enormous size—a full 12-inches—that it could only have come from a battleship. But carrying a monstrous weapon of such weight on an aeroship was impossible!

But no, the Germans relied on hydrogen gasbags for lift, not helical screws, so they had the lifting capability to mount such a giant cannon within such a small hull. It was an alarming fact to discover since just a single vessel armed with such a cannon could destroy the entire spiralifter fleet at Wei-Hai-Wei, not to mention the havoc it would wreak on the British warships of the China Station sitting in the anchorage!

The great German gun fired at the aerojunk. The shell made only a glancing hit astern, but that was enough to shatter the Chinese spiralifter's rudder and a part of her propeller, disabling her.

McWilliams had Alacrity sound her electric whistle to draw the attention of the two combatants. The signalman dropped a weighted line adorned with international code pennants out of the bottom of Alacrity's hull, the message reading STOP CARRYING OUT YOUR INTENTIONS, and I WISH TO COMMUNICATE WITH YOU.

The German seamen gawked at the Alacrity. There could be no mistaking her for anything other than a British aeroship, given that they

184

were the only ones who flew spiralifters in China.

McWilliams was engaging in a dangerous game with the Germans, for Alacrity was no match for the German aerostat. Constructed using the same process that Robur the Conqueror had developed for his first aeronef, much of Alacrity's structure was comprised of unsized paper impregnated with dextrin and starch then squeezed in hydraulic presses to form a material as hard as steel but far lighter. Yet even being as hard as steel, it was also quite thin and would do nothing to stop a 12-inch cannon shell. Indeed, Alacrity was armed with only a lightweight two-barrel flasher gun and single-shot light-ray carbines.

Which begged the question, how many of those unhappy facts were the Germans aware of?

McWilliams had a second signal-line dropped from Alacrity's belly, trailing the international code pennant for LAND IMMEDIATELY.

The Germans did not respond, save for the seamen on her open deck training their blaster-rifles on Alacrity. The damaged Chinese spiralifter was already dropping to land, but with her propeller out of action and her rudder shot away, she had no other choice.

"Turn out the flying squad," McWilliams ordered.

For once, Lord Hobart did not argue.

The pith-helmeted men in pale blue tunics and cord breeches turned to along the roof catwalk. They automatically took up firing positions with their light-ray carbines as the twin-barrel flasher was unlimbered and trained on the German gasbag. The carbines were short-range weapons intended solely for use on the ground and would hardly reach the German aerostat at this distance. And while the twin-barrel flasher had the range to hit the Germans, it did not have much of a punch, being far better suited for use on native straw-roofed huts than in

185

airborne ship-to-ship combat.

McWilliams waited, his body tensing. This was the moment.

What would the Germans do? The Royal Peninsular Constabulary had all of the appearances of a regiment of the British Army; indeed, he and Lord Hobart, while both District Inspectors (3rd Class), wore the uniforms, shoulder pauldrons, and insignia of British army lieutenants. However, despite their appearance, the RPC was a purely civilian police force—albeit a fully militarized one, with army barracks, drills, uniforms, and weapons. Most Europeans presumed they were a gendarmerie, a part of the regular army assigned policing the civil populace. Only the Americans and Canadians saw them as a civilian police force, like the Texas Rangers or the Northwest Mounted Police.

In truth, they were at best a highly trained militia or at worst bobbies with rifles; rank amateurs, facing off against blaster-armed German sailors who were professionals in the art of aerial war.

The German aerostat showed no signs of complying with his order to land, so McWilliams raised his voice to the gun crew. "Fire off one shot across his bow."

The gunners, knowing full well how outmatched they were, did as they were told, and a flasher-shot lanced out across the German's path in warning.

Now the two "friendly" foreign powers hovered opposite each other in silence for several tense moments.

The German aerostat raised the signal flag AFFIRMATIVE.

Both ships descended toward the Chinese spiralifter that had landed on the ground between them.

Kapitänleutnant Strasser, commander of the German aerostat, spoke excellent English. "I can assure you, Herr Leutnant," he told McWilliams—

or perhaps Lord Hobart, as they were standing side by side— "that we are currently within the neutrales Gebiet. You have no jurisdiction here, ja?"

"Ah," Hobart said, clearing his throat. "We—"

"Our chart," McWilliams said, "places you and I both outside the German Neutral Zone, Herr Captain-Leftenant. As such, you would have no jurisdiction here either." He waved a hand toward the grounded Chinese spiralifter. "May I ask why you were chasing this…craft?"

"Chinese scum," Strasser said. He turned and led McWilliams toward the craft, with Hobart and another German officer in their wake. "Evasion of the port tax. A purely routine matter for the German authorities, I assure you."

Not a word about the fact that the ship should not even exist, let alone that it belonged to the natives and not a European power. And something else, something in the German officer's tone, made McWilliams distrust the man's motives, but he merely smiled. "As we are both outside our zones, I would be happy to have your aid in jointly investigating the matter."

The German captain's face gave no hint of anything, but in the man's blue eyes, there was a glare that Inspector McWilliams had seen before in the eyes of a hundred guilty men.

Strasser gestured him to the aerojunk's rope boarding ladder with his own polite smile.

McWilliams listened to Strasser and Hobart question the Chinese captain, a sullen individual with the usual shaved forehead and cue of braided hair hanging down his back. While they did so, McWilliams shifted his attention from the ship's captain to the ship itself.

The modest wooden hull was very much that of a Chinese junk.

Her six metal lifting masts were in three different colors of paint, and of the 12 horizontal helical screws, seven were painted in two different colors, the remaining five being bare wood.

Strange. McWilliams opened the deck hatch and went below.

She had a single electric motor, whose manufacturer's plate identified it as having come from Birmingham, of all places. Strange, indeed! It sent power to the masts via a nest of overhead gears and pulleys, only three of which were European in origin, the remainder being hand-carved wood. Yet, apparently it worked well enough to give this aerojunk its lift through the air.

The motor, in turn, was fed power from a standard set of electrical accumulators—these too bearing manufacturer's plates identifying them as having come from England. However, the significant dents and deep scratches in them suggested they were in no way brand new. He took out a piece of paper and a pencil and scribbled notes about what he was seeing. Even with his lack of knowledge of mechanics, it was plain that all this had been set up by someone whose professional skills were sorely lacking.

Returning up to the deck, McWilliams went aft to the captain's cabin. It was dark inside, an ordinary cabin, reeking of tobacco and incense. He was about to leave when something in the corner caught his eye. He shoved the folding screen aside and beheld a Chinese girl of singular beauty kneeling on the floor. Her clean but badly torn clothing hid little of her lithe body, and though her face was streaked with dirt, her winsomeness was without question. A set of heavy, rough manacles around her wrists chained her to the spot where she sat, making her status plain.

"No one's going to hurt you," he told her. Her blank stare showed she did not understand English. "No one shall bring hurt upon you," he

188

said in Chinese. He examined her locked manacles, trying the lock. She eyed him and then indicated the far wall.

Far out of her reach hung a large iron ring with keys. He grabbed them, found the one that undid her manacles, and removed the rough-edged iron from her wrists. He helped her stand, her soft hands warm in his, and when she stood before him, her dark black eyes beheld his with a curious stare that he involuntarily returned.

It took a moment for propriety to remind him of how discourteous he was behaving, and he cleared his throat to cover his embarrassment. She cocked her head at him, no doubt waiting for his crude and angry command; such was the life of a slave. Sighing, he took hold of her smooth, supple wrist—No! Banish such thoughts, old man! —to take her out of here, when he realized that her torn clothing allowed him to see her...

Good lord!

He looked away, his face reddening. "You, you should cover yourself," he said, averting his gaze from her exposed nudity. She picked up a blanket and draped it over herself, and he led her out onto the aerojunk's deck.

She was even prettier in the sunlight, and he took her to the rail, away from Hobart and the German captain. "Who are you?" he asked her in Chinese.

"I am called 'putrid one' by my owner," she told him, the foul name typical of how a Chinese master would debase a slave girl.

"How long have you been a slave?"

"Two years. My husband sold me to pay off his gambling debts. My owner is the captain of this strange ship of the sky. I prepare his meals and work the fans night and day to cool him, and he makes me go in the hold every morning to wind a crank and appease the sky-spirit who lifts the sky-boat."

Wind a crank to appease the sky-spirit? No doubt, she cranked an electro-motor to produce electricity for the accumulators. He looked at the aerojunk's captain, whose face showed a sudden look of distrust that McWilliams recognized. So, the slave girl might well know something they could use against the fellow.

"You say you turn the crank to appease the sky-spirit. How long have you—"

"What are you doing with that native girl?" Lord Hobart asked, striding over.

"Making inquiries regarding the origins of this odd craft," McWilliams said.

Lord Hobart snorted. "I hardly think a common slave-girl would know anything about a ship's provenance."

"I would agree with your lordship," Strasser said, walking over to join them. "She is obviously kept for, shall we say, other purposes?" The German reached out and lifted the blanket with a leer across his face, and she looked silently at McWilliams for help.

He took hold of her wrist and pulled her away from the German officer. "As the Royal Peninsular Constabulary is investigating this affair, it is I, sir, who shall attend to the matter of this girl." He pointed at the boarding ladder and gestured for her to go down it.

"What are you doing?" Lord Hobart demanded. "Surely you do not intend to take this guttersnipe aboard our ship!"

"She is a woman in trouble," McWilliams declared. "It is our duty to render her aid. She may well be able to provide us with information regarding the origin and purpose of this strange aerojunk."

"You have no authority to do anything of the sort!" Lord Hobart pulled the girl free of his grip and pushed her back toward the Chinese captain, who grabbed hold of the slave girl none too gently. "She is his property, and you have no right to take her from him, even if he is a filthy Chinaman."

McWilliams looked to the slave girl, whose face broke like a dropped vase. Once more a slave, having tasted freedom for but a moment. Back to the dim cabin and the unlit hold, to slave away at day and night at the crank and the fan. McWilliams' eyes flew wide open. He shoved Hobart aside and grabbed for the Chinese girl.

Hobart spun him around, and McWilliams found himself facing his lordship's .450 Webley service revolver. "You have gone too far this time, McWilliams!" Hobart shouted. "I shall bring you up on charges! Striking a superior officer!"

"I did not strike you!" McWilliams shouted back. "And that girl—"

"Be silent!" Hobart yelled. "I am placing you under arrest. Striking a superior officer, insulting a fellow officer, attempting to take a native girl aboard the Alacrity for no doubt lewd purposes—"

"You idiot!" McWilliams countered. "Can't you see—"

"Be silent!" Hobart screamed. He cocked the hammer on his Webley and aimed it at McWilliams' face. "You are under arrest, pending court-martial. You will remain silent, or I shall shoot you down where you stand!" Lord Hobart lowered his voice to a normal tone. "You are free to go," he told the Chinese captain. "As we are so close to the German Neutral Zone, I shall escort you away from the German colony."

McWilliams opened his mouth in protest, but it was a sure bet that Hobart would shoot him dead before he got three words out. He looked at the Chinese girl and bowed his head slightly, his eyes narrowed.

The gesture was lost on Lord Hobart, who marched him off the aerojunk at gunpoint.

"... and as to the origin of the Chinese spiralifter," Lord Hobart told the officers of the court-martial, "I have no idea. I believe that it must have been sold to them by some unscrupulous Yankee trader. We all know how money-grubbing the Yankees are." He turned his attention to McWilliams, seated at the other table across from him. "As to the accused, I insist that McWilliams suffer the harshest penalty possible for his actions against a superior officer and fellow member of the service."

With that, Lord Hobart sat down, victorious. The acoustic recorder in the corner clicked, and the attending sergeant removed the wax record and installed a blank disk.

The RPC Commissioner—wearing the uniform and steel shoulder pauldron of an army colonel—waited until the new disk was in place and the recorder running, and then eyed McWilliams. "Has the prisoner anything to say in his defense?"

McWilliams stood up. "I would wish to answer the court's question regarding the origin of the Chinese spiralifter," he told them. "It was one of ours. Or rather, three of ours."

The Commissioner blinked. "What?"

McWilliams produced a folded paper from his pocket. "I took the liberty of asking one of my gaolers to check Records regarding these serial numbers I jotted down from the equipment aboard the aerojunk. The electric motor, piles, and accumulators were all previously installed on three of our spiralifters which crashed during the past year and were recently ordered destroyed." McWilliams paused. "He also informed me that it was Lord Hobart who handled the disposal of the three wrecks."

Hobart's mouth fell open, and he stared from McWilliams to the court officers, sweat breaking out on his wan face.

"Is this true, Lord Hobart?" the Commissioner asked.

"Uh...well, it would seem, I should say—"

"Did you dispose of the remains of three spiralifters by having the wreckage dumped out at sea, as ordered," his voice tightened, "or did you sell the wrecks to the Chinese?"

"Your lordship, surely such scrap could never be used—"

"Did you sell the wrecks to the Chinese?"

"I," Hobart swallowed. "Yes, my lord."

The Commissioner drew a long, angered breath, but McWilliams spoke first. "I should add, m'lord, that he also released the female bandit Shih Yang, whom I was about to take into custody, and let her go free, in possession of the aerojunk in question."

Lord Hobart gaped at him, as indeed did every man in the court.

"You had best explain yourself, Inspector," the Commissioner demanded.

"The slave girl aboard the Chinese spiralifter," McWilliams explained as if he were in the witness box rather than the prisoner's dock, "was Shih Yang in disguise." He ticked the facts off on his fingers. "First, her face and hands were streaked with dirt, yet her torn clothing was spotless. An inconsistency, m'lord. Unless, of course, she had merely quickly torn her clean clothing and smeared a little dirt upon her face and hands to camouflage her identity. And her palms were quite smooth when supposedly she was a slave who spent the past two years laboring not only in a kitchen but also in pumping a punkah fan day and night, as well as turning a crank daily to charge the piles within the spiralifter's hull. Yet her hands were soft and bore no calluses. A second inconsistency, m'lord. Unless, of course, she was lying about being a slave."

Hobart no longer looked shocked. He now looked stricken.

"And," McWilliams continued, "there is the matter of her manacles. She supposedly had worn them for years, yet her wrists were quite unblemished. A girl who had been in such shackles for years would have wrists marred by callouses and scars, but she bore no such marks. A third inconsistency, m'lord, Unless, of course, she had only put them on just two minutes before our arrival. And, lastly, her actions when I spoke to her made it clear that she was an ignorant slave-girl who did not speak English, yet in the cabin, when I told her, in English, to cover her nakedness, she immediately did so. A fourth inconsistency. Unless, of course, she did speak English and was hiding the fact to conceal her true identity."

He summed up the facts he had listed off. "Given so many inconsistencies on a vessel surely having been built illegally, it was obvious that she was not a slave girl at all, but rather the female bandit Shih Yang in disguise. That is why I moved to arrest her. However, before I could, Lord Hobart placed me under arrest on trumped-up charges, released the female pirate Shih Yang, and then escorted her, her illegal spiralifter, and her gang of bandits to safety."

His presentation to the court done, McWilliams sat down.

The Commissioner's eye twitched.

Hobart looked pleadingly at McWilliams. "Why did you not tell me?!"

"I attempted to," McWilliams pointed out, "but you threatened to shoot me if I spoke another word. I was, therefore, constrained to silence by your direct order."

Half the court face-palmed in disbelief while the other half glared in fury at Lord Hobart. The Commissioner's twitching face reddened, but he reined himself back to a modicum of composure. "Gentlemen!"

Both McWilliams and Lord Hobart stood up.

194

The Commissioner gestured vaguely at McWilliams. "District Inspector 3rd Class McWilliams, Aerial Corps, Royal Peninsular Constabulary, the case against you is dismissed. You are hereby reinstated to your previous rank and position, with all pay and benefits accorded you." He turned his attention to Hobart. "And you, Lord Hobart. This court shall be pressing charges against you for dereliction of your duty as an officer of the Royal Constabulary."

McWilliams' close friend, Inspector Andan Hamilton, was waiting for him as he left the courtroom. A smiling foil to the tight-faced McWilliams, the Canadian was also his closest friend, a fellow officer in the Constabulary's Aerial Corps and the sky-captain of the RPC spiralifter Urgent, sister-ship to McWilliams' spiralifter Alacrity.

"Good show, old man!" he said, fixing his monocular lens on McWilliams. "It is indeed gratifying to know that some measure of justice still exists." He fell into step alongside McWilliams as they walked outside into the open air of Port Edward, the colonial capital of Britain's Wei-Hai-Wei Territory. "What do you suppose they will do with old Hobarty?"

"I should think that Lord Hobart shall be made to answer for his mistakes, although in what fashion, I have no idea." McWilliams halted as a Chinese messenger boy on an electric monocycle rolled up to them, bearing a small wooden box and a clipboard. Frowning, McWilliams signed for the box and took it. He turned the box over in his hand and opened it. Inside were a pair of iron manacles, the same ones that had lain so heavy on the female pirate's wrists.

"What in the world...?" Hamilton asked.

McWilliams frowned. "A gift from Shih Yang."

Hamilton gaped. "Why, that witch! She's taunting you."

195

McWilliams raised one eyebrow. "I do not think so." He reached in and removed three orchids tied together: a purple one, a yellow one, and a red one.

"She sent you flowers?" Hamilton asked in an incredulous tone.

"Not just flowers," McWilliams said. "In China, just as in England, certain flowers convey specific meanings. A purple orchid signifies authority: a respectable person—me. The yellow orchid signifies a special friend, a new beginning—her intention toward me. And a red orchid means the joy that fills you when you spend time with the person the flower is given to. I hate to say this, but...."

"She's flirting with you?" Hamilton exclaimed.

"And implying that the next time we meet, it is I who shall be the one shall be wearing the manacles."

Hamilton broke into such roaring paroxysms of laughter that his knees buckled.

McWilliams sighed and closed the box, trying to remember if there was a Chinese flower that he could in return send to the arrogant female pirate. But there were no flowers in China that symbolized relentlessly hunting down someone to arrest them.

He pursed his lips. He would have to invent one, then.

Inspector McWilliams of the Aerial Corps walked off with the box, the sound of his best friend's uproarious laughter following behind him.

He headed for his quarters, and he was not laughing.

And the next time he met up with Shih Yang, neither would she.

AUTHOR BIO

J. F. Benedetto was born in a US Army field hospital in Germany, educated in Rome, and now lives in North America on the Appalachian Plateau, where he writes full time. His published work spans three different genres (mystery, science fiction and action/adventure) and has appeared in magazines, anthologies and short story collections from America to Australia. An expert on the opening days of the Boxer Rebellion, he nearly fell off the roof this morning but still adheres to the dictum put forth by James Bond: Follow your fate, and be satisfied with it. Those interested in his fiction can see more at his website FoulPlayWriter.com.

ARLO'S STORY:
THE LITTLE TOY AIRSHIP

JADE WILDY

Dreams of his childhood had chased sleep away from Arlo. He looked to the dark predawn sky outside the airship's port window. The window came from *The Last Hope*, an airship shot down in one of the battles in The War with the Decayer, vile creatures bent on destroying humanity. It was just one of the many battles Arlo had witnessed as a child.

He carefully closed the door to the bedroom where his wife slept and sat in a ragged old chair to reread the letter.

Dear (idiot) Brother,
Mother said I should write, and she keeps glaring at me, so I'm doing it.
We got to visit Irrtum yesterday. The old town's a trash heap, and bears
have moved in. That's kinda cool, I guess.

A smile played over Arlo's face. There was a substantial age gap between Arlo and his younger brother. Rumi was now a few years shy of the age Arlo had been when the township of Irrtum had been attacked. Back then, Rumi had been only a baby.

Our cottage is still there, mostly. Mother sat on the front wall and cried. Roses are growing everywhere, even inside the house! I wanted to get some for you, but Mother said they would probably be dead by the time we catch up. I got some for Mother instead, and they are in a bucket on the table. Mother said we can get a vase later today when we catch the sky rail to the High Street. They only just finished it. The sky rail. Not the High Street.

Arlo ran his hand through his hair. He wasn't sure he could ever return to permanently live on the surface, like his mother and brother, not after the things he had seen. He closed his eyes to the horrors that still plagued his dreams. Rumi could not appreciate the ruthless violence the surface-dwelling Decayer enacted against humanity.

The best thing was the granary. All the threshed grain has been growing for years, so it's everywhere, and you can run through it. They are thinking of walling everything off again and rebuilding the town. Would you live there if they did?

The thought of the granary caused Arlo's breath to catch in his throat, and he needed to blink back tears to be able to keep on reading.

I think Mother wants to grow things in the ground, but she hates the big

199

walled-off cities. Says they are like living behind fences for farm animals.
I dunno. I like Freya City. They have automobiles and steam carts that
can carry 30 people and a huge network of trains. I want an automobile
when I grow up. Or a train. Anyhow, Mother wants to check my spelling
now, and I want to play knucklebones with Ellie.
Goodbye.
Rumi

Arlo smiled at the scattering of corrections over Rumi's writing.
His mother's neat, precise cursive filled the bottom of the page.

My dear Arlo,
The visit to our old home in Irrtum was uplifting for the potential to
rebuild, but also painful because of everything we lost. Rumi is growing
up so fast, and it would be wonderful for him to spend time with his
brother. I hope you are doing well. When will there be grandchildren?
Love, Mother.

"Not yet, Mother." Arlo sighed to himself. He regretted that his
decision to study sigillary and engineering at an airship university meant
that he didn't see his brother grow up, but it had brought him to his wife.
Now they had airship of their own.

He leaned back in the heavy chair and thought about his life
before his family had fled to the safety of airships.

"Arlo, what's Rumi got in his mouth?" Arlo's mother called from the other
side of the garden, hand on her hip, garden snips still gripped in her
fingers.

Arlo looked around the garden for his brother and spied him on

200

the open grass patch near the front fence of their cottage rather than on the blanket he had just been placed. Arlo put down the toy he had been constructing and went to the baby.

"For someone who can't walk, you sure get around," Arlo muttered as he pulled a leaf from his brother's mouth, sparking a squawk of protest, and placed Rumi back on the blanket. Evangeline, their mother, dusted the dirt from her hands and stood to stretch her back. Neat little rows of pots now filled with rose cuttings, ready to grow and sell at the markets in a few weeks.

"I know it's only a hobby, but I do like it more than propagating food plants." She sighed deeply and wiped her forehead with the back of her hand, leaving a smudge of dirt.

Arlo had spent the afternoon building and adding sigils to a small clockwork airship from a box of parts his father, Orton, had brought back for him. He set the small toy on the blanket near Rumi and twisted its key. The airship sprang to life with a stutter of ticking cogs as its little side sails swung back and forth in much the same manner as the real airships had that occasionally drifted through the sky.

Rumi giggled.

"Looks like we have another engineer in the family. A few more years, and you'll be off to study in the sky." Evangeline smiled at her boys as she untied the apron from around her waist that protected her long skirts and kept her pruning shears and other small gardening tools close to her hand.

"Try eight more years," Arlo said. "But I don't think I'm good enough." The thought of leaving home on the ground and living on an airship left him feeling perturbed. They flew so very, very high.

The front gate clanged, breaking into Arlo's musing about

heights, and he looked up to see his father coming home. Orton's arms were full of rolls of paper filled with schematics.

He greeted them, leaned over, and kissed Evangeline's cheek. "Remind me to request a tube to carry this lot in," he remarked before heading towards the house to put the papers away. "Your scarf is askew," he said over his shoulder, laughing.

Evangeline frowned as she pulled off the scarf holding back her near-black hair and re-tied it. Arlo, like Rumi, had his father's mid-brown hair, but he was tall and slender like his mother. His eyes were also green like hers.

The absence of ticking clockworks caught Arlo's attention, and he looked down at his brother.

"Ah! Rumi! No!" Arlo pulled the airship toy from his little brother's mouth, cringing over the drool, glistening in the bright sunlight.

Orton reemerged from the house. He'd stowed his schematics and exchanged his formal jacket for a threadbare homespun jumper Evangeline had made him some years prior.

"Anyone wants to guess what the council said about my revised wall defensive design?" Orton sat on the blanket and pulled Rumi onto his lap, to the delight of the baby.

"Too expensive. Too restrictive. Never needed one before." Evangeline counted the points off on her fingers. It was the same old story.

"Yes." The corner of Orton's mouth quirked up.

Arlo's eyes narrowed. "'Yes,' that's what they said, or they said 'yes' to the designs?"

Evangeline put her hands on her hips, waiting for her husband to clarify.

Orton's eyes twinkled. "Yes, they have accepted the design."

Evangeline's eyes widened. "What made them change their mind?"

Arlo sat on the blanket next to his father, curious to see how this would go. His mother always disliked the township's walls, even though they helped keep everyone safe from Decayer raids, but Orton's plans were more than just walls. It was the first design involving heavy fortifications and a whole system of rail-mounted, moving cannons for use during an attack. While some of the bigger cities like Freya or Calenthea were open to the wonders of new technology, Irrtum had not been so progressive.

Orton bounced Rumi on his lap as the baby giggled. "There have been a lot of attacks on outlying towns, and the council has concluded that we can't trust the natural density of the forests outside our walls to provide protection anymore. I am to draft a letter to Calenthea to ask about the availability of construction machinery."

Evangeline scrunched up her nose then looked from Arlo to Rumi. "I guess it is time for an armored wall then." She sighed deeply. "And dinner."

"I'll set the boiler warming." Orton stood up and brushed little bits of leaf from his clothes. Evangeline may dislike the heavy walls, but Orton saw them as a challenge for improvement.

The sun was starting to get low in the sky. Evangeline picked up Rumi, holding him close, and turned to Arlo. "Can you grab the blanket?"

Arlo nodded, picked up the blanket and toy airship, and followed his parents back into the cottage.

Several days later, the town bell started tolling. Orton's brow creased as he stood up from where he had been seated at the table, writing his letter to the fabricators at Calenthea, and went to the window.

Evangeline stood by his side. "Wrong day for a council meeting. Is there a funeral?" She looked up at Orton, bouncing Rumi on her hip.

Orton slowly shook his head. "Not that I'm aware of."

Arlo briefly glanced up from the list of words he was copying from a book on his writing slate. It wasn't that he didn't know how to spell, but he found it helped him remember. Arlo paid little attention to his parents' concerns, instead leaning over to look at Orton's schematics that were spread out on the table. He hovered one finger over the spidery details showing how the cannons moved along the top or even up and down the vast walls' vertical face, allowing defenses to move where needed. He looked back at his book, running another finger down a list of runes, coming to rest on the sigil for strength.

"Father, would Valknut work on the tracks?"

Orton took his eyes from the window and moved behind Arlo to reflect on his notes. He tapped his finger on the schematics as he considered it.

"Valknut alone wouldn't be enough and would need to be applied every hand span or so. Try looking up amplifiers." Orton winked at Arlo and returned to stand with Evangeline, placing a loving hand on the small of her back.

Arlo frowned and went back to his book, flicking through the pages.

"Orton, it's still going," Evangeline told her husband in a hushed voice.

Something about her tone made the hair on the back of Arlo's neck stand up, and he slowly closed his book.

Orton's posture was rigid. "We won't find anything staring out from our window. I'm going to head over to the Council Chambers and see what's going on." He reached for his traveling coat that hung on a hook by the door.

"I'm coming too." Arlo started packing his writing things away.

"No." The stern tone of his father's voice made Arlo look up. "I want you to stay here with your mother and brother. If anything is interesting, I will come back and tell you."

The look in his father's eyes quelled any thought Arlo had of arguing.

Orton leaned over and whispered something to Evangeline before kissing her cheek and leaving.

She watched him from the window before turning to Arlo. "Well, let's get some things in the house in order."

Evangeline smiled, but there was a strained, concerning note in her voice. Arlo stood up slowly.

"What do you want me to do?"

"Gracious! Is my boy *offering* to help?" Evangeline's feigned surprise as she looked around, earning an eye-roll from Arlo. "A messenger tube was delivered this morning. It's by the door. Can you roll up your father's plans and stow them away?"

Arlo blinked. Evangeline was smiling. While he had been allowed to look at his father's papers, he had never been permitted to touch them, much less pack them away. His mother set Rumi down on a floor rug with some wooden blocks and busied herself setting out the packs they took when they went on foraging walks in the hills behind the town.

With a growing feeling of unease, Arlo fetched the messenger tube and rolled the plans tightly to secure them in the tube. He turned at the sound of his mother's quick steps coming down the stairs from the second floor. She had an armload of clothing that she dumped on the now-clear table.

"Can you give me a hand folding and packing these?" she asked Arlo.

"Where are we going?"

"Oh, nowhere. It's just in case we need them." Evangeline smiled, but her hands were a flurry of movement as she put clothes for each of them into packs. Her smile slowly faded as concentration got the better of her, transforming her face into a blank grimace.

As Arlo stuffed a jumper and the little toy airship into his pack, the front door flung open, and Orton dashed into the room. He was breathing heavily.

"Did you pack the bags? Raiders have attacked the town. I'm going back to defend the granary."

Arlo's heart sank.

Irrtum was in chaos. Evangeline let the front garden gate slam shut behind her as she stood with Rumi on her hip and Arlo by her side. People crowded into the streets.

"Evangeline, what's going on?" Nancy, their neighbor from across the street, called out. "Elwood went to check but hasn't come back." Nancy leaned over her front fence, looking up the road in the direction of the Council Chambers. Some neighbors were standing around in confusion, while others were leaving.

"Raiders are attacking," Evangeline called to her.

The effect was instant. Several neighbors ran back into their houses to get children and tell others. Then an explosion sent a plume of smoke into the air, confirming everyone's fears.

Irrtum had been attacked before, but this was the first time Arlo was old enough to realize what was happening. He looked at his mother.

Evangeline's eyes widened, and she took Arlo's hand and began to run away from the blast. A steam cart rattled past, carrying a group of determined-looking townsfolk towards the fray, leaving a spray of water on the cobblestones. They were heading towards the battle.

Arlo pulled on his mother's hand. "Where is Father?"

"Arlo, we need to flee."

"Father went to the granary. I want to go to him. I want to fight off the Raiders."

Evangeline shook her head. "Leave it to the adults with guns. I am not going to allow my son to run into battle." She shifted Rumi on her hip. "I need help carrying supplies and your brother. Please, Arlo. Come with me."

Arlo looked into his mother's eyes. He wanted to *do* something. He wanted to *fight*. But the fear he saw in Evangeline's eyes as she scanned the street for raiders weakened his resolve.

Someone screamed from behind, and Evangeline tugged on his hand. Even though Arlo wasn't yet fully grown, he *was* big enough that she couldn't force him to move, but the surge of screaming people running past made up his mind. He went with her.

More people joined them as they ran through the winding town streets, adding chaos. A second large explosion erupted as several horses and steam carts dashed through the crowds from the side, cutting across. It sounded like the Decayer had fired one of their infamous canons.

"Mother, Mother!" Arlo shouted, tugging her hand. "They are coming from the side."

Evangeline turned to look at Arlo as he pointed towards the direction their forces were running.

207

"Look out!" someone shouted as Decayer raiders spilled into the streets, met by townsfolk armed with whatever came to hand and city guards on horseback.

Evangeline changed direction, running towards a front garden filled with flowering bushes, clutching Rumi and dragging Arlo along with her. She crouched down as several Decayers ran down the other side of the street, chasing terrified people. A woman tripped on her long skirts and fell, and they were on her in an instant.

Arlo clamped his hands over his mouth as he watched the long-limbed raider slump the woman's limp body over his shoulder. He had never seen the raiders before, but they were always described as monsters. They truly were monsters by their behavior, but now from his hidden spot in the garden, Arlo saw their long, lumpy bodies, like demons from the wastelands. They appeared to be wearing some sort of mask over the mouth.

As reinforcements arrived, there were more shouts along the streets. Steam sprayed out from the carts, enveloping the scene in an eerie mist. One of the horses reared up and let out a terrified whinny before bringing its hooves down on the raiders in front of it. The only saving grace was that all the noise of people shouting and the sounds of the steam carts drowned out Rumi's terrified howling.

Evangeline clutched Rumi to her chest as she tried in vain to shush him. There was no way they could leave the garden now that the street was full of fighting.

Arlo clutched the straps of his hiking pack and resisted the urge to join his brother's hysterics. Instead, he looked behind them. The cottage was not unlike their own, but it was smaller, and he could see to the back fence. Nestled among ivy growing over the back wall was a gate.

He gently pulled on his mother's arm and pointed. "I think there

208

might be a back alley," he whispered.

Evangeline shifted to look over her shoulder and nodded before taking Arlo's hand once again like he was a toddler who needed guidance to cross the street.

Evangeline led Arlo to the alley beyond, but once there, her shoulders sagged. One end of the path was blocked, but the other led back towards the town center and the battlegrounds.

"It's better than here," Arlo said and started towards the center of Irrtum as a blast erupted as one of the sides set off a cannon.

The alley twisted and turned through the backstreets of Irrtum, winding behind the rows of cottages that eventually turned into industrial buildings. Arlo and his family avoided the main streets and sounds of fighting, only crossing the paths of a few frightened townsfolk who hadn't yet succeeded in their escape. Despite all the twists and turns, Arlo knew where they were. Even as a small child, he always had an uncanny sense of direction. Orton called it his 'internal compass.'

Two men came into the alleyway ahead, ushering a couple of young children with them. One of the men holding a toddler waved to Evangeline. "Hey, don't go that way. The streets are overrun."

"It's not much better back the way we came." She shifted Rumi on her hip. He had stopped crying and fallen into an exhausted sleep. "Do you know what happened?"

The man shook his head. "It was like they came out of nowhere. John here," he gestured to the other man, "was looking after the kids, and I was on patrol on the east walls. We had a runner tell us there was movement on the south walls, but they were on us just as we started to investigate. We were overrun in minutes and told to run and get the word out."

The other man, John, dropped his hand to the head of a boy who was clinging to his leg. "We all hid in the garden to wait for Paul."

"I think we were ambushed on several fronts." The guard, Paul, looked to the houses around them. "Best keep moving. It's not safe here. The word is to head to the forests on the western border."

They watched as the men and their kids made their way back along the alleyways they had just emerged.

"Come on, Arlo. We best stick with them," Evangeline said.

Arlo was about to follow when there was shouting further down the street.

"Tell anyone you encounter to get to the forests beyond the west wall. We have cleared a lot of them out, but the town is still overrun."

A second voice joined the first. "They are heading for the granary. If the raiders get to that, the town is done."

"That's Father!" Arlo set off at a run despite his mother's protests. He turned the corner and came face to face with a group of townsfolk. They were bloody, and while a few had guns, many were clearly not from the garrison and held nothing but kitchen knives and shovels.

Arlo searched person to person looking for Orton before hearing a voice behind him.

"Arlo? What in blazes are you doing here? Where is your mother?" Orton wrapped his arms around his son and held him tightly as Evangeline caught up.

"I'm sorry. I tried to get us out, but the raiders caught up," Evangeline said.

A flurry of emotion went across Orton's face as he kissed her and Rumi.

"I'm glad you are safe," Orton said.

Arlo watched a tear run down his father's cheek. "We can all go to the west forests together now. Can't we, Father?"

Orton regarded his son for a moment, then placed his hand on the messenger tube slung over Arlo's shoulder.

"I need you to keep these safe and go with your mother to the forests outside the west wall. There are no Decayer there."

"But Father—"

"No *buts*. Their attack on the town hasn't yet been successful, but from studying their tactics, we know they *will* attack the granary. We won't have a town to come back to if they do. I have to help defend it." He turned to Evangeline. "Get them to safety. I'll join you when I can."

Arlo felt his lip quiver. "Father?"

Orton knelt before Arlo. "Arlo, in that tube, you have the plans for the steam cannon rails. It is the most ambitious design I have ever made, and any city, town, or far-flung homestead fitted with them will be more than a match for the raiders. You must not let them fall into Decayer hands." He tousled Arlo's hair. "You can do this."

There was a blast and a smattering of gunfire in the distance.

"That's the granary," Orton shouted to the other townsfolk. With one last look at Arlo, Evangeline, and Rumi, he ran to join the others.

Arlo followed his mother with a growing feeling of dread in his belly. He clasped the messenger tube tightly in his hands as they made their way to the western wall and out through the gate to the forest beyond, joining other people from Irrtum.

As they followed the grim procession of townsfolk, Arlo scanned the tree line looking for any signs of Decayer raiders. The forests were

211

dense and rocky, which had been thought to form a natural barrier to the raiders and their large cannons, but clearly, this was not true.

Evangeline paused to wipe the sweat from her forehead and reposition Rumi when another explosion erupted. A plume of dirty smoke trickled into the air, becoming darker as smaller blasts rang out.

"That's that." An old man drew his cap from his head and held it to his heart.

"What do you mean?" Evangeline asked.

Arlo's usually tidy mother was red-faced, and her hair stuck out at odd angles where it had escaped the scarf she used to hold it back. Her face paled.

"That black smoke means things are burning. I'd say our last stand has been defeated, and the granary just went up. Irrtum has fallen." The man replaced his cap on his head and continued following the line of people.

Arlo looked back to where the smoke had thickened to a black cloud over the township.

"Father?" he whispered.

It was near silent in their dark little camp. They couldn't risk a fire. Instead, people warmed themselves on small boilers heated through a system of alchemic sigils and well-engineered mechanics. The townsfolk huddled together in little groups, sharing what they brought with those who had fled with nothing.

Arlo sat with Rumi in his lap and a blanket wrapped around them both. Rumi was playing with the little airship from Arlo's pack while Evangeline spoke with some of the other adults. At another time, Arlo probably would have been straining to hear what the adults were saying, but at the moment, all he could think about was his father.

Rumi shuffled around a bit, moving the messenger tube with Orton's plans for the rail-mounted wall cannons.

"Father took different versions of the plans to council for months. If they had just agreed at the start, we would have had them built by now," Arlo said to the baby.

Rumi looked up at Arlo and smiled with a big toothless grin, dribble trickling down his chin.

Arlo shook his head and wiped the baby's mouth with a handkerchief from his pocket, prompting a small giggle from Rumi that sounded out of place among the tears and hushed tones.

"Arlo?" Evangeline carefully picked her way towards the boys and sat down beside them.

"Do you think there is a chance Father survived?" Arlo looked up at his mother.

Evangeline bit her lip and looked down at her hands. "I don't want to give you false hope. Those who saw the granary go up said it was unlikely anyone survived." She knelt next to her sons.

Arlo cuddled Rumi closer, and Evangeline put her arms around both boys.

"Will we survive?" Arlo asked, staring at the moving shapes of people barely visible in the moonlight.

"I think so. Try to get some rest," Evangeline whispered.

Arlo laid down with his mother and brother, clutching his father's plans. He dreamed of Orton coming through the trees to rescue them.

Animated whispers came to Arlo's ears in the predawn light, rousing him from his restless sleep. He felt his mother carefully extract herself from around Rumi, tucking the blanket around the sleeping baby.

"Mother? What's going on?" Arlo whispered.

"I'm not sure. Stay here with Rumi, and I'll try to find out."

Arlo laid back down and listened to the hushed voices, trying to decide if they were scared or excited.

Arlo propped himself upon his arm as his mother returned. "Is it safe now? Can we go home?" Arlo hoped there would be news that Orton was fine and they could return home.

Evangeline shook her head and sat down.

"No. But we have made contact with an airship which will be landing at Rock Clearing to rescue the survivors."

Rock Clearing was an open space in the forest and a popular spot for small enough airships to land. Ships too large to land would transport passengers using hot-air balloons.

"The survivors..." Arlo repeated as the words filtered through his mind. "You don't get survivors unless you also had those that *didn't* survive. He laid back down and closed his eyes.

Evangeline gently patted his hair. "Get some rest. I expect we'll be leaving as soon as the sun gives us enough light."

Arlo followed a bleary-eyed procession of people through the trees. There was quiet talk about who had seen who, where, and what the likelihood of rebuilding was. From the way they were talking, it didn't seem likely that Irrtum would become a booming little town again any time soon. It was a known Decayer tactic to destroy what they couldn't carry off. In some cases, they even poisoned the land so nothing would grow. Though some believed they were unnatural, and their very presence poisoned things, creating wastelands. To Arlo, the most chilling stories were about the abducted townsfolk.

Lost in his thoughts, Arlo barely noticed the talking had stopped

214

until he heard a shout up ahead.

"Raiders!" someone pointed to the dense tree line.

Arlo froze, staring as the creatures pushed through the dense undergrowth of the forest and crept through the trees towards them.

"They've come to abduct people!" a man shouted. "Run!"

People dashed in all directions as the Decayer sprinted after them.

"Not if I have anything to do with it," a woman near Arlo muttered as she aimed with a gun.

The shot rang out. A raider staggered and fell. Rumi began to wail, and the sound broke through Arlo's horrified awe. Even though he wasn't sure they were human, it was the first time Arlo had ever seen somebody shot. He turned to his mother. Evangeline's face was pale, and her mouth set in a thin line of determination as she looked back at Arlo.

"Arlo, take Rumi and hide." She passed him the baby and picked up a shovel someone had dropped. "No one is taking my kids."

Arlo stood for a moment staring with horror at his mother, but a raider's monstrous shriek made up his mind. He grabbed the wailing baby and, running as fast as he could carrying Rumi, zigzagged through the trees.

Arlo left the sounds of gunfire behind him as he made his way towards a ridge that overlooked the town. He didn't know how long he ran with his baby brother in his arms, but his lungs burned with the exertion, and he staggered to a stop. His legs were scratched from the forest's blackberry bushes, and blisters had sprouted on his ankles. He waited and watched, listening for the slightest hint that they had been followed. Even Rumi seemed to know he needed to be quiet as Arlo scanned the trees.

215

There was nothing but the occasional sound of far-off gunfire and the stillness of a forest in which even the birds were silent. When he heard no signs of pursuit, Arlo let out a long sigh of relief. Aching and weary, he turned and continued to walk, following the slope of the hill. His stomach growled. Their rushed, meager breakfast seemed an age ago.

He looked at Rumi. "You are lucky Mother could fill your belly before…."

Arlo couldn't put a voice to his fears that the Decayer had killed everyone in the forest. Not even to his little brother, who couldn't understand his words. Instead, he cast his gaze on a dense thicket of brambles. He sighed. It was late in the season, and the blackberries were small and bland, but it was better than nothing.

"I miss Mother's blackberry jam." Arlo sighed, chewing a handful of blackberries, pits and all. "At least all those long hikes taught me something about getting food out here," he told the baby, who smiled in response. He didn't want to consider what would become of them if they didn't find help.

After Arlo had eaten as many blackberries as he could gather, they continued on their way. The ground had begun to slope upwards, and Arlo paused to get his bearings.

"It's the western ridge," he told Rumi as he made his way to the top of the cliff that overlooked the town.

Below the outcrop, the town lay in smoking ruins. A fire had ripped through the buildings, and there was evidence that canon blasts had carved through streets of little cottages. The granary where his father had been heading was a smoking pit.

Arlo took a stunned breath. "It's all gone. There is nothing left."

Arlo slowly eased himself to the ground in an exhausted heap. Rumi clung to the front of his shirt as if the baby was afraid of being put down, so Arlo slid his arms around his brother and gently rocked him.

"If only they had listened to Father, we could have been prepared." The boy rubbed his tear-filled eyes on his sleeve.

Fatigue took over, and he slumped where he sat, but something hard jammed into his back. It was the messenger tube that contained Orton's lifework. Arlo had studied those plans with his father. Every detail was carefully laid out in meticulous diagrams explaining how each component worked, so they could easily be installed on any wall to keep the citizens safe.

Arlo took the strap tightly in his hand. "Rumi," the baby looked up. "Whatever happens, we have to get these back, so no other city suffers what we did."

Rumi closed his mouth, making his lips pout in a way that gave the small baby a look of defiance.

Arlo hugged his brother. "I agree."

Even after a brief rest, Arlo's muscles screamed as he slowly pulled himself back onto his feet and picked up his soggy little brother. He frowned at the baby's wet pants then sighed.

"Nothing for it." He positioned the baby on his hip, making it easier to carry him. "Hopefully, we can both get a change of clothes when we make the rendezvous point." He looked toward the smoking ruins of his hometown and out into the forest.

"If the airship landed in Rock Clearing, it would be this way." He started through the forest, following his uncanny sense of direction towards the clearing, moving as quickly as he could under the weight of his brother.

While many people lived exclusively on airships, fearing the surface where the Decayer raiders had destroyed many towns and even a city over the years of the war, Arlo felt comfortable on the ground within the safety of the town walls. Even the short foraging field trips outside the town walls with his parents or growing up hearing about the attacks and destruction the raiders left behind hadn't bothered Arlo. Until now, that was.

Arlo looked up, scanning the sky through the trees. All he could think about was getting into the safety of the air with his brother.

As if seeking to confirm his fears, Arlo heard a stick snap in the forest. He froze and listened for the direction the Decayer were coming from, waiting with bated breath for what was about to befall him and Rumi.

"Ho there, boy!"

Arlo spun about to face the direction of the voice, his heart beating rapidly. It took a moment before his mind registered the approaching group looked like ordinary folk, not long-limbed monsters. Yet Arlo didn't recognize any of them.

The man who had called out stopped in front of Arlo, wheezing. "Just give me a moment to catch my breath. My old legs aren't used to hiking hills, and you were hitting quite a pace." The man took a few deep breaths.

A woman shook her head and stepped forward. "While Felix recovers," she stuck out her hand. "I am Aimee. We are from the Airship *Phoenix,* and we're looking for the townsfolk that fled into the trees. We're here to take you to safety."

"What about the raiders?" Arlo's voice shook.

"There were a few lurking in the forest, but we've sent them packing." Aimee smiled. "You are safe."

Arlo's legs buckled, and, still holding Rumi, he sank to the ground.

"Here, let me help." Felix held his arms out to Rumi, and Arlo let him take his brother while Aimee helped the boy to his feet, slipping an arm around his shoulders.

Felix held up Rumi. "Gosh, he's a little damp. Angela? Do you have anything we can use as a swaddle?"

Arlo stared at the ground as he took each grudging step. "Did you happen to see my mother?" he asked Aimee.

Aimee bit her lip. "We were hit hard, and people got scattered throughout the forest. But if she is anywhere, it will be back at the *Phoenix.*"

Arlo nodded and clutched the messenger tube. Aimee scanned the forest as they walked, and Arlo wondered if they were truly safe from the raiders.

"Want me to hold that? It looks heavy," Aimee asked.

Arlo shook his head and gripped the tube tighter. He wasn't going to let anyone take it from him until he knew it was safe.

"Ahoy!" Felix shouted.

Arlo flinched and looked up. Ahead of them was the balloon of an airship peeking through the tree branches. People around him gave a sigh of relief, and their step picked up as safety was in sight, but Arlo couldn't bring himself to feel relief. What if his mother wasn't there? What if both she and Father had died?

A cheer went up from the people grouped around the landed airship, like a mini celebration of survival as they emerged from the forest.

"A few stragglers and a couple of children," Felix answered a question called by someone near the airship.

A commotion caught Arlo's attention as someone broke from the crowd. Evangeline was coming to them at a dead run. Her head was bandaged, and her clothes bloodied, but she ran as if she thought she'd never see them again.

Arlo was wrapped in a soft blanket with his hands around warm cocoa. His mother and sleeping brother were safely beside him. He had to balance the mug on his knee as the trembles in his hand threatened to splash it all over the airship's deck. The air smelled of wood and oil rather than soil and flowers like their cottage. Every now and then, another cheer would go up as more people were found and brought to the *Phoenix.* But he knew in his bones, none of them was going to be his father.

He looked up as Felix came and sat with them and handed Arlo his little toy airship. "I believe this is yours."

Arlo took the toy from him and stared at it.

"I had a look at those plans, lad," Felix continued. "Your father was a visionary. His designs are going to save a lot of people, and you were the one that kept them safe."

"But the designs won't bring him back, will they?" Arlo said, staring at the floor while the toy airship hung loosely in his grasp.

Evangeline put her arm around him.

Felix sighed deeply. "No, it won't. Still, you were the one to keep them out of the raider's hands, and you kept your brother safe when they attacked. I believe those are things any father would be proud of." He glanced at the toy airship Arlo held. "Is that your design?"

Arlo nodded.

"Seems you aren't such a bad engineer yourself."

Arlo barely managed a shrug. He just wanted to cry.

Aimee walked up and cleared her throat. "Captain? We lift off shortly."

Arlo's head slowly came up as the identity of his rescuer dawned on him.

Felix gave a sharp nod. "I have to go. Duty calls." He slowly climbed to his feet. "You're going to go places, lad. And if you ever need a hand, you can call on old Felix."

Arlo watched him go and then turned to his mother.

"Was that the captain of the airship?" Even through his grief and aching body, he was in awe of having spoken to a real airship captain.

Evangeline smiled. "Yes. And a high ranking one at that." She gave Arlo a gentle squeeze.

Arlo leaned his head on his mother's shoulder, turning the little airship in his hands, wondering what his future life on an airship would look like.

Arlo broke from his thoughts about the day, all those years ago, that he had left both the surface and his childhood behind.

The dawn was starting to tint the sky pink as he stretched in his ragged old chair and stood, walking over to the ornate dresser in the lounge. It was heavy for an airship and too big for their bedroom, but having it made his wife happy. Assorted keepsakes were scattered across it. He picked up the little, battered toy airship from where it sat on top of an aged letter of commendation from Captain Felix that had helped Arlo get into engineering and sigillary. Arlo twisted the airship's key and watched as the little ship moved slowly, its tiny side sails swinging back and forth.

Arlo smiled and put it back on the dresser with Rumi's letter and went back to bed, hoping to steal a few more minutes of sleep before the day had to start.

AUTHOR BIO

Jade Wildy holds bachelor and master's degrees in visual arts, giving her a flair for culture. She returned to creative writing in 2020, concentrating on speculative fiction but branching out into fantasy, science fiction, and horror.

Through her writing, Jade addresses themes like death, psychological state and being different, and delights in slipping in the unexpected. She believes in the power of storytelling as a motivator for change, and her writing has been included in numerous publications internationally.

A self-confessed wallflower, Jade lives in South Australia on the traditional lands of the Kaurna People and can be frequently be found writing or drawing in the local cafes. Visit Jade online at www.jadewildywordsmith.com.

MA BELLE

C.L. SPILLARD

Normal.

He could hear the Friday racket from inside of the Saloon. The cheerful shouts: a bashed-out tune on the ancient piano.

That's it: gotta look normal.

Same as last week, last month, last year, even. Before he'd known all this stuff, learned about the upgrade. This stuff was dynamite— dynamite with added nuclear waste from that time way back, before the Black Flash. When it was said, you could send news around the world in a split second.

He caught a spur against his bags as he dismounted. He was thinking too much.

Just act natural. Same old, same old. C'mon, it's Friday. Booked the weekend off, not unusual. Do watcha always do, two doubles at the bar and fend off Ma Belle. No sweat.

He led Old Faithful to the hitching-post—made sure she could reach the trough. Hundred and ten it had topped today, blasting him as he rode from the desert back into town. That dry-out heat wasn't kind to the old girl, and she had a long night ahead.

Did she know? Could she tell? Feel it, maybe even smell it?

The reins slipped in his hands as he fumbled to tie them.

Sure she knew. He patted her. Thank the Lord a horse can't talk.

Dust kicked up from the dried-out wooden steps—rust-colored clouds in the low, burnt-orange sun.

He pulled the neckerchief down from his face, took off his hat, and pushed in through the rickety swing-doors, scuffing his boots on the worn mat.

His first double waited for him on the bar.

Ma Belle hovered nearby—crazy brown curls around a tight-drawn face. The only woman who dared set foot in the place. Often, from one week's end to the next, the only woman he saw at all.

He caught the barman's eye.

"Say, how d'ya know I'd be here?"

"Word gets about."

He picked up the glass.

"First one's on me."

"Cheers, Frank."

He raised his glass and downed it in one. Normal.

Ma Belle bustled over with her usual Port and Introduction.

He complimented her burgundy dress and deflected the latest match-making offer with some polite chatter—same old, same old.

"Only way you'll ever meet a good woman."

Only way he'd meet any other woman at all, this place was so dry

225

of them. Hell, the whole country parched dry of them. And he might even know why.

He recalled the reason behind Frank's free double.

Month's end: pay up his tab.

He pulled out a roll of frayed bills and counted over the usual total.

"Month don't end 'til next week." Frank smiled as he took the bills. "What's up?"

Sweat.

"I gotta pay raise."

Frank expressed no surprise.

Hell, he must know then.

About the promotion. About the two new hires three months back, in the spring. Sure, they must've shown their shiny new faces in this place from time to time, and Frank never forgot a face.

He would have known.

About the shooting. One of the new faces, a Negro gifted in math, had been mistaken for a wanted man from another county. And damn it, the second guy—a whizzkid engineer—had been run down by the Mayor's steam car only ten days later.

All of which carnage had left him, Harry B. Neville, alone in charge once more. In charge and—once he'd discovered from his boss the real reason for the new hires and realized what the upgrade really meant—in shock.

Hell, but he could use a third double right now.

And maybe even some company, a silent confidante. Even a lady silent confidante would do, if such a supernatural thing existed. This stuff was too much for one mind.

He noticed the newspaperman come in, pull the green eyeshade from his balding head and set it down on the bar to order a beer. He saw him lift the tankard. Off-white shirtsleeves, pulled back from their grimy work by dull metal sleeve garters.

If that guy only knew what was waiting for him in his mailbox on Monday morning.

The upgrade.

Every telegram...

"Got somethin' on your mind?" Ma Belle had reappeared, likely not sounding as sympathetic as she'd hoped.

The newsman looked over, right at him. Had he already seen? Looked-in on his mail this late in the day?

"Just work. You know how it is."

"Work. Sure."

Every freaking letter...

He'd never been able to make out the color of her eyes. Or the lines of her dress where the bodice met the skirts. But he saw now. Sensitive, from being so on-edge—because he had to notice stuff now, for his survival.

He wasn't the only guy around here with something to hide.

Every goddamned record card...

"Guess I'd better head on home."

But he didn't go home.

He rode on under clear stars out in the dry, treeless plain. The empty darkness creeped him out. He fumbled for his goggles. With them, there'd be light. Grey and without depth for sure, but hey, light.

The grainy images played in his eyes. Like a hiss, but one you see, not hear. Was that movement? He strained for details, but none came into focus. And the sound, the way it carried: as if it came from nearby, but also far away. The whole landscape—light and sound—went on forever, to the horizon and beyond.

Was that a sound behind him?

He turned around to look. Nothing.

Like little warnings, restless whorls of wind stirred the sand on the track ahead. The dust storm, the one that would hide his flight, had just begun to extinguish the lowest stars in the sky ahead.

He heard it before he saw it—hadn't realized how much noise a dirigible made, grounded and tethered, even over the rising wind—the low hiss of the gas; the whistling of the storm in the stays. The rig waited unlit, all but invisible in the blur of sand and grit. The Pilot, chafing at the tether point by a large boulder, waved in salute as he dismounted. He couldn't help noticing how slight the little guy was as he approached to shake hands.

He nodded toward Old Faithful, went back to unbuckle the bags, and hunched them onto his shoulders. The little guy raised his goggles and pulled back the leather hood on his—

No, wait.

"Betcha weren't expecting that, eh?"

A round, freckled, and very female face grinned up at him.

He didn't know what to do with his hands.

"Ever flown before?"

Wind and dust whipped her hair, which he thought might've been ginger, but he wasn't sure in the dusty wind.

He raised his goggles and pulled down his neckerchief, instantly regretting both decisions as his eyes and teeth ground dry in blown grit.

"Sure. Flight Club. Twenty hours of flight time, plus lift-off, landing, emergency procedures, and basic maintenance."

It had cost him all his savings. Flight Club attracted the preppy types: golden-haired sons of industrialists and criminal masterminds.

"Strip."

"Git—"

"Strip, mister."

The decals on the revolver gleamed.

"We don't usually git your sort out here."

The voice softened a little with the explanation.

"Dudes."

So, the rumors were true. OutLine's fugitives were all women who had escaped to Canada, where the laws treated them kinder. Cracking OutLine, and stopping it draining his country of women, the talk had it, had been one of the spurs for the upgrade. And, with a neat twist, it had been the upgrade that had enabled Harry to contact OutLine's fugitives.

"You're not exactly gonna be in need of a termination, are ya?"

His face must've asked the question for him.

She indicated with the shooter.

Indiana Roulette.

He tugged off his boots and started to unfasten his outer clothes. Grit dried out his skin and caught him in sensitive places. He could see the flight suit, a substantial all-in-one, draped over the edge of the gondola.

He stood naked but for his underpants as she handed the flight suit to him. He wrestled it on—hitched it up, and pushed his arms into the sleeves. She moved to help him with the buckles at the collar—

"Drop it!"

They both looked around to the deep shadow by the rock.

Ma Belle stood there; the revolver pointed at the petite Canadian redhead.

Wind and dust lashed the unwanted intruder's hair.

It tore it right off in one piece.

Well, I'll be...

Ma Belle disappeared in a dust-devil formed by a sudden eddy in the lee of the rock. Two shots burst out from behind him. The dust-devil dispersed, revealing the inert body.

The redhead turned to him and studied his face for a long time before speaking.

"My name's Cody. Pleased to meetcha."

She nodded towards the gondola, and Harry threw his bags in. He noticed the tether straining as the storm buffeted the envelope.

"You gotta say goodbye to your horse."

The revolver again.

"Don't—"

"She rides good, I saw. My colleague will pick her up later." Cody smiled. "Extra reward for helpin' ya."

He'd already paid a hundred in silver.

Guess you couldn't argue.

"Let's git, then."

"Shit, it's cold up here."

The icy wind cut its way into his neck, his face, and his wrists. He'd never given it much thought before: that some clouds were made of ice, that the rest soaked everything they touched, or that upstairs was always at least thirty degrees cooler than down below.

Ice clung to the stays, the controls, and the ledge of the gondola.

230

"Welcome to Canada!" Cody grinned, indicating the forested shore of a long lake that stretched out far below them.

"We can't land right now."

"Huh?"

"Wind's too strong downstairs. See those trees?"

She made to pass him the eyeglasses. Maybe she was expecting him to take his eyes from her and concentrate his gaze over the gondola rail so she could catch him off-guard….

He took the glasses. He had no choice; he was unarmed. Working his numb hands with difficulty, he turned the knurled brass wheel to focus and saw the branches bending.

"You know, you never told me why you wanted to git."

He lowered the eyeglasses and studied her face.

She'd be able to see right through a lie—any lie—else she wouldn't be in this line of work. He'd have to come clean.

"I want something stopped. Something that's grown outta hand."

"So ya <u>do</u> want a termination!" She almost laughed.

"I guess I do."

She held his gaze. Beyond and below her stretched the silver lake and the trees...

"The Enhanced Difference Engine."

She said nothing.

"Ever hear of it?"

"Can't say I have."

It had been set up for the weather and obtained readings from all across the Continental States on swarms, pests, diseases, and more. The system was wired into the center where the girls on the lower floor would type the reports on paper-tape. The Girls left their jobs when they

231

married or lost their honor—had to, by law—but the paper records lived on in the desiccated air forever. Records from Greater Nevada and all over the Old Country: Cascadia, Lakeland, New England, and Dixie. Even Greater Mexico, now the truce was finally holding.

Records processed into patterns, correlations, and predictions, by the device whose design he had worked to perfect: The Enhanced Difference Engine. Its gears, its valves, its gleaming brass details, precision-machined and assembled by the team of engineers working by gaslight day and night deep in the mined-out mountain where the temperature never varied.

The device he had hoped would help reunite his old country whose flag, with its bold stripes and clean stars—a little silk one—he always carried in his breast pocket.

The device would have helped every state predict and protect against pests, disease, and violent weather. But with the upgrade, the device would also, in short order, turn his fractured country into one giant prison.

"And they're after you guys, saying you're outlaws."

"Well, we are outlaws." She stood straight, fists on hips, proud of the fact. "Least, south of the Line we are."

Her eyes turned thoughtful, gazing down as if tracing her country's border through the trees. "Have you gone public with this?"

"I left file-loads of papers with our town's newsman. I wanted the story out there. The same day I got the signal from you guys, so I had to git before I had proper time to talk to him alone and take him through it piece by piece."

He had to hope Bill would understand it—that the documents he'd left there would speak for themselves. That he'd publish.

"Safer this way, though." Cody sounded matter-of-fact.

"I guess so."

"'specially as someone must've told the guy in drag what you'd done."

Ma Belle.

No wonder there'd always been this thing about getting him paired up. Ma Belle had wanted him paired up with someone who'd get him spilling any talk that could be used against him: either his work or his plan to leave.

Pillow talk. Oldest trick in the book.

He studied Cody's face.

"I'm guessin' here, but I reckon it was your newsman told him. And the guys with the Engine, your place, with the secrets, I bet they've some kinda bounty pledged for findin' anyone who snitches. So he came out alone, the greedy S.O.B."

He said nothing. He felt stunned, betrayed.

"If you kept it all quiet like you said, your newsman would've been the only one who had anything to tell, eh?"

Cody had started the dirigible on its descent.

"'Part from me, that is."

He couldn't go on alone.

He'd need help now, in Canada, if he wanted to be sure to get the story out. And he wanted to go public—needed it.

His head hurt with puzzling it through in the thin, cold air—air that pierced his vision with tiny white points.

After what he's told her, Cody – OutLine – would surely want the story out there, too.

How about that silent confidante?

He noticed the ice on the stays had begun to melt.

AUTHOR BIO

C L Spillard was born just in time to endure the U.K.'s coldest winter on record. A physicist by profession, she also writes science fiction, fantasy and crime.

She has been mistaken for an arms-smuggler, a sex-worker, a Mason, a gentleman, and an Australian.

She lives in York, U.K. - within walking distance of mediaeval streets and Roman ruins - with her Russian husband, two almost-bilingual children, one vegetable allotment and nine solar panels.

She is author of several short stories and the Verity Player fantasy adventures 'The Price of Time' and 'The Evening Lands'.

Visit CL Spillard online at CSpillardWriter.co.uk

THREE NICKELS AND THE
INMATES OF THE TRANSCONTINENTAL
RAILROAD

DANIEL SCHULZ

They used tiny doses of dynamite to burst cracks inside the rock. Then they used some more to bust them wide open. You could hear heavy machinery moving towards the boulders—the workers in their surrogate bodies. And behind them, a quietly ticking mechanism behind the cloud of dust slowly settling to the ground, the overseer with his rifle and his mechanical heart.

It was a marvel to behold those monstrosities, the giant mechanical bodies cleaning up the debris and that thin line of humanity casting its shadow behind them. They were on the clock quite literally, both the workdolls and their overseer. You could see it, the way he held his watch up to stop the sun, the way his pacemaker clicked, mechanically. Two sides of the same coin, the machines that were half-human and the human being that was half machine, the watch in his hand echoing the sound of the clock someone had once installed into his chest.

They were ten miles into the mountain now, plowing through the granite wilderness of an indifferent landscape. The first transcontinental railway was not only a vision of scope but also of speed and ingenuity. That was what all of this was about, not only social progress for all but prestige for all those who had invested in this project.

Ten miles in, 150 to go.

They were on track for now. Unless, of course, someone did not get their calculations right, which happened. There was a delicate balance in place here, a well-coordinated dance of steam power and political power at play, one facilitating the other. One was giving the green light, the other running the race. Who the horses were on which this race was won was of no significance to either party.

Time seemed to move slower as Churchill felt the hands of his clock slowly cutting into his chest, almost becoming stiff. Waving his hand, he signaled his deputy to take his place, packed in his watch and turned his horse around, riding with speed to the railway encampment, to his boss, the financial manager.

Underway he could feel his heart palpitating. His left arm going stiff, he held tighter to the reins in his hand and the handle of his saddle. It was as if his veins were growing denser and denser, as if the blood in his veins was unable to get through to the other parts of his body, slowing down to the point that it almost felt as though everything else in the world was standing still. Death, it seemed, was a bubble in time. How much longer could he endure being locked into it? Down there at the horizon, his destitute hope was coming into sight. Gaining speed, he held onto his saddle only to kick in the breaks. Out there, on the porch of his coach, a shadow stood waiting for him.

He took off his hat and combed through his head. Pearls of sweat were dripping from his forehead. The manager smiled at him as if he was some kind of treasure. Churchill stared back at him, bleak.

"I need my payment," he said.

The manager remained motionless, then suddenly, his body set into action, though his face seemed to remain in place, just smiling, asking him to unbutton his shirt. "A nickel," the manager replied, holding a coin up to the heavens like a host before he submerged it into the slot inside Churchill's chest.

The overseer sighed as the coin rolled down and clicked into place. The clock hands loosened.

"You owe me a dollar," he sighed.

"You have to earn that money," the manager replied, the smile still frozen on his face. He looked like a walking advertisement. Churchill scowled.

"Don't forget you owe me," the manager replied, "Don't forget you owe me for everything I did."

The man stood before him like a monument, like he could move the world. He didn't flinch, didn't stare. He just looked at him with an ever mysterious smile.

Turning his horse back around, the overseer went back to work to earn a living. There was no way out of this predicament now. The rhythm of his heartbeat had been subdued to the machine's rhythm. Ten mechanical bodies ran back from the explosives they had just planted, then removed the debris they ignited with fifty more lending them their hands, earning their wages. The dead-end they were working through, their pathway. There was no escape from the task they were set out to do. A group of men with rifles made sure of that on horseback. This was his primal purpose: to exploit others to keep himself alive.

"You wanted adventure," one of his deputies smiled at him, almost grinning, "Here you got it."

The company, it seemed, was everywhere.

The crowd cheered, rifles in the air, while the two work dolls fought it out between them. Observing the spectacle from the margins, Churchill made his rounds. Some of the people inside those mechanical bodies were former convicts, others victims of unsurmountable accidents, and victims who, incidentally, could not pay their hospital bills. This is where the company came in, providing them a new life, a second chance to start over again, the bodies they were wearing. The limbs they used to propel themselves were company property, a debt they were required to work off. Everybody, after all, has dreams.

The crowd cheered once more. The doll with the red flag waving like a banner on his back battled the doll with the white flag, a highly symbolic spectacle meant to entertain the gunmen.

In some ways, you could even say the fights were rigged. The boss made sure of that. The red flag lost more often than it won. You could not give people the idea that leftist politics, anarchists, communists, and unions were worth fighting for. People needed a strongman that represented their freedom. They needed to believe in something that represented their liberty. Someone that represented everything they wanted to be. The bodies, of course, were company property, a means to provide their workers with some amusement, leisure time amid the wilderness where everything was always at stake.

The crowds cheered at the punches being thrown, a hook exchanged for an undercut. The red flag was getting the better of the white one. Extremely agile in his heavy body, he ducked and delivered

238

another punch, which his enemy evaded, only to be hit by a right hook.

There was a delicate dance at play here, a dance between the powers that be. Steam fumed from the dual chimneys on the backs of the two fighters, circling each other in order to make a living, while the flags in between those chimneys waved ideology. Who would conquer whose? This wasn't a simple box match. This was Capture the Flag.

Churchill unscrewed the jar mounted inside his back and poured the money out on the table. His body was the absurdity of his current situation. He needed to make more money to keep himself alive. He needed to place a bet. He needed to spend more than he actually had. Providing for your living with money only to then spend money to provide yourself with drinks and food was the paradox he found himself caught in, as every cent of wealth he made flowed through his fingers like quicksand.

Maybe this day would be different. Maybe today, he would win. The red one seemed to be delivering quite a fight. Against better knowledge, he placed his bets on the body that was about to lose.

Whenever one of the workers disapproved of being paid more with coals than with coins, the manager would reply to them, "But how else will you keep your heart warm?"

The liquor in his mouth tasted bitter. He only had a nickel left to keep his pacemaker running until noon. With some luck, he could borrow some money. The pennies in his hand wouldn't suffice. The machinery was specific to a specific type of coin that could be inserted into the slot: nickels, dimes, and quarters. One nickel left and besides that pennies. Churchill made a fist and stared at the horizon. How could he have been so stupid to have placed that bet?

239

In the background, his men were celebrating their winnings, cheering themselves on with drinks, giving each other toasts to the thrill of the evening. Music sounded from the salon coach as women surrounded the men who had won the most cash. You could tell what they worked by the clocks they had installed into their hearts. A way to keep time. A way to keep the men in line.

"Want another beer?"

The overseer didn't respond. He didn't recognize the voice calling him until Jared put his hand on his shoulder and handed him another bottle.

"Why did you bet on the red one?" he asked. His friend shrugged, staring to the horizon, wondering how long he could keep this up. There was a word on his lips that could answer Jared's question, but he preferred not to say, "Hope."

"Cheers," Jared said, clinking his beer bottle to Churchill's. Jared was one of his best men, and the only one on the whole transcontinental railroad that actually enjoyed his silence. He was a guy who did his work instead of letting himself be distracted by others. He was someone who did his job orderly, concentrated.

"By the way, I thought this might come in handy," he added, pressing three nickels into Churchill's hand. "One of us, after all, knows how to place his bets."

"Cheers," Churchill said.

One gang of workers started installing the rails, while the other gang plowed through the granite right in front of them. Remove the debris, plant the explosives, ignite.

When the granite cracked, they blew it up again, trying to maintain a controlled demolition of the mountain. It was this routine that had been advertised to them as an adventure, a brand new life, and a possibility to start over again. In reality, it was the endless repetition of cleaning up after other people's mess, of doing the dirty work for other people's visionary plans, and of working wages where others earned percentages and interest.

The dolls didn't earn much money. They earned less than the overseers did. There was a good reason for this. They didn't have to pay for meals after all. A nutritional cocktail was injected into their tanks in the same way their organs were re-installed into their bodies every morning, and when they came back from work their organic selves were extracted from their steel bodies and put on the hook of a conveniently heated boxcar. That way, the workers could sleep in peace instead of being kept awake by the steel creaking motion of their own bodies, the noise of a mechanical motor never coming to rest, because it, unlike its operators, didn't have a mind in need of rest. So, at night, they hung from the meat hooks of their coach and when the first rays of light fell through the coach's windows, they were taken off the hooks, their flesh bags of meat served up to the customer and installed into bodies of steel.

Churchill watched their silhouettes hang there in the balance in the morning. He felt just like them, sometimes.

He heard his gunmen rhythmically hit the buts of their rifle against the steel frames of the workers. This was the way they escorted them to their coaches, kindly admonishing them to keep each other in check, not break out of formation, or pursue any activity of their own desire, for there was a clock ticking in the background, keeping time. Churchill's pacemaker was a peacemaker, an admonishment to everyone whose time they were wasting if they did not stay on track with their daily schedule. It annoyed the workers to be treated that way, but they had no other choice than to comply, unmoved by the comments that some of their guards spat at them.

Churchill watched them march off, sitting in the saddle of his steam-engine horse. It did not matter to him what motivated the workers. What mattered to him was that they kept themselves in line.

The manager could not stand the dolls that believed they had privileges just because they were lauded for their good work. He could not stand it when workers thought they had rights.

Of course, this is where Jared got his cut from, the little favors he provided some of the workers under his care. As handy as their steel hands were for carrying rocks and boulders, they still were not nimble enough to hold a pencil and write a letter. You could sometimes see dolls dictating letters to others, wasting away the little they had just to get word to their family or provide them with money for the winter. It was the reason some of them agreed to attend the fights. Money was their prison. A door that promised them an escape but never opened wide enough to let them through. And so, they hung in their coach in the mornings, bags of meat slumped down on their hooks like bait, promises of a better life and the pursuit of happiness.

It was up to them to keep the peace, to make sure that this operation went as smoothly as possible without disrupting the plans of that visionary to which they owed everything.

He heard the butt of the rifle hit cold steel and turned around, only to watch one of his deputies flying against the rocks. The metal frame of the worker turned around, looking at him, undecided if he should run towards him, put his hands up, or flee.

Putting his hand on his rifle, Churchill looked into the dark

cavities in which the worker's eyes rested. His body was a cave out of
which he wanted to claw himself but couldn't. Slowly but surely, the doll
put up its hands, surrounded by a dozen other deputies taking aim. The
man who had just hit the rocks was dead.

He couldn't identify who it was exactly. His face had swollen up,
bloody like a raw piece of beaten down meat. He looked at the doll who
had just killed his man. The body was numbered *101*. He looked into the
eyes of the machine as if looking into the eyes of a ghost. For some
reason, he felt as if he had lost someone close to him. He could feel his
pacemaker tightening, the clock ticking away as he stared into the abyss
of that metal skull. Searching around for another dime, he found one of
the nickels Jared had lent him, inserted it into his chest. The pain slowly
withered away. The overseer took a deep breath.

They carried the corpse to the medic to verify no signs of life
remained, and they escorted the doll to his coach, where he was
disembodied, hung up, and exhibited for scientific observation.

They still weren't sure who the worker had just killed. Churchill
did not care for the reason. What he cared most about was that the
workers kept themselves in line.

With the rest of the workers disembodied for the rest of the night, he had
his men all stand in line and accounted for. Three were missing, one of
them Jared. The identity of the corpse they had just dragged into the
hospital tent was still not clear by sunset. They would have to wait until
the following day to see who was missing, which of the men appeared for
work, and which of them didn't.

Grim suspicion weighed on the shoulders of the overseer as he
walked toward the saloon. He could have spared his money that evening,

but his feelings got the better of him. Unscrewing the jar stuck in his torso, he spread out his earnings on the counter and bought himself a whiskey. He didn't want to think about what happened today, did not want to think about death, did not want to think about how his friend was missing, how the corpse they had dragged in might have been his friend. He let his hand sink into his pocket. He still had two of the three nickels Jared had lent him. He still had a little time in reserve if things went wry. He swallowed his whiskey in one gulp and ordered another.

What was he living for?

The question crossed his mind as he stared at the coins spread out on the counter. Was this all his life was going to be? His head began to spin. It wasn't clear if it was the whiskey or his thoughts that were disorienting him.

Of all the men he had been stuck with, Jared was the one he trusted most. Was all lost? They were stuck in the middle of nowhere with nowhere else to go but where their job took them. Looking at himself, he realized how his clothing reflected the position he worked, the endless repetition of the same old same old.

Who could ever recognize a person if he was nothing but his clothing, and his clothing, like his work, was always the same as everyone else's? How could you distinguish the dancer from the dance?

The build of the body he dragged in had been diminished by the punch that the working doll thrust. The steam power accelerated his engines for whatever reason there was. Had its actions been accidental, or were they intentional? Churchill looked around. How could you distinguish the dancer from the dance?

The question repeated itself out on the streets as he found himself staggering through the mud of this bloody encampment. How could you distinguish the dancer from the dance?

His feet gave in next to the railroad tracks, the spine of this encampment. The clock hands of his pacemaker were once again coming to a standstill, wringing out the life of his heart. Taking a nickel out of his pocket, he realized this was all he had left, two nickels and a few pennies, inserting the second of three into his chest. The mechanism eased up and went back into motion.

Tears flowed from his eyes as he stood up from the mud he had just dropped into. Getting up from the ground, he headed toward the hospital tent, the address to which they delivered the corpse like a package ready to be unboxed from its mortal coil, covered in silt.

He held himself up by a pole that held up the entrance and looked around. There was a dim light in the background and some people occupying the beds. The doctor looked up from his desk with curiosity.

"Have you seen Jared?" the overseer gurgled, trying his utmost best to form a clear and articulated sentence, a sentence quite the contrary to him, a sober sound of language. "He's been missing,"

The doctor looked at him with a sad sigh, his white coat covered in bloodstains. "Don't worry," he said, putting his hand on Churchill's shoulder, "He's alright. No need to be concerned anymore. He's fine."

Churchill felt an air of relief fill his lungs. He was glad that Jared, wherever he had been, had returned. However, watching the rainfall, another question came to mind. "Then who was the corpse we dragged in?" The medic looked at him, both dumbfounded and surprised.

"Oh, never mind," Churchill replied and turned around, feeling dizzy. Two eyes glared at him from behind a mask of dirt and mud, shaking a cup in front of his face that rattled change. It was as if he was looking into the mirror, or so it seemed.

"Mister Churchill," the doctor intervened, "may I introduce you

245

to Mister Taylor? You remember Mister Taylor, don't you? Mister Taylor has recently lost his store here on the railway. He'll be staying here for some time, as he has nowhere else to go."

Churchill nodded, feeling the loose change in his pocket. "And I have nothing left to give," he replied with a smile of bitterness that almost kept him upright as he staggered out the door.

Tilting his head, the overseer looked back at the doctor and nodded before silently passing the beggar.

"My, my," the doctor said, "You two really do look alike."

As the first rays of light fell onto his face, a hard slap knocked him off his ass and onto the floor.

"Well, well, well, Mister Churchill, haven't you got work to do?"

The overseer squinted. Someone was smiling down on him. He blinked until his eyes adapted to the brightness. It was the manager standing tall in front of him, hands on his hips.

"Here," he said, "a nickel to show how invested I am in you. I believe if you weren't in such a drunk and hung-over state, you might find the present day to be full of pleasant surprises. Happy workday."

The manager turned around on his heels and walked off as the nickel slowly fell down the slot, releasing the tension building up in his pacemaker, that clockwork he had installed into Churchill's heart. The working man put it in his pocket. He had exactly one nickel left for himself.

Chain gangs of heavy steel marched past the wagon he had slumped against last night. Their heavy steps disturbed the drowsiness which he was slowly shaking off. Sitting there for a while, the rifleman watched the metal giants pass by him, the smoke of their chimneys waving like flags in the wind. They were marching past him, number by number, 97, 98, 99, 100, 101...

"Hey, Hey!" he sprang up, waving his hands to his men, "Hold it!
Hold it!"

Firing a shot into the air, he made the line come to a standstill
and looked in awe at the work doll before him, out his mind with rage as
he heard himself yelling, "Can anyone explain to me what this guy is doing
here? 101, what is he doing here? He just killed one of our own yesterday!
He doesn't belong in here!"

And as the machine turned toward them, a hundred rifles locked
themselves onto the accused.

"You're mistaken," he replied, with a voice part human, part tin
can, "And I would even go as far as to say that you owe me exactly three
nickels."

The overseer felt his rifle fall to his side. Bodies in this world were
exchangeable, just like people.

"So that's what the doctor meant when he said you were okay..."

Looking into the caves of Jared's eyes, he stroked his metal cheek
with silent contrition flowing down his face.

"I'm sorry," he said, "I'm sorry."

Then suddenly, one of the deputies fired a gunshot. "Okay,
people, back in line! We're headed out to the mountain! Go!" And the
parade of steel marched onwards past him, indifferent to his tears.

"I must truly say, I'm sorry for the man," he heard the manager
standing behind him, "But you of all people should know how it is, Lewis.
A life for a life."

Looking back at him, Churchill could not help but scowl at his
boss.

"You could assassinate me, you know," the businessman smirked,

"I mean, after all, I gave you the time to do that, didn't I? Out of my own pocket even."

"You can't help but keep me in your debt, can you?" the gunman growled.

"What can I say? I'm a humanitarian. I believe everybody should have a second chance."

In the background, you could hear the clock ticking, that clock that ruled all. The manager had installed it into the thoughts and hearts of his employees.

Ripping the jar out of his back, Churchill threw the money his boss had given him back into his lap and left.

"If you don't do time, you'll die," a voice behind him echoed as the overseer headed back down the tracks, tired of running away from his fate.

Outside one of the tents to his right, a mud-stained figure crouched on the side of the road, begging for some cents since he had recently lost his store. Digging into his pockets what he had left, Churchill let one last nickel fall into the cup the man held up, the cup that seemed so similar to the jar he had just torn out of his own back.

As he passed, he could hear the beggar speak, "Thou preparest a table before me in the presence of my enemies; thou anointest my head with oil; my cup runneth over."

And as he passed into the desert, the overseer looked back and murmured, "I should never have taken a bullet for that man and his company. I should never have let him cut it out."

AUTHOR BIO

Daniel Schulz is a U.S.-German author based in Cologne. He is best known for his short story collection *Schrei* (Formidabel 2016) and his work as curator of the Kathy Acker Reading Room at the University of Cologne. In 2019 he co-organized and curated an exhibition for the Goethe Institute in Seattle for which he edited the book *Katy Acke in Seattle* (Misfit Lit 2020). He also worked as co-editor of *Gender Forum's* special edition *Kathy Acker: Portrait of an Eye/I* (2019). His works have appeared in the journals *Der Federkiel, Luftruinen, Die Novelle, The Transnational, Electronic Book Review, Mirage #5, Gender Forum, Fragmented Voices, Divanova, Kunst-Kulut-Literatur Magazin, Versification, Salut L'absure, Café Irreal* and *Cacti Fur* as well as the anthologies *Tin Soldier* (Sarturia 2020), *Corona-Schnee* (Salon29 2021), *Jahrbuch der Poesie 2021* (AG Literatur 2021), and *Home* (Fragmented Voices 2021).

Thank you for Reading this Book!

Please take a moment and leave a book review on Amazon, Goodreads, another venue, or (if you are amazing & have the time) multiple sites.

Honest reviews help our books gain visibility to other readers who may be interested, and they are always appreciated by both Madhouse Books and our featured authors.

Please also take a moment to visit Madhouse Books online for information on

news and upcoming releases!

MadhouseBooks.com

CPSIA information can be obtained
at www.ICGtesting.com
Printed in the USA
BVHW051759030423
661673BV00027B/763